I0600983

The Elephant's Tooth, Crime in Alice Springs

Sustainable Justice Australia

Written and researched by Suzanne Visser

Edited by Jonathan Smith

External advisor: Eric Turner

Image on cover: Luxstorm/Pixabay

ISBN Ebook: 978-0-6456547-2-1

ISBN Print: 978-0-6456547-3-8

Clear Mind Press, Australia

Copyright © Suzanne Visser

Legal deposit in the National Library of Australia

Design and layout: Clear Mind Press

Clear Mind Press: www.clearmindpress.com

Typesetting: Clear Mind Press - Baskerville 12

Cover Design: Clear Mind Press

The Elephant's Tooth

Crime in Alice Springs

Suzanne Visser

Sustainable Justice Australia

Clear Mind Press

Research and written by
Suzanne Visser LLM

for
Sustainable Justice Australia

Edited by Jonathan Smith

Aboriginal consultant: Eric Turner

About the book

Between August 2020 and January 2023, independent research into the root causes of crime in Alice Springs was undertaken by Sustainable Justice Australia. Hundreds of people from all walks of life were consulted informally through conversation and story. From these conversations, a way forward emerged. An open model, the lychee model, is presented as one way toward sustainable justice.

The study examines how we think about crime, problems within the law, and trauma in the community and lists the hurdles we have to overcome to solve this highly complex problem.

The reader is invited to participate in several thought experiments that use stories about animals, trees and inanimate things in nature.

Animals and lifeless things were brought before courts of law on criminal charges in the distant and not-too-distant past. In ancient Greece, waves of the sea were punished with whip lashings after a storm had sunk a ship. Rocks and trees that had killed people appeared before a court and were trialled, convicted and stricken with hammers or axes as punishments.

As recent as 1916, circus elephant Mary was publicly hanged from a railroad crane in Tennessee as a punishment for murder. She had killed her handler after he had prodded her on the left cheek. The coroner who examined Mary after her death found that she had a severely infected tooth in the spot where her minder had prodded her.
We no longer put waves, rocks, trees, or animals on trial for reasons that are clear to all of us. We have come a long way. We have become so much more enlightened, but have we, really?

This is the questions this book tries to answer. A just justice system should be crystal clear about the origins of human behaviour. Punishing people, especially young people, because they deserve it makes as little sense as punishing a wave, a rock, a tree, or an elephant.

What is sustainable justice?

Sustainable justice combines sustainability's three-pronged approach: environment, society and economics.

It wants to make sure that criminal laws, institutions and policies achieve just justice outcomes and result in a just society.

When such justice is achieved, it makes sure criminal laws and criminal justice institutions, policies, and practices that achieve justice in the present do not compromise the ability of future generations to have the benefits of a just society.

Introduction

Truth and justice

In October 2022, the opera *Olive Pink* by Anne Boyd was performed at the botanical gardens in Alice Springs, in collaboration with the Central Australian Aboriginal Women's Choir. The stage, under a gum tree, was positioned on the site where Olive Pink had once lived in a tent. On the stage was a white house-shaped tent from which white smoke drifted upwards. The night fell while the opera was in progress. The moon was full, lighting up the white trunks of the gum trees. Olive's white laundry on a line flapped in the wind, bringing us the scent of freshly burned gum leaves. It was an unforgettable night.

Alice Springs, this red-hot bleeding heart of ours, is a surprisingly robust society, largely because of its community-driven collaborations. The town features truly iconic creative and sports events: the Parrtjima light festival, the Anaconda mountain-bike race, the Finke Desert Race, the Beanie Festival, the NT Writers' Festival, the Bush Bands Bash, Desert Mob, Desert Song and the Desert Festival.

In the opera *Olive Pink*, the actor who plays the anthropologist Ted Strehlow sings: "The Northern Territory, where truth and justice are always just out of reach."

Justice and truth in the Northern Territory form the subject of this book. It is about the future and what it *can* be when we walk the path of sustainable justice and stay on track. Sustainability is not only about the economy and environmental pollution and the ultimate effects on the climate: it is also about justice, and seeing truth, and having a vision from a clear mind. Only sustainable justice can repair this hot, wild, bleeding heart of ours. Just as with our climate, we need to be quick and sharp and not sluggish and dull. Our kids are burning down the town because they cannot feel its warmth. It will take a village....

A town councillor tried to declare a state of emergency, only to find out that town councils cannot declare an emergency. A few weeks later, the same councillor was forced to withdraw a motion to privately finance street guards with dogs – in other words, to take vigilante action – because of the number of concerned community members present. Was this councillor seriously suggesting a private army? Precious time was lost. The town showed its concern. It may be ready for sustainable justice instead of the revolving-door justice that has been practised up to now.

Clear Mind Press 2022

One person!

I have lived in Alice Springs for 22 years. In my younger years, I worked in remote communities for several NGOs. I left for a few years during my law studies at Charles Darwin University and went to Hervey Bay, where I was offered cheap accommodation to help me finish my studies. When I returned to Alice Springs for the summer holiday of 2019, I noticed how crime-ridden the town was. I saw that kids were the main offenders and that little was being done to tackle the problem. I drew up a plan of action, contacted the Gap Youth Centre, arranged to have the use of an empty shop for five weeks in Yeperenye Shopping Centre, and, with the help of youth workers – one of them the multi-talented artist Tamara Cornthwaite – offered art workshops to kids, along with fruit and water. It was a great success. More than a hundred kids a day passed through and shared with us their ideas, thoughts and stories, along with their anger and sadness. One project was called Dreams in Motion. We made Tibetan wish flags: every kid painted a wish on a flag. At the end of the project, the flags were strung onto a rope and suspended between trees outside so that all the wishes of the kids of Alice Springs were released into the wind. It was a project of hope. There were more than three hundred flags.

During the third week, we painted a large series of concentric circles entitled My Town. In the centre was a sports field. Around that was a circle showing back yards with animals and toys. Next came a circle with houses and people. Then came the streets; then the bush.

While they were painting the flags, over a period of two weeks, and the giant mandala over a week, the kids expressed their worries and their aspirations.

We then embarked on a week of Japanese calligraphy. We drew large kanji characters in black ink. The kids were good at it (kids often love learning kanji) and were eager to learn as many characters and their meanings as they could.

In the final week, we constructed a wall with sculpted animals. The project was titled Wrapped Animals. We wrapped old and broken stuffed toys in masking tape, tightly so that the shapes of the animals changed into absurd forms. We taped them all together and had a good laugh while we were doing it.

All the kids were just that: kids. Cheeky, lovable, annoying, curious, and in need of love and encouragement. Some came in agitated but calmed down soon enough. I made painting aprons, with the same pattern for everyone. This gave us all a feeling of belonging.

So I know many of the kids who roam our streets, and many who don't. Some of them I've seen grow up.

The key difference between kids who offend and those who don't seems to be that those who do not roam our streets have at least one person who cares about them. I have heard of academic research showing that one person can make the difference between offending or not offending, between success and catastrophe. I have searched for this research ever since and am still looking for it; it is a needle in a haystack. It was used in a presentation for Bath Street Day Care Centre employees, but when I asked an employee they could not retrieve it. Yet the idea has never left me. One person can make a difference. The difference. It is a powerful and hopeful idea.

I saw myself as unqualified to write this multi-layered book. I have a background in law. I am also an artist and a business owner. However, this is not the first time I have been unqualified to write a book and succeeded. In the 1980s, while running a company in Amsterdam typesetting Japanese and Chinese text, I wrote a book in Dutch about a series of crimes in Tokyo, Japan. I had no qualifications in that field. Nevertheless, it was published in Dutch by a reputable publisher, received many good reviews, and was translated into three other languages.

I also wrote a book about love, set in Alice Springs. This was also published. Again, I cannot think of anybody who knows less about love than I do, but then, who knows anything about love? The same counts for crime; we all know everything and nothing about it. We mainly have opinions about it.

The facts, figures and narratives I have used in

this book are not my opinions. They point to possible approaches – dare I say, possible solutions? They advocate for a more sustainable justice system in the Northern Territory.

What motivated me to choose such a complex subject as crime in Alice Springs, the trauma that brings it about, and the trauma it causes, in a seemingly endless cycle of cause and effect? Whom am I trying to help? Who is this book written for? Why was it written?

When a writer sets out to write, if they are a professional, they supposedly know the target audience.

I wrote this book to see if I could lay out some of the basic principles of sustainable justice regarding trauma and crime, in the hope that by writing them, I would get better at applying them to my own life in my crime-ridden community. However, if this book finds its way into anyone else's hands, I hope they will find it of value and worth the time spent reading it, and will use it to help improve our community.

While writing this book I could make no claim to being an expert in the field. I therefore adopted an attitude of listening deeply to members of the community with diverse backgrounds: Aboriginal, Chinese, Indian, European, American, South American, Middle Eastern, Asian and African, and followed the advice of Benjamin Disraeli, the 19-century British Prime Minister, that "The best way to learn about a subject is to write about it." I also bore in mind the Russian journalist Pjotr Ouspensky's dictum that sometimes the best way to understand something well is by trying to explain it to others. Putting my research findings down on paper and trying to explain them to myself and others has given the ideas a solidity they could not have had by just talking about them.

We talk endlessly in our community about the "crime crisis" and what should be done about it. We are all experts, or at least we think we are. We all have an opinion. It is one of these subjects that is never left only to the experts.

When I know nothing about a subject, this becomes apparent when I try to put it down on paper. In writing this book, I had to dig deeply into the concepts that it deals with. Whether I have got it right will, in the final analysis, be shown by whether there is a change in my community towards sustainable justice.

I am addressing a problem that is part of our shared story: trauma. This trauma divides us, but it also has the potential to unite us, just as our cultural and sports collaborations unite us.

There is one other point I want to make about this book. As the graphic below shows, all the concepts in it are interdependent. Therefore, when the ideas are discussed, instead of thinking of them as a straight line, it is better to think of them as a circle. Some key ideas are reiterated as the book develops. This is because when I write about a new topic, it will often be related to the ones I have already discussed. A reader can start anywhere in the research, and this will lead on to other related ideas: the concepts that I start with at the beginning could in principle have appeared later in the book, and vice-versa.

I lived and worked with remote-living men and women and their children early in the latter half of my life, during the beginning of the Intervention. When I returned to Alice Springs, I had many questions; for example: is the Community Development Program (CDP), a work-for-the-dole program, even legal? It was part of the Intervention and caused increased poverty and food insecurity in remote communities. It was forced upon these men and women. I could not find answers to these questions and decided to study law at Charles Darwin University to find the answers. During my master's degree, I was finally able to start answering some of the questions that had plagued me. I demonstrated in a paper that the CDP was discriminatory and a form of modern-day slavery. The paper received a High Distinction. The research for this book is a continuation of this search for meaning and justice within my community. In my old age, I want to give back to the community that has given me so much for more than two decades and about which I care deeply. My dream is to establish a Centre of Sustainable Justice in Australia, preferably in Alice Springs.

Suzanne Visser LLM

Figure 1: How the issues in this book are interrelated
Source: Author's original graphic

The problem

Since the Intervention, crime has gradually increased in Alice Springs, with a dip in 2020 because of pandemic lockdowns and a sharp rise since the lockdowns. Many call it a "youth crime crisis". We don't know, and cannot know, whether the Intervention caused the spike in crime; however, it is widely known that the Intervention caused more food insecurity and less self-determination and, therefore, increased feelings of disempowerment to those who were the subjects of the intervention: disadvantaged people in remote communities.

In the daytime and at night, between 100 and 150 children and young adults, male and female, roam around Alice Springs in groups. They often harass and intimidate passers-by; throw rocks; steal from shops, cars, businesses, and houses; steal cars and (dirt) bikes and go joyriding; ram-raid buildings; break the windows of cars; break into businesses and homes; and vandalise public spaces and businesses. Sometimes they are involved in severe assaults, often of vulnerable inhabitants such as the elderly and the disabled.

Some of the children committing these crimes are as young as seven. Some are equipped with weapons; some with tools for breaking and entering. They display gang-like behaviour, such as organising people to stand watch while others check doors and windows. This puts them at significant risk of becoming subject to the laws of complicity combined with mandatory sentencing. This is an extremely troubled field of law with very bad outcomes for offenders, especially if the crime is serious, as will be explained later with reference to the Zach Grieve case. They differ from other gangs in that they already had a relationship before they formed the gang: they are either family, or are from the same town camp or remote community, or both.

All offenders identify as Aboriginal. Most are highly transient and move around between remote communities and houses in Alice Springs. For most, the street is the safest option. For many, the street is the only option. Most suffer from the impact of severe cultural trauma and severe adverse childhood experiences.

To tackle this public-health problem with privately-funded guards accompanied by dogs or by cruel incarceration, Northern Territory-style, seems absurd. However, expecting the offenders to attend programs at NGOs is also absurd. Their lives are in too much chaos to regularly attend programs.

The criminal justice and law enforcement systems in the Northern Territory cause extremely high reoffending figures and an immeasurable amount of suffering and trauma to all involved: victims, offenders, witnesses, police officers, lawyers, judges, magistrates, prison workers and the families of all these people. We are truly united in trauma through the crime problem in Alice Springs.

Since the end of the cashless debit card and the alcohol restrictions in remote communities in July 2022, an older cohort of troublemakers are regularly seen on our streets again too, often after having consumed copious amounts of alcohol or, if no money for alcohol was around, hand sanitiser, with all the problematic behaviours that come with it. A video of a seriously intoxicated naked man who jumped on the roof of a taxi, kicked in the windscreen with his bare feet and then rode the top of the cab while fondling his genitals went viral in September 2022. The incident occurred in broad daylight in one of the most people-dense areas of the town, where parents were walking with their children. After the incident, Senator Jacinta Price and Labour member for Lingiari Marion Scrymgour, called for bringing back the ban on alcohol in remote communities.

Young offenders eventually come before the court and are processed through a justice system which is meant to help heal the community from the wounds of crime and to teach the offenders to change their ways. Alas, instead it exacerbates the wounds. Offenders come out at the other end reoffending; victims feel unheard and abandoned; and lawyers, police and prison workers are frustrated, to say the least

Victims of crime are calling for a variety of actions. A Facebook page named Action for Alice 2020 gives them a voice. The usual "tougher measures", "hold the parents responsible", "a curfew", "more CCTV cameras" frequently come up as solutions in this forum. These measures have proven to be challenging to implement or not to work at all to reduce crime and reoffending. Nevertheless, some people want "to give them a go." The question is whether giving something "a go" without first analysing the problem to its core has a high enough success rate. It seems instead a hit-and-miss approach that is doomed to disappoint and cost millions. The problem is seldom thought through from its very roots until the end.

Both the right and the left need to respond more thoughtfully to this problem. I attempted to think the problem through from its roots. This book is the result. It began as a PhD thesis, but meaningful research for it was systematically blocked by the ethics committee. I will tell the reader more about this in the chapter about identity politics, tokenism, and the infantilisation of Aboriginal people, which is one of the 31 hurdles this book describes that we must overcome to solve the problem of youth crime in our town.

This book proposes a bipartisan solution: one that is based on science and was developed by talking informally with many people in the community.

Need rather than greed

Figures from the Bureau of Statistics show that theft and burglary are the most common offences committed by young people. An important study published in the journal Youth Justice interviewed 50 children between the ages of 11 and 17 who had committed burglary. The study showed that the children rarely planned burglaries, but rather decided to burgle on the spur of the moment with a group of friends, to steal food or drugs, out of boredom or while drunk or high. The time spent selecting the target was minimal. Most groups chose an empty home (one with no cars in the driveway). This was tested by one child knocking on a door. The children saw something they wanted through the windows or in the garden. The reason why they burgled was out of need rather than greed. Eight of the fifty children only stole fresh food from the fridge and frozen or tinned items to take home to family. When asked why they stole, one child said: I had nothing to eat. Another said: I got stuff from the freezer. I go for the food, but I didn't take anything else. Other stolen items included money, drugs, jewellery, food, and mobile phones. Most kept the items or gifted them to friends or family. Items that were not kept were sold to drug dealers. Many reported stealing to get drugs or the money to buy drugs. Others burgled because they were intoxicated. The majority were opportunistic burglars. So called "searchers" said that they would roam the streets looking for a house. Although the intention to burgle was present, planning was minimal.

The lives of these children were often chaotic. Most were not attending school regularly, if at all. Most learned to burgle from family members. Most committed burglaries in groups with friends (78%) or family members (10%). These findings strongly support the case for measures to address the underlying behaviours that contribute to criminal behaviours. We need holistic interventions that address the disadvantages that drive children to burgle.

The causes

When we listen carefully to the offenders, their youth workers, social workers, and psychologists, we learn that certain factors feature strongly in their lives. These include intergenerational trauma, adverse childhood experiences, lack of parenting and care, a high level of transiency, lack of meaningful education, depression and other mental health issues, FASD, homelessness, alcohol, and drug issues, and/or violence. Once on the streets, gang and peer pressure take over, and ringleaders set the rules. Anger over disadvantage fuels the situation.

Adequate housing has long been a problem in Alice

Springs. It is expensive, and there are long waiting lists for public housing. Houses in the town camps are often overcrowded and unsafe for the young. Those who come out of prison often have difficulties finding housing, despite numerous agencies to address the issue, and soon find themselves back on the streets and reoffending.

The way that houses in the suburbs of Alice Springs are protected against trespassing adds to the crime problem. The many high fences made from corrugated iron offer a labyrinth of hidden lanes and back alleyways. It is easy to climb these fences unseen, gather together and hide, go through bags of stolen goods, and dump unwanted loot.

When we see crime as the triangle of (1) the desire of an offender to commit a crime; (2) the target of the desire; and (3) the opportunity for the crime to be committed, one way of breaking this triangle is by not giving the offender the opportunity. The architecture and town planning of Alice Springs, or rather their deficiencies, offer a major opportunity to the offenders. Thus, what is intended to protect against crime facilitates it instead.

Better town planning would help and make the town more attractive. A meaningful fence policy for the suburbs would be a start.

Figure 2: The triangle of crime: desire, target, opportunity
Source: Author's original graphic

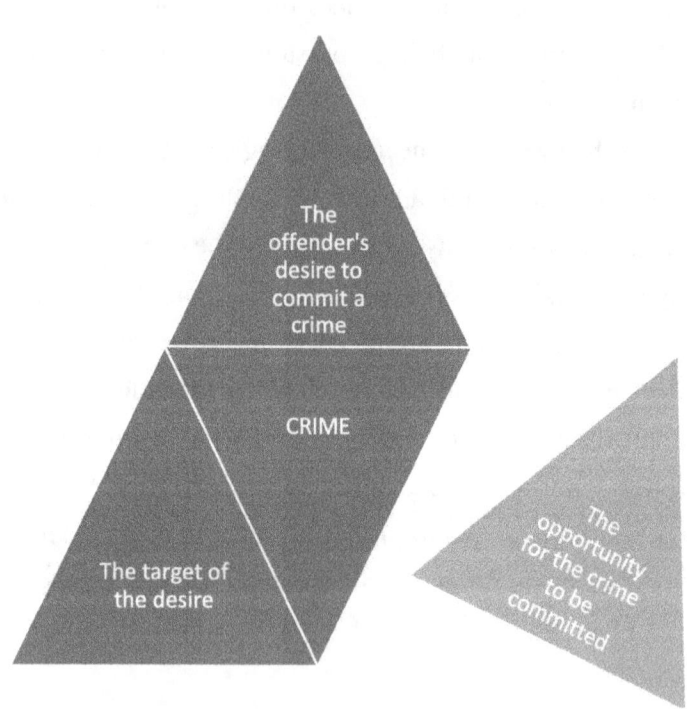

Searching for solutions

The literature review for this book identified 31 obstacles that we must overcome to begin to solve the problem of (youth) crime in Alice Springs. These can be divided into three groups:

- The way we think about the problem
- Problems within the law
- Trauma-related problems

The widely-publicised Dylan Voller case illustrates how the problem develops into revolving-door-justice and counterproductive prisons that are absurd, traumatising, vicariously traumatising, and extremely expensive to run. The Zak Grieve case illustrates how the combination of mandatory sentencing and the laws of complicity put young and vulnerable offenders and the public at risk. The still-evolving Zak Rolfe and Dylan Voller cases illustrate how trauma in offenders, victims, and law enforcement causes volatile situations that put the whole community at risk. The Dylan Voller case and the 'case of Mick' illustrate that most prisoners want "a normal life" and would benefit from the *normality principle* used in Scandinavian and Greenlandic humane prisons.

Community members of all cultural backgrounds

have been consulted for ideas as to how to solve the problem.

What if

Through the exposure of Dylan Voller's treatment in detention by Four Corners and the subsequent Royal Commission into the Protection and Detention of Children in the Northern Territory in 2016, Australians have come to understand that the Northern Territory has notoriously cruel prisons, where children as young as ten are locked up under appalling conditions and where young adults suffer unspeakable wrongs, such as being locked up for 23 hours a day with little or no daylight.[1] The high number of suicide attempts bears witness to these conditions.

These prisons exist to punish. They are built around the premise that people have the freedom to decide their actions, and thus wrongful deeds should be discouraged by punishment. It is a view of human behaviour that assumes a rational agent carefully weighing several options and then pursuing the most favourable option. However, what if this assumption, and therefore the entire criminal justice system built upon it, is incorrect? What if human behaviour is not based on a centralised self with free will and that humans act not out of freedom but are following predisposed influences that act upon their unconscious minds?

Modern empirical research, beginning with the experiments of Benjamin Libet in the 1980s (which showed that the brain/body makes decisions before they become conscious and then, when they rise to consciousness, we take credit for them), has shown time after time that the 'self' that we experience as solid, sitting behind our eyes making decisions, is, in fact, more like an orchestra. When one listens to an orchestra, one has a sense of there being a single piece of music. We hear it as one harmonious whole, but we also know that this is only because the different musicians and instruments are performing their separate tasks. There is no single entity distinct from its components . The same can be said about the 'self'. The orchestra is a collection; brains and consciousness can be said to work like an orchestra. Different systems work together and create a sense of oneness because they harmonise. When one of the instruments is damaged (receives trauma), the orchestra plays a little out of tune. When more than one instrument is damaged, the orchestra cannot function. A traumatised brain is like an orchestra playing with damaged instruments.

Pjotr Ouspensky, who was an experienced meditator and, therefore, an observer of the mind, said, in his *In Search of the Miraculous*: "We say, "'I' did this," "'I' think this," "'I' want to do this" — but this is a mistake. There is no such 'I'... there are hundreds, thousands of little 'I's in every one of us…" "Each minute, each moment, man is saying or thinking 'I.' And each time his I is different. Just now it was a thought, now it is a desire, now a sensation, now another thought, and so on, endlessly. Man is a plurality. Man's name is legion." [2]

Aims

This book has several aims. Firstly, I hope to create a framework for thinking clearly about crime in Alice Springs because such a framework seems lacking. Secondly, I aim to add meaningfully to the growing body of therapeutic jurisprudence, which is part of sustainable justice. Thirdly, I hope to help the community of Alice Springs find sustainable solutions for the complex crime problem. Lastly, I hope to help "to turn bad into good" as is described in the Charter of Sustainable Justice.[3]

This book also aims to consider seriously the idea that our actions are not freely chosen and that instead, unchosen factors such as genetic make-up, arising emotions, arising thoughts, arising desires, arising sensations, parenting styles we are exposed to, environments we are exposed to, neighbourhoods we are exposed to, our schooling or the lack thereof, and trauma to body and brains, are the main drivers of our actions. This research considers what effects such an idea would have on the current criminal justice system and on crime responses such as prisons.

Criminal justice policy should be based on known scientific evidence and not on opinions, feelings, religious beliefs, assumptions, or folklore. The criminal justice system should be crystal clear about the origins of human behaviour.[4] Retribution, punishing people because they deserve it, makes as little sense as punishing a rock, a branch of a tree, or an animal, as humans used to do in the past, as will be recounted later in this book. It was not so long ago that the circus elephant Mary (the inspiration for the title of the book) was prosecuted, convicted and sentenced to be publicly hanged from a railway crane as a punishment for having lashed out at her handler. At the autopsy, it turned out that Mary had had a severely infected tooth where her handler had prodded her.[5]

We do not publicly hang elephants any more. We would find such a practice bizarre now. We think we have become so much more civilised; but have we, really?

If policy were to be based on rigorously obtained, peer-reviewed empirical evidence, then the way that the criminal justice system and police, courts and prisons operate may have to change radically. In fact, in the author's view this is long overdue. There will come a point in history when we look back on today's court practices as bizarre, cruel and inhumane.

One visit to Alice Springs' Lower Court on a typical day reveals that lawyers and judges still resemble the coloniser, with their wigs, gowns, and use of formal language. A day of listening to the verdicts in this court informs us that the libertarian view of the centralised self with free will is very much alive, and the driver of how we treat the crime problem in our community –with catastrophic consequences.

Research questions

My research attempted to answer the following questions:

1. What obstacles do we have to overcome to solve the problem of youth crime in Alice Springs?
2. In the light of neuroscience and neurolaw, are our beliefs in free will and a centralised self still useful?
3. Should libertarian views play a role in criminal justice?
4. How can we apply the Charter of Sustainable Justice to Alice Springs?
5. Why do Scandinavian countries and Spain do much better in reducing crime?
6. When we look at our criminal justice system, can we call ourselves "civilised"?
7. What are the roads to a sustainable solution open to us?
8. What are our unifying stories?

The short answers to these questions are:

1. See the 31 obstacles identified
2. Deterministic free-will-skepticism is the only respectable framework to work from
3. Libertarian views are outdated and not congruent with scientific findings
4. See chapter: The Charter revisited
5. Humane 'nosirps', public health approach, normality principle, the principle of least infringement, the lychee model.
6. The justice system should be clear about the origins of human behaviour
7. See chapter: Community ideas
8. Trauma, sports and the arts

Scope

The scope of this book concerns offenders aged 10 to 26 who are processed through the justice system, from arrest to release. Although I acknowledge that prevention and after-care are as important, if not more important, they are not part of this book. This book aims to improve the offender's journey from the police office, through the courtroom and prison – for the sake of the safety of the community, the victims, and the offenders. It advocates for swift and thorough trauma-focused public health approaches. The ages 10 to 26 were chosen because ten is the age of criminal responsibility (at the time of this writing), and 26 is the age when the brain is assumed to be mature, by neuroscientists and the UN alike. Some academics consider the age of maturity to be even higher.

Perspective

The perspective of this book is one of deterministic free-will-skepticism and, in the broader sense, of naturalism. The author believes that such methods are more reliable and more objective than those based on feeling, intuition, revelation, religious authority, or sacred texts. When one does not believe in anything supernatural such as gods, ghosts, immaterial souls, and spirits, one subscribes to naturalism, which is the idea that nature is all there is. Then empirical, evidence-based science is the way to observe such a reality.

Methods

I used a mixed approach of methods for my research. Mixed methods research combines qualitative and quantitative analysis. The result is a more holistic approach combining and analysing statistical data with deeper contextualised insights.

Indigenous style research

I used some of the principles of Indigenous research and methodologies. Because Indigenous knowledge is relational, Indigenous research methodology requires the researcher to locate herself within the context of the community from which the Indigenous knowledge stems, emerge herself in it, and co-create stories. I engaged with knowledge holders in the community and built on the strength of relationships.

Indigenous research is reciprocal. The exchange between me and my consultants was co-created and reciprocal and should always be beneficial to the community. In co-creating knowledge, I sought to apply an Aboriginal lens to interpret the data sometimes.

Aboriginal knowledge is collectively held. Methods of learning presented in stories and in the reflections upon those stories informed my writing and data analysis.

I aimed to help restore wholeness to Indigenous knowledge systems. I interpreted my data through a decolonising lens while drawing an understanding of how Aboriginal people have continuously learned in and from their locus of interaction with the environment.

Trauma-centred research requires this reciprocity and respect for cultural knowledge and the sharing and representation of that knowledge. I drew from ignored knowledge systems on this ancient land: Mparntwe. I aimed to create better relationships and our relationships with this place where we all live together, Alice Springs.

The principles of sustainable justice used in this book were formed after extensive research with the help of Indigenous populations in Australia and elsewhere in the world.[6]

Decolonising theory

Decolonising theory addresses the concerns about Western historical research in Indigenous settings. I understood and acknowledged the historical and detrimental effects of previous research methods on Aboriginal communities, strongly question the ethics and conduct of such research and instead advocated for research that offers Aboriginal peoples real opportunities to voice their perspectives and knowledge.

I applied research practices that are sensitive in Aboriginal and mixed cultures to benefit the whole community. I hope to help strengthen Aboriginal peoples to address social injustices and promote well-being in the community.

This does not imply that Western research methods were unsuitable. I adapted my methods to resonate with Aboriginal perspectives in the community. I did this by being intimately connected to the practices and needs of the community by living and functioning gently in it.

I adopted my protocols and did not see myself as the source of discovery. Like many Aboriginal peoples, I considered the knowledge I worked with as residing in nature, in the bodies and brains of humans and the community; knowledge thus can be uncovered but not discovered. I did not prioritise the scientific findings I uncovered over Aboriginal knowledge and recognise that Aboriginal knowledge has evolved over many centuries to help communities live sustainably. I consider this scientific research too.

Realist ontology

Ontology refers to the nature of reality. It asks: do objects or concepts exist outside of our mind (the realist position) or not? I ask this question: is the solid self with free will real or not? And if it is not, as is becoming increasingly clear through empirical evidence, what are the consequences for the criminal justice system? What are alternative thinking frameworks, and do they stand against determinism?

The qualitative approach of pragmatism

I want to effect change in the criminal justice system and/ or find alternatives for it in public health. The aim is to solve a problem: the public health problem of crime in Alice Springs. I collected and analysed both quantitative data, that is, numbers, for example, to show the rise of crime, and qualitative data, that is, words, in acts and other legislation, case law, scientific journals, the media and social media (the latter only as a gauge of public opinion and political will).

Consultation

I involved several Aboriginal community members, whom I know personally. Only Eric wanted to be mentioned:

Eric Turner

Eric is an Alice Springs-based Arrernte man who has lived and worked in remote and urban Aboriginal communities across the Northern Territory, South Australia and Western Australia for the past 36 years. Eric has worked for state and federal governments in the NT and Canberra, the Aboriginal Community Controlled Health sector, and NGOs. These include management, policy development, planning and implementation, community development, and project management. Eric's passions are empowering Aboriginal people to determine their own goals and futures through engagement, information sharing and enabling tools.

They agreed to meet with me informally two or three times per year to act as consultants and advisors. Their knowledge informed the research.

They are acknowledged and greatly appreciated for their role in walking alongside my research process in the final book and in any publications that may result. Both people kept me sharp; they pointed out any flaws in the research frankly, and they indicated where they wanted the research to be focused.

The power of story

I recognise the power of stories and use stories, particularly about animals, plants, and inanimate natural objects. In this research, I use these stories as thought experiments about blameworthiness to show how courts in the past worked. I see the yellow rabbit sculpture in front of the Supreme Court as one symbol of our confusion about crime and justice.

Centre for sustainable justice

I have established Sustainable Justice, Australia, an organisation that researches and advocates for the philosophy, concept and principles of sustainable justice.

www.sustainablejusticeaustralia.com

A note on names and usage

In the Northern Territory, members of Aboriginal peoples' groups usually refer to themselves in English as 'Aboriginal'. This book also follows this practice. The term 'Indigenous' is often used in government and other official contexts and in statistical reporting; this book follows their lead. Members of Aboriginal peoples' groups do not use the given name of a deceased person. Instead, they use a bereavement name. In accordance with this, this book has not used the given names of deceased Aboriginal people. Instead, it has used the bereavement name Kwementyaye for Arrernte people or Kumunjayi for Warlpiri people.

Endnotes

1 See generally the work of senior lawyer John Lawrence. He protests every Friday in front of the new Don Dale prison, which is located in the condemned Berimah adult prison building.

2 Ouspensky, PD 1949, In Search of the Miraculous: Fragments of an Unknown Teaching Rare Treasures, Kindle edition edn., Harcourt Brace. P 130.

3 https://www.sustainablejustice.org/documenten/Charter-en.pdf

4 Sam Harris in his book Free Will and in several podcasts.

5 Olson, T 2009, The hanging of Mary, a circus elephant, University of Tennessee Press.

6 Research by Alexander de Savornin Lohman, director of the Center of Sustainable Justice, Utrecht, the Netherlands.

The Telethon Kids Institute survey[1]

The Western Australian Aboriginal Child Health Survey was the largest and most comprehensive survey ever undertaken into the health, well-being, and development of Western Australian Aboriginal and Torres Strait Islander children. The survey was designed to develop preventative strategies to promote and maintain the healthy growth and the social, emotional, academic, and vocational well-being of Aboriginal and Torres Strait Islander children and young people. It was a collaborative effort by the Telethon Institute, the Kulunga Research Network and Curtin University through the Centre for Developmental Health.

In this critical study, most of the children assessed were found to have some form of neurocognitive impairment. Because of the difficulty of diagnosis, it was hard to establish the precise extent of the role of maternal alcohol use in those children. However, in the result, the researchers assessed 36% of all children as suffering FASD. This is the highest recorded incidence of FASD in the world. The children assessed had feeble general health, often showing signs of physical trauma - scars and poorly healed injuries from risky behaviours or self-harm, hearing loss and difficulty sleeping. A very high percentage had a history of trauma, such as incarcerated family members, single or no parents, substance abuse and chronic illness within the family. 25% to 30% of participants had a motor skill impairment. 50% had severe language disorders. [2]

The fact that many who live in Alice Springs are not surprised by these results shows how desensitised we have become to the disadvantage and dysfunction experienced by young Aboriginal people. We will return to this matter in How we Think about Crime.

A justice system worthy of the name and a society that claims to provide equal justice to all cannot do otherwise than respond compassionately and effectively to the needs of these young people. "Effectively" can only mean a response that identifies the complex needs of each young person and answer to those needs in a way that will reduce the risk of escalation in offending and improve the prospect of that child living a fulfilling life as a responsible member of the community.

Linguistic disadvantage

Language is a significant disadvantage for Aboriginal people caught up in the justice system. The Northern Territory has, thanks to efforts by Russell Goldflam and others, good Interpreter Services. The issues arising from linguistic disadvantage were analysed by Forster J in R v Anunga,[3] resulting in the Anunga Rules, discussed in the chapter Problems within the law.

Mental impairment

There have been several cases where people actually convicted of a lesser offence have served significantly more extended periods in prison than they would have served if they had been convicted of the offence with which they were charged. Two of the most publicised of those cases involve Aboriginal people,[4] one of whom is a young woman from Alice Springs.

The Community Affairs References Committee of Senate[5] conducted an inquiry in 2016 into the indefinite detention of people with cognitive and psychiatric impairment. It recommended that the FASD diagnosis tool be provided as a support and resource to police, courts, Legal Aid, and other related groups.; and that COAG ensure a consistent legislative approach concerning limiting terms for forensic patients in all Australian jurisdictions. It also recommended that the Australian government work closely with the Northern Territory government to: "plan, fund, and construct non-prison forensic secure care facilities and acquire supportive accommodation options in communities, and ensure that all forensic facilities are appropriately staffed; and ensure that its operating procedures for forensic patients have clear objectives of transitioning a forensic patient from prison to secure care, and where appropriate, from secure care to the community": and specifically aimed at the

Northern Territory, to transition forensic patients held in prison to relevant secure care facilities as a matter of urgency.[6] It seems pertinent that we should extend these recommendations to all Aboriginal young people in custody.

Unless we improve the services dramatically, the rate of Aboriginal imprisonment will continue to increase, and much of our resources will be spent imprisoning Aboriginal men, women, and children. There is something that is neither costly nor difficult that we all can, and need to do; that is, to work in a genuinely collaborative way with Aboriginal people who continue to tell us that nothing will change otherwise.

Aboriginal people come before the court suffering from disabilities caused by no fault of their own: disabilities caused even before they are born, exacerbated by adverse childhood experiences, and/or anti-social behavioural patterns associated with chronic substance abuse, which is associated with the inter-generational trauma visited upon Aboriginal people.

The law does not discriminate because of race, but it is still somewhat blind to disadvantage.

Why do parents and Elders feel powerless to discipline their children?

Aboriginal families and Elders feel powerless to discipline children for fear of intervention by child protection services or reprisals from other families, the Coronial inquest after the Rolfe trial heard. Giving evidence, Sergeant Smith told the court that after break-ins to both shops, after which the community had had enough, the offenders were lined up, and their responsible adult smacked them. After such one incident, a complaint of child abuse was made. Elders felt "the government took away the power to discipline their children" during the Intervention. The Warlpiri Youth Development Aboriginal Corporation filed a complaint against the Elders.[7]

Physical correction of a child is, within limits, lawful. The practice in Yuendumu was a mixture of physical punishment and shaming.

Sergeant Hand said the combination of community-controlled councils into "super shires" at about the same time as the Intervention had also disempowered Elders. "I think that's got a lot to do with it, but also society, mobile phones and social media, YouTube, TikTok, they're moving towards what you would call an American-style society in many of these communities. It's moving away from culture, from that traditional culture, but you're right, the Elders also are feeling a little bit disempowered because they don't have that local control anymore."[8]

Endnotes

1   https://www.telethonkids.org.au/our-research/aboriginal-health/waachs/

2   Martin, W 2017, 'Unequal Justice for Indigenous Australians', paper presented to Criminal Lawyers' Association of the Northern Territory Biennial Conference 2017, Bali, Indonesia.

3   R v Anunga (1976) 11 ALR 412.

4   Mr Marlon Noble and Ms Rosie Fulton (Martin 2017).

5   Senate Community Affairs References Committee 2016, Indefinite detention of people with cognitive and psychiatric impairment in Australia.

6   Recommendations 20, 22 & 26. Martin, W 2017, 'Unequal Justice for Indigenous Australians', paper presented to Criminal Lawyers' Association of the Northern Territory Biennial Conference 2017, Bali, Indonesia.

7   Walls, J 2022, 'Kumanjayi Walker inquest hears Yuendumu elders concerned to discipline kids for fear of intervention, 'tribal payback'', NT News, 19 September.

8   Walls, J 2022a, 'Kumanjayi Walker inquest hears Yuendumu elders concerned to discipline kids for fear of intervention, 'tribal payback'', NT News, 19 September.

Walls, J 2022b, 'Yuendumu shooting death 'a result of brutal, structural, racial violence by NT Police', court hears', *NT News*, 21 September.

The economic cost of crime in Alice Springs

Below I investigate the approximate economic cost of crime in Alice Springs at the time of this writing: 2022. Firstly, I look at pre-tax spending; out-of-pocket expenses related to crime. Secondly, I look at the costs of the justice system. I look at the cost of domestic violence separately. I am not an economist; I do these calculations in a way a lawyer would do them. Lawyers use blunt tools.

According to the calculations below, the total cost of crime in Alice Springs currently stands at approximately:

$148,613,338 per year on crime
$73,814,733 per year on domestic violence

These figures do not take into consideration hidden costs, such as, in some categories, unreported crime, because they are not known or knowable. "Pain and suffering" is not calculated for domestic violence because this type of cost is different from case to case. Hence, the figures above are minimums. The basis for the estimates is shown below. As noted above, I invite anyone to improve on these calculations, and I will be happy to adjust them. This is an eBook and adjustments are easy to make.

Pre-tax spending

Before we pay taxes to keep the criminal justice system working, there are pre-tax out-of-pocket expenses related to crime to be considered. The table below is an attempt to calculate these as clearly as possible.

I used the following statistics from the NT Police Force:

Table 1: NT crime statistics

CRIME	2020-21	2021-22	% change
Assault	1882	2126	12.96
DV related assault	1158	1337	15.46
Alcohol related assault	918	1020	11.11
Sexual assault	93	79	15.05
House break-ins	713	1035	45.16
Commercial break-ins	423	700	65.48
Motor vehicle theft	320	437	36.56
Property damage	2166	2635	21.65

Source: NT Police Force

To calculate the out-of-pocket cost of crime in Alice Springs, the public crime statistics published by The NT Police, Fire and Emergency Services were used for the first and second columns of Figure 4 below. Domestic Violence was not taken into consideration.

The 2008 *Costs of crime, crime facts info no.169* of the Australian Institute of Criminology were used for the first six of the seven types of crime in the 3rd column. Car theft was calculated separately.

According to the Australian Institute of Criminology, assault costs Australia in 2008, $1.4b per year, with an average of $1,700 per assault; sexual assault costs $720m overall, with an average cost of $7,500 per incident; burglary costs $2.2b overall and $2,900 per incident; and the average unit cost for property damage was $350 per incident.[1]

Car theft leaves the insured with around $5,000 in out-of-pocket expenses, according to the National Motor Vehicle Theft Reduction Council.[2]

Figure 4 takes the average cost per instance of crime and multiplies it by the Alice Springs figures. It then adjusts the outcome for 2022 (as the averages by the Australian Institute were calculated in 2018).

For the calculation 2008 to 2022, the Inflation Calculator of the Reserve Bank Australia was used.[3] Since this calculator extends only to 2021, the 2021 rate was used for the final calculations in 2022.

The unreported assault figures were calculated as being 25 per cent by the NT Police Association in 2019.[4]

The population of Alice Springs was estimated at

31,000.

I did not calculate the economic consequences of unreported break-ins, property damage and domestic violence, as no reliable estimates could be found.

Table 2: Estimated economic cost of crime in Alice Springs: total and per-capita

Type of crime	Annual figures	Total cost, 2008, calculated from average costs	Total cost, 2021, calculated from average costs
Assaults, reported	2,126	$3,614,200.00	
Assaults, unreported (25%)	531	$903,550.00	
Alcohol-related assaults	1,020	$1,734,000.00	
Alcohol-related assaults, unreported (25%)	255	$433,500.00	
Sexual assaults	79	$592,500.00	
Sexual assaults, unreported (25%)	20	$150,000.00	

Type of crime	Annual figures	Total cost, 2008, calculated from average costs	Total cost, 2021, calculated from average costs
House break-ins	1,035	$3,001,500.00	
Commercial break-ins	700	$2,030,000.00	
Property damage	2,635	$922,250.00	
Motor vehicle theft	437		$2,185,000.00
SUB-TOTAL		$13,381500.00	$17,417,827.00
TOTAL			**$19,602,827.00**
Population of Alice Springs	31,000	Cost per person	$632.35

Source: Author's calculations from publicly available data

From the table above, we learn that the consequences of crime cost the community nearly $20 million per year. This is around six hundred and thirty dollars per inhabitant. Part of this is absorbed by insurance companies and Medicare.

Note that the above estimate is conservative because:
- the percentage of unreported cases is known only for the 'assault' categories:
- the related intangible costs of a crime – expenses such

as the loss of time and the damage to one's mental health – are not taken into consideration. These are likely to comprise about one-third of total losses, even with a conservative approach to cost.[5]

Example: A broken passenger-side window

Let us consider the petty crime of smashing a car window – a daily occurrence in Alice Springs. The incident happens in broad daylight on a residential street in front of the victim's workplace, which is in a residential area. The victim had accidentally left an empty folded shopping bag on the passenger seat. This bag was found on the ground next to the vehicle and was the reason why the window was smashed. There were no valuables in the car. It cost the victim $470 to replace the window. Glaziers are extremely busy in Alice Springs and run out of windows regularly, so the victim must wait. The victim could not use her car for five days. She had to take taxis to and from work, which cost her $150. It took an hour and a half to clean up her car and the area around it and an hour to take the vehicle to the workshop and back. It took two hours to go to the police station , wait, and report the incident. While she cleaned up the glass, she hurt her hand. If we calculate this at her hourly salary at work, the cost of her time is $225. The total cost of this petty crime, which was committed in a minute or less, now stands at $845. It was not worth claiming on insurance because the insurance premium would have gone up if she had made a claim.

We have yet to calculate pain and suffering.

The victim is now scared that every time she parks her car in front of her workplace, her window will be broken again. She now leaves her vehicle unlocked. However, this has led several times to attempts to steal her car (she found several plastic parts of the dashboard on the floor). This causes her to be scared that her car will be stolen or set to fire. Her salary is not very large and she is considering giving up her job.

How lawyers calculate pain and suffering

After an incident that causes harm, in a civil lawsuit for personal injury, financial compensation for all losses stemming from the at-fault party's wrongdoing can be demanded from the offender in a court of law. These losses are called "damages." In most personal injury cases in courts, the victim will be entitled to compensation for two kinds of damages: economic and non-economic. Economic damages include medical bills and lost income, while non-economic damages cover the less quantifiable effects on the victim. The legal term for non-economic damages is "pain and suffering."

The author does not recommend suing a youth from our streets in civil court because there is no point in doing so; the kids have no money.

Material costs, as we have seen in the broken window example, are easy to calculate. Time and effort are irretrievably lost, but we can still attempt to put a price on them. We aptly call these "irretrievable losses." We have already done this in the above calculation.

The type and seriousness of a personal injury determine the monetary value that can be put on it. The amount of money the victim spent having their injuries assessed and treated is called "medical special damages". This is the indicator used by insurance companies. The more painful the injury, the higher the number that gets fed into the formula to measure pain and suffering, connecting types of injuries with pain levels. In our example, the physical injury is zero because the victim did not go to a doctor.

Physical injuries are typically divided into two categories: *soft injury*, which consists of the description of discomfort by the victim, and *hard injury*, which is an injury that can be detected through a medical examination. A strained back, neck, knee, or ankle is considered a soft injury because it involves only muscles and other soft tissue. These injuries attract a damages formula multiplier between 1.5 and 3 because they are not permanent or dangerous.

Hard injuries are more serious and attract a damages formula multiplier of 4 to 5 and sometimes higher. This is the case for injuries observed by an X-ray, or a medical description of the injury; for example, a compressed or pinched nerve. An injury requiring repair or intrusive medical treatment, such as stitching a wound or setting a bone, increases the damages formula multiplier. Examples of *hard injuries* are broken bones, head injuries, wounds, and spinal injuries.

Vandalism, break-ins and assaults cause significant *psychological* suffering. In legal injury cases, "pain and suffering" encompasses emotional and mental injuries such as fear, insomnia, grief, worry, inconvenience, and the loss of the enjoyment of life. In these cases, the victim may be able to recover an amount, and sometimes a large amount, for pain and suffering damages. Especially in cases involving severe injury, pain and suffering can be a significant part of a personal injury victim's losses.

Two methods of calculating the victim's loss through pain and suffering are the most common. The first method is to multiply the actual damages by a "reasonable" number between 1.5 and 5 (depending on the severity of the injury). For example, if a victim incurs $3,000 in bills, she may multiply that by three and state that $9,000 represents a reasonable amount for pain and suffering. Sometimes, the top multiplier of 5 is not high enough. In those claims, the multiplier may be increased to up to 10 times special damages. The second method uses a *per diem* approach where a certain amount, say $100, is assigned to every day from the day of the incident until the person reaches full recovery.

If we use the first method, let us assign the smashed window incident a seriousness of 2. 2 x $845 = $1,690 in pain and suffering + $845 in irretrievable loss and actual costs. The broken car window has now cost us $2,535.

If we unleashed these calculations on the above table of the costs of crime in Alice Springs, the costs would at least triple.

Domestic violence

Domestic violence must be calculated separately as the parameters differ from other crimes. It was estimated in 2014-15 that women experiencing physical violence, sexual violence and emotional abuse by a partner will incur an on average cost of approximately $27,000 per person.[6] This is approximately $29,950 in 2021.

Table 3: Domestic violence pre-tax spending

Reported DV cases	2014-15	2021	Per victim in 2021
1337	$27,000 per victim	$40,043,150	$29,950
Total			$40,043,150

Source: Author's calculations from publicly available data

Domestic violence post-tax spending

Australian Governments (National, State and Territory) bore costs of domestic violence to the tune of of an estimated $7.8 billion a year in 2014-15[7] ; an average of $26,780.20 per victim.

Table 4: Domestic violence post-tax spending

Cases in AS	2014-15	2021	TOTAL
1137	$26,780 per victim	$29,702 per victim	$33,771,583
TOTAL			$33,771,583

Source: Author's calculations from publicly available data

This brings the total cost of domestic violence in Alice Springs to $73,814,733 per year. This does not take into consideration unreported cases and pain and suffering.

Post-tax spending on crime (not DV)

The rate of (re)offending in the Northern Territory comes at a huge post-tax cost. The government spends about $338 per adult prisoner per day to house roughly 1,749 inmates across the Territory, according to the Attorney-General department's 2020-21 annual report.[8] That is nearly $600,000 per day. The incarceration of an adult prisoner in the NT is estimated to cost $317.73 per day. The cost increases significantly for NT youth in detention, estimated to be $2,038.05 per day.[9]

On 31 January 2022 there were 626 prisoners in The Alice Springs Correctional Centre.[10]

The average juvenile in detention in Alice Springs on 25 July 2022 was 16.[11] Territorians are the most heavily policed in Australia, with about eight officers for every 1000 people. A 2022 report by the Productivity Commission shows that the Northern Territory police has the highest average staffing costs and the most expensive police force per person in the country. Despite this, Territorians feel the least safe compared with other Australian policing jurisdictions. The NT force costs each Territorian $1,807, more than four times the cost of police in the ACT and three times the cost for West Australians. The average staffing cost per officer in the Northern Territory was $212,323.[12]

The population of Alice Springs was estimated at 31,000.

For the calculation 2008 to 2022, the Inflation Calculator of the Reserve Bank of Australia was used.[13] Since this calculator extends only to 2021, the 2021 rate was used for the final calculations in 2022.

Table 5: Cost of the justice system in Alice Springs

			2008 cost	2021 cost	2021 per capita
Adults in prison 2020-2021 on an average day	626	Cost per day $317		$71,439,120	$2304
Young offenders in prison 2020-2021 on an average day	16	Cost per day $2,038		$11,738,880	379
Police Cost 2021 (70% on crime)				$39,215,000	70% of $1807 =$1265
Court Admin Cost			$5,084,000	$6,617,511	$213
TOTAL				**$129,010,511**	**$4,161**

Source: Author's calculations from publicly available data

A total minimum of $148,613,338 is spent per year on crime and its consequences and a minimum of $73,814,733 on domestic violence. We have not even considered the cost of prevention, such as CCTV cameras, dogs, alarm systems and human security, and diversion programs for offenders. Victims of Crime expenses were not calculated. The cost of domestic violence was not calculated.

In Australia, crime prevention is primarily the responsibility of state and territory governments. Local government must play a significant role in delivering crime prevention at the community level. Councils have long been involved in helping to create safer communities. Most crime of immediate concern to communities is local: for example, property crime, antisocial behaviour, and vandalism. Thus, the primary focus for preventive action should also be local.[14]

The focus on local government in creating safe communities was first described by Gilbert Bonnemaison, a deputy in the French national parliament and mayor of a town near Paris in post-WWII France. The Bonnemaison model stresses that prevention strategies should focus on addressing the problems experienced by disadvantaged community members by striving to (re)integrate these people into their local communities, thereby reducing the likelihood that they will participate in crime. The Bonnemaison model became a prototype for local crime prevention action in countries across the world, including Australia.[15]

This emphasis on the role of local governments in crime prevention is, in turn, strongly encouraged by international organisations such as the UN Office on Drugs and Crime, the UN-Habitat's Safer Cities Program and the World Health Organisation through its Safer Communities Program. Good governance, combined with strong and consistent leadership, should provide a framework within which evidence-based crime prevention policies and programs can flourish. The Northern Territory is and *is seen* to fail consistently to do this, whether under right-wing or left-wing leadership. The blame game between the two does not help us move forward. What is needed is long-term, robust, bi-partisan cooperation. This was recognised long ago by long-term resident Phil Walcott, a local counselling psychologist, and was enshrined in his Youth Engagement Strategy NT (YESNT).[16]

Endnotes

1   The Cost of Crime; Crime facts info 169, 2008.

2   https://carsafe.com.au/car-theft

3   https://www.rba.gov.au/calculator/annualDecimal.html

4   Chlanda, E 2020, 'Can Alice Springs crime statistics be trusted? ', Alice Springs News, February 17.

5   AIC 2010, Australian crime: Facts and figures 2010.

6   PwC, PA 2015, A high price to pay: The economic case for preventing violence against women.

7   PwC, PA 2015, A high price to pay: The economic case for preventing violence against women.

8   NT Attorney-General department's 2020-21 annual report.

9   https://justice.nt.gov.au/__data/assets/pdf_file/0010/728164/aim1-Reduce-reoffending-and-imprisonment.pdf

10 Perera, A & Roberts, L 2022, 'COVID-19 outbreak grows at Alice Springs prison as almost half of all inmates test positive', ABC News, 1 February.

11 Department of Territory Families, Housing, and Communities, 2022, Youth detention census.

12 https://www.ntnews.com.au/truecrimeaustralia/police-courts-nt/nt-police-ratios-highest-in-the-

nation-yet-territorians-still-feel-unsafe/news-story/
fe1bc0ed34759a07b946c085c27a0b3f

13 https://www.rba.gov.au/calculator/
annualDecimal.html

14 Homel, P 2005, 'A short history of crime
prevention in Australia', Canadian Criminal Journal of
Criminology and Criminal Justice 47(2):355-36; Sutton,
A, Cherney, A & White, R 2008, Crime prevention:
Principles, perspectives and practices, Cambridge
University Press.

15 Homel, P 2009, 'Lessons for Canadian crime
prevention from recent international experience', APC
Review, 3:13-39.

16 YESNT.org

Chapter one - Literature review

To understand a problem, one must read about it. And read I did. The following literature review was conducted from August 2020 to August 2022. It contains three sections.

How we think about the problem of crime
Problems within the la
Trauma

How we think about the problem of crime

The Elephant's Tooth

In the distant, and indeed and not-too-distant past, animals and inanimate things were brought before courts of law on criminal charges. In ancient Greece, the waves of the sea were punished by being lashed with whips after a storm had sunk a ship. Rocks and trees that had killed people were brought before a court and were shattered or cut down as a punishment.[1]

In 1916, a circus elephant called Mary was publicly hanged from a railroad crane in Tennessee as a punishment for murder after she had killed her handler, who had prodded her on her cheek. Later it was found that she had had a severely infected tooth.[2]

We do not put waves, rocks, trees, or animals on trial anymore, for reasons that are clear to all of us. We have become so much more enlightened – but have we, really? This is the question that this book puts under scrutiny and tries to answer. It might well be that punishing people, especially young people "because they deserve it", makes as little sense as punishing a wave, a rock, a tree, or a rat.

We all have opinions on the issues of offending and how the criminal justice system should deal with it; about rehabilitation and punishment; whether offenders are like us, or are moral strangers; and whether they deserve a chance at a better life.

There seems no end to the expertise of the layman when it comes to crime, especially when young offenders are involved. Opinions are expressed very confidently; there is an expectation that crime and its prevention are community matters and should not simply be left to the professionals. Such confidence about the expertise of the layperson is rarely seen in other disciplines.

The narrative of the youth worker

Below are observations by Rainer Chlanda, an Alice Springs-born youth worker and winner of the Fitzgerald Youth Award and the NT Human Rights Awards 2018. He has worked for several NGOs in Alice Springs as a case manager and program coordinator. He was the program coordinator of *Shields for Living, Tools for Life*, funded by the NT Government's Territory Families *Back on Track* initiative provided by Creating a Safe and Supportive Environment (CASSE). He publishes occasionally in the *Alice Springs News*.

"Most offenders are extremely troubled young people who are falling through all cracks. Many have no safe homes to go to and move around between overcrowded houses in town, the streets, and the remote communities. Many have witnessed violence and family dysfunction from a very young age and are extremely traumatised."

"These young people gravitate towards anti-social behaviour for several reasons. They may first stay out late at night in the streets where safety and guidance can be found in peers. They are introduced to petty crime, such as stealing food or clothing, to meet their basic needs. Their tactics become brazen quickly. Thus, a street culture develops from peer solidarity, self-expression, and a sense of identity. Most crimes, such as joyriding in a stolen car, rock throwing or property damage, have no gain at all. They can be best understood as acts of protest against the disadvantage they find themselves in. The group offers a sense of belonging and the thrill of law-breaking is a way of expressing anger and a call to the adult world to see their disadvantage. These actions are ways of asserting control over their lives if those responsible don't meet their basic needs."

"Anger is a natural response to youth crime (and much of it can be found amongst the victims of crime on the *Action for Alice 2020* page, Eds,) where it results in urgent calls for a better justice system and (vigilante) action. The often-mentioned curfew may result in a never-ending game of cat and mouse. "Taking coppers for a run" on foot or in a car, is seen as fun. Once caught by the police, resisting arrest earns peer admiration. Having been detained is seen as a rite of passage. Prison, however awful, gives stability and regularity in the form of a bed to sleep on, three meals a day and a day-to-day routine. It is often better than home."

"We are taught in trauma-informed practice that this behaviour should be understood as acting out unmet needs where the offender doesn't have the capacity to express these needs in words. If we understand this, we should also be able to understand that any policy or measure of discipline that is aimed at correcting this behaviour is futile."

"Holding parents to account," is a constantly-flogged dead horse. People in Alice Springs keep repeating it and hanging on to it as if it were a policy instead of just a slogan.[3] There is ample evidence showing that impoverished communities have high rates of dysfunction, incarceration, drug and alcohol abuse, and violence, so why would furthering their poverty help foster responsible caregiving?"

"Caregivers are often unable to provide the supervision and care needed either because their resources and energy are exhausted by the demands of large families in overcrowded houses and the pressures of their struggling community and their own history of trauma. Any effort to encourage responsible caregiving that isn't aimed at correcting these underlying causes is futile in a fundamental way."[4]

A problem rooted in history

The phenomenon of (youth) crime in Alice Springs is deeply embedded, of course, in Australia's colonial past and the declaration of *Terra Nullius*. That Terra Nullius was a fallacy was proven in the famous *Mabo* case.[5] But just as the *Jogee* case,[6] which is discussed in the context of complicity laws, did not prevent over-criminalisation in cases of complicity (which is relevant in cases of gang/ group behaviour), *Mabo* did not change our views of moral responsibility when it comes to the Aboriginal offenders who make up 84 per cent of the Northern Territory prison populations. Youth detention centres often even contain 100% Aboriginal offenders.

Numerous studies that have compared harsh prisons and 'humane prisons' have found overwhelming evidence that humane prisons work much better to reduce recidivism. Once it had been established that harsher punishment was ineffective, it should have fallen out of favour. Instead, in the years following the publication of these studies, the number of harsh punishments in the Northern Territory went up.

There are many reasons for what is now called a "youth crime crisis", among them a lack of better treatment options for offenders, the increasing rates and seriousness of youth crime and the rate of re-offending. However, to a large degree it is because we are attached to the idea that we are all endowed with a solid central self that possesses free will. The result is that we keep trying to fix the wrong things – even when that means ignoring the science. Meanwhile, the costs of crime and incarceration have never been so high. The perception of crime in the community brings about renewed calls for vigilante action. Trust in the justice system has plummeted. Fed-up citizens are arming themselves with paint guns, baseball bats, pitbull terriers, and security cameras.[7]

We need a fresh approach to offending by children and young adults – a new way forward. For decades now, we have all suffered the consequences of measures that have manifestly proven ineffective. The details of Dylan Voller's story are specific to the Northern Territory justice system and are still fresh in our minds.

While crime rates are going down in many parts of the world[8] and in Australia as a whole, in the Northern Territory they are not. Recidivism rates in the Northern Territory are among the highest in the world.

Free will and the law

The public and many community leaders are quick to blame crime on the "bad character" of the offender, as if offenders chose their behaviour consciously and freely and then put it into effect, making them blameworthy and punishable. But it is quite obvious that there is no freedom to choose when it comes to the family we grow up in, the neighbourhoods we live in as a child, the abuse or disadvantage we experience, our genetic make-up, and the schools we attend or do not attend. Most readers of this book will have been relatively privileged, and / or lucky. This is not to deny that they may also have worked hard to get where they are. But it is worth asking ourselves, "If I had grown up in a chaotic environment where alcohol and drugs were rife; where I didn't know where I would sleep from one night to the next; where my role models obtained what they wanted by stealing it; where no-one showed me how to work or provided guidance and stability and consistency; where my schooling was fragmented; and even the food I ate lacked some of the nutrients that we know are necessary for young brains to develop – where would I be now?"

For an overview of the debate around free will, *The Routledge Companion to Free Will*[9] and the *Oxford Handbook of Free Will*[10] are good companions.

The question of whether we have free will has been debated since the dawn of Western philosophy. However, very interestingly, in classic Eastern philosophy, this subject is largely absent.

In Western philosophy, the matter is broadly divided into three streams: determinism, compatibilism, and libertarianism (examined further below). The contemporary debate between these produces thousands of scholarly papers a year worldwide. This book focuses on those scholars that I consider most cutting-edge: the American neuroscientist and determinist Sam Harris; the

American philosopher and compatibilist Daniel Dennett; the Australian legal scholar and libertarian David Hodgson; and the American determinist Greg Caruso.

Harris, Dennett and Caruso debate the issue of free will regularly. David Hodgson is interesting because he was an Australian, was a judge most of his life, and had a keen interest in the matter of free will in connection with the law.

Sam Harris's bestseller *Free Will*[11] and the conversations Harris has had with the compatibilist Daniel Dennett on his podcast *Making Sense* were influential in the research for this book, as were Harris's podcast and App *Waking Up*, which frequently releases publications and interviews with a variety of scholars on subjects such as free will and the self.

Compatibilism is the reigning view among philosophers, just over 59 per cent, with libertarians coming second at 13 per cent and hard determinists at only 12 per cent.[12]

Determinism

Harris and Dennett; two of the four horsemen of the new atheism

In 2007, at the beginning of the new atheist movement, the philosophers who later became known as "the four horsemen" or "the heralds of religions' unravelling" – Christopher Hitchens, Richard Dawkins, Sam Harris, and Daniel Dennett – met for a conversation. This exchange was filmed, and the video went viral on YouTube.[13] The transcript of the famous conversation was bundled in a book, with essays by three of the participants, Dawkins, Harris, and Dennett, and an introduction by Stephen Fry.[14] Hitchens had died before the book was published. The surviving philosophers have continued to meet for debates on the causes of human behaviour.

Before I state that the solid self with the free will to choose is an illusion, we must define what we mean by 'illusion' and by 'the self' and by 'will'.

According to Jay L. Garfield[15] in an interview with Sam Harris, an illusion is something that exists in one way, but it appears in another way. For example, a mirage exists as a pattern of refracted light but appears to be water. Studying the self is like studying how deep the water of a mirage is. We must also define what we usually mean when we say: 'self'. The self is the thing we think we are, the 'me' that owns our body and mind, the 'me' that is the subject of mental states, and the 'me' that acts upon the world but is not from this world. The self-illusion is the feeling that we are a passenger in the body, a sense that we are behind our eyes, in the head, as a centre; the feeling that experiences and actions happen in inner space only. It is, therefore, better to think of ourselves as 'persons', rather than selves; things that are part of the world, act upon the world, embedded in the world, interdependent, causal conditioned, and interacting with others. Why is this important? Because, morally, the self-illusion functions as the foundation of moral reactive attitudes such as blame and anger: we forget about causal relationships. The free-will-illusion is part of the self-illusion. Will is seen as exempted from causality.[16]

Sam Harris, Free Will

In *Free Will*, Sam Harris states that neuroscientific findings give us clear reason to believe that we do not have free will. This counts not only for important decisions we must make but also smaller ones, such as choosing between tea and coffee in the morning (p. 7). (Harris argues that we have "the sense that we are the conscious authors of our actions" (p. 9) and "some moments before you are aware of what you will do next [is] a time in which you subjectively appear to have complete freedom to behave however you please. But "[f]ree will is an illusion." (p. 9). Harris seems to find the thought rather distressing at first "because it touches nearly everything we care about. Morality, law, politics, religion, public policy, intimate relationships, feelings of guilt and personal accomplishment—most of what is distinctly human about our lives seems to depend upon our viewing one another as autonomous persons, capable of free choice." (p. 1). Later the tone of concern vanishes, and Harris explains how losing the sense of free will may increase one's sense of compassion and forgiveness toward others (p. 45).

In *United States v Grayson*[17], the Supreme Court in the USA has called free will a 'universal and persistent' foundation for our system of law, distinct from "a deterministic view of human conduct that is inconsistent with the underlying precepts of our criminal justice system". (p. 48). This conception of free will rests on two false assumptions: that humans are free to think and act differently from the way they did in the past; and that we are the conscious source of our thoughts and actions in the present. Our sense of deciding what to do in each moment seems to be the actual origin of our subsequent behaviour. Offenders against the law, in Harris' view, are "poorly calibrated clockwork" who do not deserve blame or punishment)"[..] Those of us who work hard and follow the rules do not 'deserve' our success in any deep sense." (p. 1). Harris despises compatibilism. It is "not the free will that most people feel they have" (p. 16), and the vast amount of literature produced in its defence "resembles theology." (p. 18).

The compatibilist Daniel Dennett has answered this critique with several essays that were subsequently published by Harris on the Making Sense podcast website under the titles: *Reflections on Free Will, Stop Telling People That They Don't Have Free Will,*[18] and *The Nefarious Surgeon,* which was first published on the website *The Big Think.* [19]

Harris states that "the idea of free will emerges from a felt experience. "I just drank a glass of water and feel absolutely at peace with the decision to do so. I was thirsty, and drinking water is fully congruent with my vision of who I want to be when in need of a drink. Where is the freedom in this? It may be true that if I had wanted to do otherwise, I would have, but I am nevertheless compelled to do what I effectively want. Choices, efforts, intentions, and reasoning influence our behaviour—they are themselves part of a chain of causes that precede conscious awareness and over which we exert no conscious control. There is a regress here that always ends in darkness." (p 15).

With a discussion of desert, praise and blame, at the end of *Free Will*, Harris goes back to where he began: "those of us who work hard and follow the rules [do] not 'deserve' our success in any deep sense. (p.1). It is not an accident that most people find these conclusions abhorrent." (p.1).

Benjamin Libet

Harris relies heavily on experiments by Benjamin Libet: (pp. 8, 72, 73, 81, 106). "The physiologist Benjamin Libet famously used EEG to show that activity in the brain's motor cortex can be detected some 300 milliseconds before a person feels that he has decided to move. Another lab extended this work using functional magnetic resonance imaging (fMRI): Subjects were asked to press one of two buttons while watching a clock composed of a random sequence of letters appearing on the screen. They reported which letter was visible when they decided to press one button or the other. One fact now seems indisputable: some brief time before you are aware of what you will do next — a time in which you subjectively appear to have complete freedom to behave however you please — your brain has already determined what you will do. You then become conscious of this "decision" and believe that you are in the process of making it." (p. 8).

Compatibilism

Dennett, The Nefarious Neurosurgeon

Daniel Dennett subscribes to the belief that free will and determinism *can* coexist. In this compatibilist view, agents are morally responsible for their actions; thieves are accountable for their crime if they were not coerced and even if their crime was a direct consequence of their genetic makeup, upbringing, socioeconomic status, or other factors outside of their control. After all, Dennett argues, if the thief isn't responsible for his crime, then who is?

In the video *Stop Telling People They Don't Have Free Will*, Dennett accuses neuroscientists like Harris of misinforming the public and doing real harm. Dennett explores whether people are better off believing in free will, for the sake of society and their own peace of mind, regardless of the accuracy of that belief, by engaging in a thought experiment titled *The Nefarious Neurosurgeon*. It is designed to irritate neuroscientists like Sam Harris, who tell people they have no free will.

This nefarious neurosurgeon implants a microchip in the brain of a patient to treat obsessive-compulsive disorder (OCD). When the patient wakes up, the surgeon tells him: "We have your OCD under control. From now on, you will be monitored day and night, and we control everything you do. You will think you have free will. You will think you are making your own decisions, but really you won't. Free will is an illusion that we will maintain while controlling you." The patient now accepts that he no longer has free will. He becomes self-indulgent, aggressive, and negligent and starts committing crimes. He is arrested and brought to trial and pleads innocent, explaining how the surgeon took away his free will. The evil surgeon then declares before the court that it was all just a joke – she wasn't really controlling the patient.

Dennett seems to think that neuroscientists who say that we don't have free will are like this evil surgeon. To explain why the patient suddenly turns to bad behaviour and crime when he thinks he has no free will, Dennett uses an experiment by Vohs and Schooler, in which subjects who were given written statements claiming that humans "are biological computers; designed by evolution, built through genetics, and programmed by the environment" were more likely to cheat in a game with monetary rewards. In that same paper, however, the authors caution: "Although the study reported here raises concerns about the possible impact of deterministic views on moral behaviour, it is important not to overinterpret our findings. Our experiments measured only modest forms of ethical behaviour, and whether or not free-will beliefs have the same effect on more significant moral and ethical infractions is unknown."[20] Hence, it seems that Dennett is willing to do the very thing he warns neuroscientists not to do: overgeneralise the results of scientific research.

Moreover, the argument of people suddenly turning to crime is also often used of people who have lost their faith by Christians, a group that Dennett openly despises and criticizes for what he sees as their unfounded beliefs and insane reasoning. In *The Nefarious Neuroscientist*, the neuroscientist *lies* to her patient. Neuroscientists are not lying when they claim humans do not have free will, nor are they trying to deceive the public. Should free-will-scepticism have negative consequences, the position that neuroscientists should refrain from voicing their anti-free-will beliefs is one Dennett himself is unwilling to take on other issues, for example, when it comes to the existence of God. In an interview with *The Philosophers' Magazine*, Dennett defends his fellow "horsemen" against the charge that they are rude and intemperate: "There is no polite way of asking somebody: have you considered the possibility that your entire life has been devoted to a delusion? But that is a good question to ask. Of course, we should ask that question, and of course it is going to offend people. Tough."[21]

Dennett is willing to tell us what he believes is the truth, even if that truth is painful to hear, when it comes to beliefs about God, but he is not prepared to do so when it concerns our belief in free will. This is a weakness in his reasoning.

Dennett versus Harris

Unsurprisingly, Dennett has attempted to shred Harris's book *Free Will* to pieces. He agrees that the incoherence of the free-will illusion has been demonstrated and that Harris is not alone in concluding that the idea of free will is not simply confused but also a significant obstacle to social reform, but that is where the agreement ends. Dennett calls Harris's book "stupid" and "a museum of mistakes". He finishes his critique of Harris and determinism with the following polemic:

Harris, like the other scientists who have recently mounted a campaign to convince the world that free will is an illusion, has a laudable motive: to launder the ancient stain of Sin and Guilt out of our culture, and abolish the cruel and all too usual punishments that we zestfully mete out to the Guilty. As they point out, our zealous search for "justice" is often little more than our instinctual yearning for retaliation dressed up to look respectable. The result, especially in the United States, is a barbaric system of imprisonment—to say nothing of capital punishment—that should make all citizens ashamed. By all means, let's join hands and reform the legal system, reduce its excesses and restore a measure of dignity—and freedom!—to those whom the state must punish. But the idea that all punishment is, in the end, unjustifiable and should be *abolished* because nobody is ever *really* responsible, because nobody has "real" free will is not only not supported by science or philosophical argument; it is blind to the chilling lessons of the not so distant past. Do we want to medicalize all violators of the laws, giving them indefinitely large amounts of involuntary "therapy" in "asylums" (the poor dears, they aren't responsible, but for the good of the society we have to institutionalize them)? I hope not. (Dennett, 2006).

"The poor dears, they aren't responsible, but for the good of the society we have to institutionalize them." Similar words and tone are heard often regarding crime committed by young people in Alice Springs: "poor little darlings", "misunderstood little treasures", etc.[22]

"Hi, please put a warning out for to all the delivery drivers in Alice Springs. Gunner's little darlings are now targeting delivery trucks. Driver left his truck idling whilst unloading at the rear and had a little darling open the cab door and attempt to steal. Got caught by driver then too off. Maybe it's time for a boycott!" *Action for Alice*, 13 April 2022.

"This month started by me being attacked in the Coles car park by 8 kids at 2.57pm. After one little darling failed to steal my wallet and phone out of my hands I proceeded to take photos of them all." *Action for Alice*, 25 May 2021.

"Told these little cherubs to bugger off after attempting to snatch my bag while walking to Epilogue after being dropped at the end of Mall." *Action for Alice*, 6 February 2020.

Such expressions of disdain do not help us much to think clearly about a way forward, and they keep the revolving doors of our justice system turning.

Dennett versus Caruso

In *Just deserts: debating free will*, Dennett debates with the determinist Caruso, who proposes a public-health model to treat offenders. Dennett is known for his view that we should make free will into something that is "worth wanting by a species that has a capacity for being rational and mature." Caruso defines free will as "the control in action required for attributions of desert in its basic form", as do several other participants in the current debate. In the basic form of desert, someone who has acted wrongly deserves to be blamed and perhaps punished just because s/he has acted for morally bad reasons, and someone who has acted rightly deserves credit or praise and perhaps reward just because s/he has acted for morally good reasons. Such desert is basic because these desert claims are fundamental in their justification; they are not justified by further considerations, such as any anticipated good consequences of implementing them." [23]

Dennett uses a thought-experiment that is based on the work of Immanuel Kant, in which there are no good consequences to punishing a wrongdoer: "Consider that someone on an isolated island brutally murders everyone else on that island and that he is not capable of moral reform, due to his inner hatred and rage. Add that it is not possible for him to escape the island, and no one else will ever visit because it's too remote. There is no longer a society on the island whose rules might be determined by a social contract aimed at good consequences, since the society has been disbanded. Do we have the intuition that this murderer still deserves to be punished? If so, then punishment would be basically deserved if the example in fact, does eliminate the options for non-basic desert, as it seems to." Caruso frequently quotes Derk Pereboom, who, in his *Living without free will,* argues: "If, in order to protect society, we have the right to quarantine people who are carriers of severe communicable diseases, then we also have the right to isolate the criminally dangerous to protect society."[24]

Libertarianism

David Hodgson

McCay and Sevel's collection *Free Will and the Law* consists of a series of essays by various writers about the libertarian theory of free will of the Australian philosopher and jurist David Hodgson (1939–2012).[25]

Hodgson was an appellate judge for nearly three decades, and was described by James Allsop, Chief Justice of the Federal Court of Australia, as "one of the finest judges who ever graced a court in this country."[26] He had a keen interest in the problem of free will in a legal context and wrote several books on the subject, the best-known being *The Mind Matters* [27] and *Rationality + Consciousness = Free Will* [28] in which he sets out his argument for the view that despite determinism being true, we make real decisions that are not determined, but are in a fundamental way only down to us.

In addition to the collection by McCay and Sevel, several other books and papers have been written about Hodgson's work, most notably by Deery, Keaton, and Levy.[29] Despite these many analyses of his work, what Hodgson argues throughout his body of work can be summed up fairly simply as follows: our consciousness operates separately from our body (brain) in some way. The choices we make are informed by a capacity that this consciousness gives us, and we are, therefore, at least partly responsible for what we do and for our own character. Punishment is not primitive or inhumane but is needed as the basis for human rights. If we do not punish offenders because they are guilty, there is less reason not to punish people when they are innocent. In true libertarian spirit, Hodgson believes that offenders must recognise their own responsibility for their conduct, and at least partially for their own character. He therefore, proposes that we argue that, even if neuroscience refutes free will completely, we should act as if this had *not* happened. We should hold that, even if free will is a dead concept, we must *pretend* it is not. It is easy to see why this reasoning is flawed. "We should ignore what we don't like" is a problematic concept for obvious reasons.

Eastern philosophy and free will

Chinese perspectives on free will by Marchal and Wenzel[30] and *Free will and freedom in Indian philosophies* (by Chakrabarti[31] provide good short essays on free will in Eastern philosophical traditions. Interestingly, the problem of free will is absent in ancient Chinese thought. Only after Chinese scholars began translating modern Western philosophers in the late 19th century did free will emerge as a philosophical problem. Problems of fate, predetermination, agency, moral responsibility, choice, and chance are discussed in Confucian, Daoist, and Buddhist thought. However, events are not seen as being linearly connected, as cause and effect, but as reciprocal dependencies and interrelations.

In the early Upanishads and the Mahābhārata of ancient India, there is no synonym for free will; nor is there a phrase or word for it in Sanskrit, Pali, or Prakrit. A libertarianism-like view arose in the eighth century as a rejection of the more fatalistic interpretation of karma.[32]

The Buddha too, rejected the fatalism of karma thought. *Karma* in Jainism means "dirt accumulating on the soul", which must be washed off by the practice of self-control and non-violence. Gandhi was deeply influenced by this concept. However, Gandhi was also profoundly influenced by Ralph Waldo Emerson, who appealed strongly to the human capacity of freely choosing between violence and non-violence. Finally, in 1896, Swami Vivekananda, a Hindu monk known for introducing Adviata Vedanta and yoga to the Western world, said in a lecture in New York that "free will is a misnomer. It means nothing, sheer nonsense." [33]

Hunger for revenge and punishment

Judgements of blame are not always based on a rational and balanced assessment of free will, as the law presumes. We decide how much control or freedom a person possesses based upon our automatic negative responses to harmful consequences. The psychologist Mark Alicke finds that "we simply don't want to excuse people who do horrible things, regardless of how disordered their cognitive states may be." In other words: when offenders do bad things, we are eager to look for evidence that supports blaming them and to downplay evidence that might excuse them by showing that they lacked free will.[34]

Herbert Packer, in his *The Limits of the Criminal Sanction*, formulates this choice of the common law as follows:

"The idea of free will in relation to conduct is not, in the legal system, a statement of fact, but rather a value preference having very little to do with the metaphysics of determinism or free will.... Very simply, the law treats man's conduct as autonomous and willed, not because it is, but because it is desirable to proceed as if it were." [35]

Meir Dan-Cohen, in his *Responsibility and the Boundaries of the Self*, notes that:

"The core of criminal law doctrine, centred around the concept of mens rea and the variety of criminal excuses, probably comes closer than any other set of social practices to an instantiation of the Kantian conception of the responsible human subject as the noumenal self, characterized exclusively by a rational free will unencumbered by character, temperament, and circumstance."

The free-will assumption is convenient for the easy administration of justice. It allows criminal jurisprudence to focus on the responsibility of a centralised self. Not only does this allow courts to avoid the task of determining the true roots of human behaviours, but it also justifies attributing blame to individuals.[36] The concept of blame allows society to rationalize its infliction of punishment in the form of mental and physical pain on offenders.[37]Such punishment can only be justified when the individual truly deserves it. Society would consider it wrong to inflict pain and suffering on the blameless. By assuming that offenders possess free will, the necessary level of culpability and blameworthiness is met.[38] However, causing mental and physical pain to offenders is obviously traumatising them, setting them up to re-offend, not to mention the barbarity and stupidity of these actions.

Belief in quick fixes

Richard Mendel, in *What Works in the Prevention of Youth Crime*, shows that, as a quick fix, short-term shock incarceration such as boot camps or job training does not reduce criminality. Neither traditional psychotherapy nor behaviour modification has shown great promise. Scare-oriented programs or programs that place groups of youth offenders together actually seem to worsen participants' behaviour.

We need to develop and implement prevention and rehabilitation programs and learn quickly from experience through solid empirical research and evaluation. To help young people grow into functioning adults, they must be loved, supervised, supported, educated, encouraged, cared for, given opportunities to contribute and be given opportunities for recreation, exploration, and personal growth. For those from high-risk families and communities, cognitive skills training and family counselling will also be required. To be effective, these treatments must be carefully crafted, research-based, and effectively implemented. [39]

Signalling: Naming & shaming on social media and prison architecture

The right to humane treatment in detention requires that offenders be treated with dignity. This right complements the prohibition on torture and cruel, inhuman, or degrading treatment or punishment but is engaged by a broader range of less serious mistreatment. Mistreatment may amount to a violation of article 10 of the International

Covenant on Civil and Political Rights,[40] even if it does not rise to the level of torture or cruel, inhuman, or degrading treatment or punishment. Numerous international instruments establish standards to be observed in treating persons in detention.

Prison design is a component of humane treatment and rehabilitating prisoners successfully back into our community. Examples of innovative humane prison designs are: Halden Prison in Norway, Leoben in Austria, Enner Mark in Denmark, Ny Anstalt prison in Nuuk, Greenland, and the Norwegian prison island of Bastoy. These prisons are designed to reduce crime by providing positive opportunities for offenders and by building a sense of optimism for their future. They are designed to reflect the environments in the community. The design treats inmates not as prisoners but as community members, with all the social, vocational, and emotional responsibility that this entails. [41]

Scandinavian countries have pioneered humane prison design because their societies are characterized by a strong welfare state and relatively high levels of trust, according to Yvonne Jewkes, professor of criminology at the UK's University of Kent. In Scandinavia, beauty is believed to have a healing and civilizing influence. Whether it's a coffee cup or a prison, Scandi design is always stylish. In prison design, this means light, airy, non-institutional spaces. A prison like this helps foster a sense of purpose, citizenship and hope for the future, which is essential because at some point, the offenders will be released back into the community.

Problems within the law

The following chapter describes problems found in the literature concerning the law as it touches the lives of people in the Northern Territory .

The concept of *mens rea* in criminal law

Mens rea is one of two pillars our criminal law is built upon. The concept of *mens rea*, Latin for "guilty mind," allows the criminal justice system to distinguish someone who set out with the intention to commit a crime from someone who did not mean to commit a crime. *Mens rea* refers to what the offender was thinking and his intent at the time the crime was committed. The concept was first used in the writings of the English jurist Edward Coke between 1860-1865. Coke promoted that an act does not make a person guilty of a crime unless their mind is also guilty.

The phrase first appeared in the *Leges Henrici Primi or Laws of Henry I*, a legal treatise, written around 1115, that records the legal customs of medieval England, in the description of perjury. *Reum non facit nisi mens rea* (an act is not necessarily a guilty act unless the accused has the necessary state of mind required for that offence) was taken from a sermon by St. Augustine, which is also thought to be the source of a similar maxim in Coke's *Third Institutes*, the first major study of English criminal law: *"actus non facit reum nisi mens sit rea"* (the act is not guilty unless the mind is guilty) [42]

Mens rea is the mental element of a crime. It developed from the growing realisation that offenders could not be found guilty of a crime if they had an innocent mind, for example, if they had made a mistake. It is often called "criminal intent" and has become a required element of most criminal offences in most law systems. In Australia, it is reflected in section 5.6 of the Criminal Code, which creates a rebuttable presumption that to establish guilt, fault must be proven for each physical element of a Commonwealth offence.[43]

In *He Kaw Teh v R* in 1985, Judge Brennan explained: "It is implied as an element of the offence that, at the time when the person who commits the *actus reus* does the physical act involved, he either knows the circumstances which make the doing of that act an offence; or does not believe honestly and on reasonable grounds that the circumstances which are attendant on the doing of that act are such as to make the doing of that act innocent."[44]

The connection between trauma in the brain, because of disadvantage, and mens rea is seldom mentioned. The consequence of free-will-skepticism is that mens rea becomes the Achilles heel of criminal law. Mens Rea defences are automatism, duress, mistake, lawful correction, mental illness, necessity, and self-defence. Note that trauma is not on this list. This is a problem. Someone who behaves in an anti-social manner as the result of trauma in the brain may be acting automatically because of that trauma. They may be acting under duress of that trauma, but such reasoning is not likely to be accepted in courts. Someone who is traumatised is not insane or mentally ill. Hence, the full weight of criminal law comes down on the young and vulnerable, traumatising them further and setting them up for further catastrophe.

This is why Michal Zacharski in *Mens rea, the Achilles' Heel of Criminal Law* asks: "How is it possible that contemporary jurisprudence has not developed a more dependable legal means of recognising a defendant's state of mind?

The division between criminal law and civil law

In civil-law cases, an offender is being sued by a victim and is required to pay damages or otherwise make right the harm done; the plaintiff must prove the defendant liable on the balance of probabilities based on the evidence. The underlying harmful act is the same in criminal and tort cases, so why are the two treated differently? The answer most often given is: civil cases are concerned with the violation of individual rights, while criminal cases are concerned with societal rights; criminal cases should not be initiated by victims since vindication of public policy should not depend on an individual victim's decision to institute legal proceedings. Excluding victims' interests from criminal cases does not repair the damage caused by crime.

Randy Barnett and John Hagel, advocates of restitution, argue for replacing criminal law with the civil law of torts. They argue that a specific action is defined as criminal only if it violates the right of one or more identifiable victims to person and property. Only the victims, not the State, acquire the right to demand restitution from the criminal. This does not deny the fact that criminal acts have harmful effects on other individuals besides the victims. It *does* deny that a harmful effect may vest rights in a third party. Barnett and Hagel define crime by examining not the offender's behaviour but the victim's rights: "the fundamental right of all individuals to be free in their person and property from the initiated use of force by others." They find that settling the private dispute will "vindicate the rights of the aggrieved party and thereby vindicate the rights of all persons. There can be no victimless crimes."[45] Vindicating the rights of victims alone, however, does not vindicate the rights of all other persons: secondary victims *in the community* are also injured by crime:[46]

"[C]rime imposes three distinct kinds of costs on its indirect victims. There are, first, the *avoidance costs* that are incurred by anyone who takes steps to minimize his chances of becoming the direct victim of crime. Installing locks and burglar alarms, avoiding unsafe areas, and paying for police protection, whether private or public, all fall into this category. Indirect victims may also have to pay *insurance costs* - costs that increase as the rate of crime in an area increases. And, finally, as crime gives rise to fear, apprehension, insecurity, and social divisiveness, indirect victims are forced to bear the *attitudinal costs* of crime."[47]

Criminal law also deals with the accused for intolerable social behaviour. In *Retributive Hatred*, Jeffrie Murphy finds that crime arouses "feelings of anger, resentment, and even hatred [..] toward wrongdoers."[48]. He argues that criminal justice should restrain these feelings.

"Rational and moral beings... want a world not utterly free of retributive hatred, but one where this passion is both respected and seen as potentially dangerous, as in great need of reflective and institutional restraint." [49]

There are advantages to criminal cases prosecuted by the government. The victim lacks the expertise, financial resources, and time to prosecute. The goals of consistency, fairness, and efficiency can best be pursued by public prosecutors who weigh decisions against policies. Prosecutors are less influenced than victims by the wish for revenge. However, prosecution by the government comes with its own set of administrative, political, investigative, and adjudicative limitations, which often lead prosecutors to focus less on a just resolution and more on the effective use of limited resources.[50] Moreover, political forces may lead prosecutors to cater to, rather than restrain, retributive impulses in the community. [51]

The age of criminal responsibility

Dr Mick Creati, paediatrician and spokesperson for the Royal Australia College of Physicians, said in an interview with SBS News in 2020: "Incarcerating children at the age of ten, according to medical evidence, is damaging. The latest neuroscience shows clearly that the human brain is not fully developed until the age of twenty-five years. And in many cases, incarcerated children are already battling mental health issues, pre-existing trauma or in some cases, foetal alcohol spectrum disorder. We have a clear choice of whether we see these kids as vulnerable or as criminal."[52]

Best interest of the child

When a young person goes into detention, it is the responsibility of the state that this child is cared for adequately and that the best interest of the young person is paramount. The principle of the best interests of the child is set out in the United Nations Convention on the Rights of the Child and was ratified by Australia in 1990. According to this Convention, the best interests of the child should at least be a primary consideration and paramount, in most cases, in actions and decisions concerning children. Article 3 states: "In all actions concerning children, whether undertaken by public or private social welfare institutions, courts of law, administrative authorities or legislative bodies, the best interests of the child shall be a primary consideration." The Convention defines "children" as everyone under 18 years.[53]

The Convention is not considered part of Australian law but it *is* scheduled to the Human Rights and *Equal Opportunity Commission Act*.[54] This gives the Commission power to investigate complaints about whether the Convention's rights have been violated, but only in the exercise of discretion or in abuse of power. Where legislation requires the child's right to be set aside, the Commission can only advise the Parliament that the legislation should be amended.

The High Court has enacted an obligation to consider human rights in cases of discretionary administrative decision-making. In the case of *Ah Hin Teoh*, the majority held that Australia's ratification had given rise to a legitimate expectation that decision-makers would take its provisions into account. Where legislation permits discretion, that discretion should be exercised in conformity with Australia's international treaty obligations.[55]

The Australian *Family Law Act* requires the court to regard "the need to protect the rights of children and to promote their welfare" in any matter with which it deals under the Act. The best interests of the child should be the paramount consideration. The aim of the *Family Law Act* with respect to children is "…to ensure that children receive adequate and proper parenting to help them achieve their full potential, and to ensure that parents fulfil their duties, and meet their responsibilities, concerning the care, welfare and development of their children."[56]

When this counts for parents, it should count for the

state: the child's health concerns must be addressed, and the child must receive a proper education. The state, by putting children in derelict detention centres such as the current Don Dale (the old, condemned Berrimah prison) is clearly in violation of these principles.

When it comes to the right to humane treatment in detention, Australia has ratified the International Covenant on Civil and Political Rights, which complements the prohibition on torture and cruel, inhuman, or degrading treatment or punishment, by adding a wider range of less serious mistreatment. Thus, mistreatment violates article 10 of the Covenant, even if it does not rise to the level of torture or cruel, inhuman, or degrading treatment or punishment.[57]

'Child neglect' is defined as any serious omissions or commissions by a person having the care of a child which, within the bounds of cultural tradition, constitute a failure to provide conditions that are essential for the healthy physical and emotional development of a child. 'Child maltreatment' is defined as child abuse and/or neglect. The terms 'child maltreatment', 'child abuse' and 'child neglect; are used interchangeably.[58]

The laws of complicity

The laws of complicity are triggered by crimes committed by groups and are highly complex. These laws have been criticized heavily for quite some time now, because of the unbalanced justice they produce, especially in combination with mandatory sentencing. We discuss the Northern Territory case of Zac Grieve below, in which this occurred. Zac Grieve was very much like the offenders on our streets: He identifies as Aboriginal, he was young, and was "hanging with the wrong crowd".

When thinking about the problem of the laws of complicity, I have relied heavily but not solely on the work of my former lecturer, Felicity Gerry QC, who is an expert in vulnerable offenders and in the laws of complicity. I have written about the subject for my master's degree in law, and much of what follows is derived from that essay. It reports on complicity in criminal law in common-law jurisdictions by focussing on the Petition for Mercy[59] of Zac Grieve, submitted to the Administrator of the Northern Territory. Based on this case, the operation of accessorial liability in common law countries is looked at by examining the history, legislation, and impact of criminal accessorial liability. The paper concludes that, notwithstanding the contemporary developments from *Chan Wing-Siu to Jogee*, we seem to be hardly a step further than in the 16th-century case of *Saunders and Archer*, when

Petitions of Mercy had to be written to get accessories with life sentences lower sentences. This indicates that there is still a long way to go to make our criminal justice system equal, balanced, and fair.[60]

In the Grieve case, the facts are as follows: four people, Grieve, Malyschko, Halfpenny and Buttery, planned the killing of a man in 2011. The body was transported to a campsite outside Katherine, where it was found the following day. Halfpenny pleaded guilty to murder and testified that Grieve, Malyschko and Buttery had all physically participated. On this basis, the Crown asked the jury to accept that Grieve was physically involved in the crime. This was despite the evidence of both Grieve and Malyschko that Grieve had not been present but had gone home because he "could not do it". CCTV footage of his vehicle confirmed this. Grieve was at home asleep when the murder was committed, but he was convicted of murder and sentenced to the mandatory minimum sentence of life imprisonment with a non-parole period of 20 years. This was the heaviest sentence among all those convicted, while he had been the only one of the four to abandon the murder plan.[61]

The Northern Territory legislation[62] describes one form of accessorial liability for minor offences and another for more serious offences. For more serious offences, it requires reasonable steps to withdraw.[63] The question was: did Grieve withdraw from the murder plan sufficiently? The criteria for 'withdrawal' and 'reasonable steps' are not precise enough. This lack of certainty is a considerable risk to equal justice. [64]

The Commonwealth Criminal Code began its existence with the same terminology as the NT Criminal Code, but was later amended to reflect the position that the common law took until *Jogee*, (which involved two separate cases; *R v Jogee*[65] and *Ruddock v The Queen*)[66], to incorporate extensions of criminal liability. Originally, an accessory at common law was a person who acted intentionally to assist or encourage the offence. Later there was the development of extensions known in England and Wales as "joint enterprise", and in Australia as "extended joint common purpose", whereby a secondary party could be convicted if they merely foresaw that a principal offender might commit a crime.

S 11.2 of the Criminal Code 1995 (Cth) combines complicity and common purpose into one section, thereby restricting the reach of common purpose. Even with the later insertion of s 11.2A "Joint Commission", provisions remain restricted because of the definition of 'recklessness'. In addition, just as in the NT Criminal Code, the treatment of 'withdrawal' is not precise enough.[67]

It was the case of *Chan Wing-Siu*[68] that in 1985 considerably widened the application of the law of joint enterprise liability. *Jogee*, in 2017, reset the doctrine back to pre-*Chan Wing-Siu* and the latter was widely considered a mistake. While later cases still followed *Chan Wing-Siu*, the Criminal Code became infected by these mistakes; errors were made for reasons of policies in the context of gang violence and other types of group violence, which in turn made young and black people more vulnerable under these laws.

In 2006, in the case of *Clayton*[69], this development was criticised strongly by a dissenting Michael Kirby in the High Court of Australia, and later arose again in 2016 in the case of *Miller*, where a low test was applied despite *Jogee*.

Kirby J was a single voice between *Clayton* and *Jogee*, dissenting against the attitude of the courts regarding the fault element of accessorial liability. Stephen Odgers SC has also spoken out in Australia numerous times about extensions to accessorial liability by foreseeability. He finds that one of the most regressive High Court judgements was in the case of *McAuliffe*, which followed from *Clayton*, and was maintained in *Miller*.

These decisions significantly increased the risks of over-criminalization. There is no research into how the DPP across the States of Australia are exercising their decisions to prosecute. This itself is worth another book, but does not belong in this one. It is sufficient to state that the current laws put the public and offenders at risk; they are laws that the public (and therefore juries) can neither understand nor agree with.

There is still a long way to go to make our criminal justice system balanced and fair, on the Territory level, and on the Commonwealth level. The question is on which level the change should begin.

Silence and gratuitous concurrence in legal proceedings

When police apprehend one offender of a group offence, this person must assist the police in finding the others.

Aboriginal people are likely to have low literacy and numeracy skills and a limited understanding of English. They may have significant linguistic and social disadvantages, including gratuitous concurrence, which means that they will say "yes" or appear to agree with a proposition when they have no understanding of what has been said, or they will remain silent.

In *Silence, joint enterprise and the legal trap*, Hulley and Young[70] describe how the so-called wall of silence put up by peers in joint enterprise presents a threat to successful police investigations and criminal trials.

Street narratives include distrust in the police and a no-snitching culture. Drawing on a study of severe multi-handed violence and joint enterprise as a legal response, this article highlights the role of the law and law enforcement in generating silence among young suspects whose primary concern is the legal risks of talking and the protection of their peers. These young people face a dangerous trap, as their silence can be interpreted as guilt. The article concludes that to avoid overcharging, structural change is needed. The system must reverse the legal rules regarding silence and reform the law on secondary liability to reduce the legal risks of talking. Gratuitous concurrence, the tendency to say 'yes' to any question or 'no' to any negative question regardless of whether the person agrees with the question or even understands it, is a characteristic Aboriginal strategy for dealing with interviews, particularly in situations of serious power imbalance, according to D. Eades in *Cross-examination of Aboriginal children: The Pinkenba case*,[71] and may result in false confessions.

Mandatory sentencing

Zac Grieve received the harshest punishment of all offenders: twenty years in prison without parole. In his case, the combination of complicity laws and mandatory sentencing laws caused unbalanced, unequal justice. The judge stated that if it were not for the existence of a mandatory minimum sentence, a 12-year non-parole period would have been imposed.

Grieve appealed against both his conviction and sentence, but appeals were dismissed.

In December 2018, Grieve received a letter from the Administrator of the Northern Territory informing him that the prerogative of mercy was being exercised in his favour. His non-parole period would be reduced from the statutory minimum of twenty years to twelve years.[72] This decision could only be made because a Petition for Mercy was submitted.[73]

The impact of irrelevant factors on judicial decisions

Magistrates are exposed to an endless line being processed through the justice system and although they must be stoic, this *must* have an impact. The jurist Jerome Frank stated as early as 1930: "Uniquely individual factors often are more important causes of judgments than anything which could be described as political, economic, or moral views".[74]

How judges are influenced by irrelevant factors is described by Dan Priel in *What the judge had for breakfast*.[75] Recent work in cognitive science provides strong evidence for a link between emotion and moral judgment.[76] For example, Danziger et al. in *Extraneous factors in judicial decisions*,[77] and Chen and Loecher in *Mood and the Malleability of Moral Reasoning: The Impact of Irrelevant Factors on Judicial Decisions*.[78]

Aboriginal people in particular are reported to have low levels of trust in the justice system, because of the role that the legal system played in dispossession and still plays in over-incarceration, and because of the removal of Aboriginal children from their families in the past. Deadly Connections has suggested that judgments should be subject to implicit bias analysis and that this information should be used to inform cultural competence programs and bias training for magistrates and judges.[79]

According to a 2022 Australian Law Reform Commission report into (federal) judicial impartiality, developments in behavioural psychology teach us that bias and interference can influence decisions. Its recommendations involve change to how judges are appointed, monitoring of judicial diversity, more judicial education, and the creation of an independent avenue to deal with complaints against the federal judiciary – in short, criteria that are in place in most other workplaces. The report voices concerns that there may be misunderstanding of the test for bias among the judiciary, the legal profession, and the public. It recommends changes to the process whereby judges must determine their own bias, which is in opposition to behavioural psychology. It also recommends that the Australian government develop a more transparent process for judicial appointments. This would involve the publication of criteria for an appointment, public calls for expressions of interest, and a commitment to promoting diversity in the judiciary. These reforms should bring Australia into line with international standards and trends. Most importantly, the commission identified the topics for additional education of judges as: emotional awareness and emotion management; trauma-informed approaches; cultural competency; cultural humility and understanding diversity; reflective practice; mental health and well-being; critical reflection on social and cultural bias. A separate recommendation calls for a structured and ongoing program of Aboriginal and Torres Strait Islander cross-cultural education. This would be led by Aboriginal and Torres Strait Islander people and organisations.[80]

There are indications that a more radical solution for the problem of bias is nearing: a great equalizer for decentralized justice in the form of justice using blockchain. De Filippi and Wright, in *Blockchain and the Law: The Rule of Code*,[81] describe how Blockchain may be used to improve the criminal justice system using a distributed ledger architecture. Criminal charges may be shared and tracked in a ledger that law enforcement, prosecution, courts, probation, defense attorneys, and corrections organisations can access. When charges are added or dropped by law enforcement, prosecution, or courts, that information is posted to the ledger. The result is a faster, more efficient administration of justice. In later stages, the judge or magistrate may become largely obsolete, and unbiased justice should result. England and Wales are already moving towards this system, and The Council of Europe's Committee for the Efficiency of Justice has adopted the charter: *'Ethical Principles Relating to the Use of Artificial Intelligence (AI) in Judicial Systems'*. [82]

A truly revolutionary system is in place in New York, USA. In Youth Courts in Harlem, the Bronx, Staten Island and Newark N.J., positive peer pressure is used to ensure that young offenders pay back the community and receive the help they need to avoid further involvement in the justice system. These courts hear a range of crimes that would otherwise wind up in Family Court or Criminal Court. The courts handle cases involving young people, ages 10 to 18, who have been charged with vandalism, assault, and truancy. Teen volunteers lead hearings or restorative circles, assign sanctions, and provide mentoring to youth offenders. They receive referrals from schools, the Police Department, the Department of Probation, Family and Criminal Courts. The courts incorporate several features of **restorative justice:** participation is voluntary and requires offenders to take ownership of their actions. Through the hearing or restorative circle, the respondent can tell their story and answer questions posed by the jury. Sanctions typically include community service, letters of apology and skill-building workshops. Successful completion of sanctions results in a favourable disposition of the case by the referring agency.

Adult staff members make an initial assessment of each respondent. Offenders are given the opportunity to cultivate their leadership skills and are exposed to a range of education and career opportunities. Young people with previous judicial involvement are strongly encouraged to apply. Youth court members receive 30-40 hours of training before serving.[83]

Revolving-door justice

It is not because of a lack of expert recommendations that the Northern Territory justice system suffers from revolving-door justice that worsens the problem of (youth) crime. There are no fewer than five reports on the table of the Government: the final report of the Royal Commission; the Aboriginal Justice Agreement[84]; the Northern Territory Law Reform Committee Reports on Mandatory Sentencing and Community-Based Sentencing Options; and *The Recognition of Local Aboriginal laws in Sentencing and Bail*. Together they contain more than 300 expert recommendations. They involve consideration of restorative or therapeutic sentencing dispositions or hearings before a community court. Although these recommendations do not go far enough to put an end to youth crime in Alice Springs, if all recommendations were turned into legislation, we might see a change for the benefit and safety of the community and tackle some of the hurdles that we must overcome to solve the crime situation in Alice Springs. The latest "document of hope" is the *Northern Territory Youth Detention Centres Model of Care*,[85] which already ignores the recommendation not to build juvenile detention centres next to adult prisons. The hype-like promotion of the project does indeed seem to offer hope, but will the government deliver and switch from being one of the most backward jurisdictions in the world when it comes to vulnerable people and crime to being one of the most enlightened? It seems too good to be true.

All-white juries

Regarding more serious crimes, the Zachary Rolfe case[86] in 2021 has hammered home the fact that all-white juries are a problem in the Northern Territory. In this case, police constable Rolfe shot the disabled nineteen-year-old Aboriginal man, Kumanyaji Walker, in Yuendumu during Walker's arrest and was charged with murder, but was found not guilty. The case raised the question of why all jury members were white and why there were no Aboriginal people on the jury. The family of Walker voiced this concern in the media immediately after the trial. This concern is not new.

Russel Goldflam raised the issue in his paper *The white elephant in the room: juries, jury arrays and race*,[87] where he describes how the problem arose in the cases of *R v Woods* in 2009.[88] This case revolved around the fatal stabbing of Ed Hargrave in Alice Springs and the two Aboriginal men, Graham Woods and Julian Williams, who were arrested and charged with his murder. Some weeks later, five non-Aboriginal young men were charged with the murder of an Aboriginal man. Because the second case was widely publicised in the national media, Woods and Williams doubted that they could get a fair trial by a local jury who they thought, correctly, would be all-white. They argued, also correctly, that because 21 per cent of the Alice Springs population and 83 per cent of the Northern Territory prison population are Aboriginal, a disproportionate number of Aboriginal people were excluded from jury duty. This raised the question of whether the Juries Act[89] was inconsistent with section 10 of the Racial Discrimination Act[90], which states the right of persons of a particular race to enjoy a right to the same extent as persons of another race, notwithstanding a provision of a Northern Territory law. The court rejected their reasoning as follows:

"To impose some overriding requirement to the effect that a jury, once randomly selected in this way, has to be racially balanced or proportionate would be the antibook of an impartially selected jury, not to mention the enormous practical difficulties that would be associated with attempting to meet such a requirement, particularly as it is not an easy matter to identify who is, or is not, a member of a particular racial group."[91]

The Northern Territory Law Reform Committee released reports on the issue in 2013[92], 2020[93] and 2021[94]Several reports have recommended more Aboriginal representation on juries and relaxing the requirement for jurors to be able to read, write and speak the English language; relaxing the rules that disqualify people from being on juries if they have committed crimes that have resulted in imprisonment; and using text messages and social media to summons jurors instead of sending letters.

Justice Graham Hiley, in his conference paper *Trial by Peers?*, suggested that courts should be assisted by one or more witnesses with appropriate expertise in relation to a particular cultural issue involved. "This may well involve other Aboriginal witnesses who might have appropriate seniority, knowledge, and experience to be called as experts in relation to a particular matter. Alternatively, a party might seek to call a linguist or anthropologist with relevant expertise." "Aboriginal people, particularly those who live in remote communities, should be consulted and their opinions and suggestions sought as to how their particular cultural and other issues could be better accommodated within the criminal justice system." [95]

Anthony and Longman in *Blinded by the white: A comparative analysis of jury challenges on racial grounds*, found that Aboriginal people rarely face a jury that comes from the community in which they belong.'[96]

There should be ongoing efforts to encourage Aboriginal people to get onto the Electoral Roll. Practical and regulatory barriers to participation on juries by Aboriginal people should be removed. This is an enormous task as it seems impracticable to extend the jury districts to the remote areas where most Aboriginal Territorians live. The tyranny of distance is real in this respect. Another barrier includes the ineffective service of juror summonses.[97]. Despite their complex nature, these obstacles must be addressed rather sooner than later. In this way, the hurdle of all-white juries raises yet more hurdles.

The closure of Bush Courts & the steady defunding of community-based mediation services

To hold Bush Courts, the Northern Territory's Circuit Court used to send lawyers, judges and court staff from

Alice Springs and Darwin to remote communities once a month to hold court hearings.

Most defendants in the bush courts are represented by the North Australian Aboriginal Justice Agency (NAAJA), but where NAAJA has a conflict of interest, they must refer people to another legal service. They can no longer do so. This means that vulnerable remote Northern Territory residents, including children, are forced to represent themselves in criminal matters because as of April 2022, Legal Aid will no longer accept Bush Court files.[98] This denial of legal rights means that a fundamental human right is taken away.

The lack of diversion out bush

Arresting offenders does not address the boredom or the disadvantage that lead offenders to offend. Arrests will not reduce crime. Unless we respond to the root causes of why offenders take to the street, (youth) crime is here to stay. A lack of diversion programs in remote communities because there are no remote providers is a serious concern, according to Kirsten Wilson from Central Australian Youth Justice.[99]

Trauma

Trauma is no longer a subject discussed only by experts. Books about trauma have now become number-one bestsellers. In recent years, Dr Gabor Maté became world-famous with his *In the Realm of Hungry Ghosts*, about the link between drug use and trauma, and *When the Body Says No*, about the connection between trauma and physical health.[100]

When the Body Says No presents research into the physiological connection between life's stresses and emotions and the body's systems governing nerves, the immune system, and hormones.

In the Realm of Hungry Ghosts recounts stories of treating drug addicts in Vancouver's notorious Downtown Eastside, with legislative reform in mind. The book is a call-to-arms for the decriminalisation of drugs and for a more informed view of addiction. "Those whom we dismiss as 'junkies' are not creatures from a different world, only men and women mired at the end of a continuum on which, here or there, all of us might well locate ourselves." *In the Realm of Hungry Ghosts* begins by introducing many of Maté's patients. They steal, cheat, sell sex, and otherwise harm themselves for their next hit. He looks to the root causes of addiction and trauma, applying a clinical and psychological view to the physical manifestation and offering some answers to why people inflict such catastrophe on themselves.

Similarly, *The Body Keeps the Score*, by Bessel van der Kolk, contains case studies of trauma from the author's clinical practice, autobiographical reflections, and sharp critiques of mainstream practices. The book begins with a discussion of the neuroscience of trauma, explaining brain anatomy and function and how they underpin reactions to threats. Traumatic reactions, van der Kolk, explains, are not simply disturbances of fear and anxiety: the amygdala in the traumatised brain triggers people into fight-or-flight reactions. This severely disrupts interpersonal relationships.

Van der Kolk explains how hormonal influences and the vagus nerve result in trauma having significant effects throughout the body. Traumatised people may lose a sense of bodily ownership, connection to others, and even of being alive. Recovering a sense of personal agency and bodily ownership – what he refers to as 'befriending the body' – is key to recovery.

He then explores childhood trauma. His focus is on violent family environments that produce children who lack a secure sense of connection to others and suffer a heightened risk of illness and re-traumatisation. These children are more likely than their peers to experience and perpetrate violence when they get older, to engage in self-damaging behaviour, and to experience a range of mental-health conditions.

He advocates for policy responses that address disadvantage and vulnerability and for better recognition and understanding by the medical profession of the impacts of trauma. He proposes diagnoses that recognise the outcomes of repeated childhood trauma, such as Complex PTSD and Developmental Trauma Disorder, to be included in the DSM. However, these efforts were rebutted by the DSM-IV (1994) and DSM-5 (2013).

The Body Keeps the Score ends with an exploration of forms of treatment other than medication. It advocates for using neurofeedback, somatic psychotherapies, yoga, theatre, and eye movement desensitisation and reprocessing (EMDR). The book is a hopeful one. Although it acknowledges the enormous impact of traumatic experiences, it argues that post-traumatic distress *can* be healed.

Van der Kolk pays attention to sexual abuse and violence as sources of trauma that affect women and girls. In doing so, he is making the psychology of trauma, once focussed on soldiers coming home from combat, more inclusive of the experiences of female trauma survivors.

PTSD is not only described as the traditional set of symptoms, such as flashbacks, nightmares, and hyper-vigilance, but also as the cause of relationship problems, emotional disturbances, and forms of acting out, such as rebellious, defiant, impulsive, and inattentive behaviour.

The range of events that lead to trauma is considerably widened in this book to include unpleasant events witnessed indirectly (vicarious trauma).[101]

Closer to home, Australia's National Research Organisation for Women's Safety developed the emerging theory that a high percentage of Aboriginal women incarcerated for violent crime may have a diagnosis of complex trauma. It found that these women had experienced multiple life stressors, many of which involved abuse beginning in early childhood, which may contribute to the women's victimisation and offending, but also to the incredible resilience the women display. The study identified common complex trauma enablers[102] that the women experience, such as broken mother-child, family and community relationships; communication disconnect; impacts of the legal and policy environments; and barriers to health, housing and support services; and systemic failures.[103]

The relationship between harm and juvenile detention

According to the Office of the Children's Commissioner in the Northern Territory's *Annual Report 2020-2021,* harm to children in detention in the Northern Territory has significantly increased. Children under fourteen in juvenile detention often experienced "significant and detrimental cumulative harm from when they were very young" and a "lack of support provided to the children and their families." Most issues related to offenders' treatment by staff, where 'treatment' refers to physical restraint, use of force, separation, at-risk procedures, searches, behaviour management system, access to therapeutic programs and interventions, leaving detention planning and education. (Media Statement, 2021 p1).

According to a Department of Territory Families, Housing and Community spokeswoman, there is no centralised data system to measure harm. The system does not record the data about a child's harm to themselves as a 'mandatory field' and therefore data regarding rates of attempted suicide could not be 'extracted for reporting purposes.' Two children in the care of Government died by suicide between 2017 and 2021. In the annual report and monitoring reports, serious concerns about the Northern Territory Government's transparency in reporting were raised. "Northern Territory children bear the consequences of a fragmented service system that does not adequately meet their unique support needs."[104]

The Office of the Children's Commissioner in the Northern Territory released a monitoring report about the conditions in Don Dale Youth Detention Centre that highlighted the fact that youth "are living in a cage-like setting with minimal trauma-informed responses from Youth Justice Officers" six years after the Royal Commission. Staff shortages result in those children being confined in their cells for 23 hours and 45 minutes per day." Some children at risk of self-harm did not receive medical attention for up to three days. Separations, which place a young person in isolation, were used regularly. In at least three instances, force was used for the purpose of separation. Complaints about youth in detention currently make up 70 per cent of the Office of the Children's Commission's workload.[105]

In *The Impact of Poverty on the Developing Child: A Narrative View*, Monks, Mandzufas, and Cross found that disadvantage, social exclusion, and poverty significantly harm children's development, health and educational success. Because of the sensitivity of the young brain, poverty causes an ongoing stress reaction which leads to the child responding to adversity in an ineffective manner. The child's brain is likely to develop less executive function, which forms the basis for learning, when experiencing poverty. Moreover, if parents fail to provide a low-stress environment due to their own stress as a result of poverty, this can significantly harm the child.[106]

Trauma and neurolaw

The Telethon Kids Institute study in 2018 in Western Australia's Banksia Hill juvenile detention centre showed that nine out of ten offenders have at least one form of severe brain impairment, 65% have at least three forms of severe brain impairment, 23% have five or more forms of severe brain impairment, and 36 per cent were diagnosed with Fetal Alcohol Spectrum Disorder (FADS). [107]

Note that trauma is not mentioned. Neither was there any measurement of Adverse Childhood Experiences (ACEs).

Neurolaw connects neuroscientific research findings to the law and legal practices. It is a fast-developing field that attracts substantial funding, for example for the EU's *Human Brain Project*, which aims to advance brain simulation and neuro-informatics, and the *Brain Initiative* in the USA, which seeks to improve treatment, prevention and cures for disorders of the brain. Australia is the home of the *Neurolaw Database*, a website that facilitates research into neurolaw cases in Australian courts and tribunals.[108]

Offenders' intergenerational trauma

Michael Halloran states in *Cultural maintenance and trauma in Indigenous Australia*[109] that one effect of intergenerational cultural trauma is that carriers experience high levels of anxiety, which is translated into maladaptive coping strategies and a form of collective helplessness. These practices may become normative, increasing the likelihood that cultural trauma and its effects are carried forth into the next generation.

The problem of (youth) crime in Alice Springs is deeply embedded in Australia's colonial past and the trauma and disadvantage this has left. The symptoms of this trauma are visible in Alice Springs to even the briefest observer. (Youth) crime is not new in Alice Springs, but the scale of it that we are seeing today is a relatively recent phenomenon, often involving large groups of children. The author of this book had partly to rely on newspaper articles and other secondary sources, such as reports by government, NGOs and youth workers, to describe this phenomenon. She also observed the Magistrate's Court.

Adverse childhood experiences of offenders

In prisons in the USA, the powerful *Step Inside the Circle* exercise, which is part of the *Compassion Prison Project* designed by Fritzi Horstman, makes it clear to offenders and bystanders alike that nearly all offenders in prison report a multitude of adverse childhood experiences. Understanding the shame and dehumanization that results from both child abuse and incarceration, the participants were helped by the *Step Inside the Circle* workshop to make amends to themselves, the people they'd harmed and their communities. They learned what it means to have compassion for themselves and others.[110]

Trauma in police

Policing officers face potentially traumatic situations and witness the trauma of others. As a result, they are known to have elevated rates of PTSD, depression, and suicidal thoughts and actions. Due to their work culture this subject has been quite taboo. In August 2016, a Four Corners exposé titled *Insult to Injury* revealed how police officers' claims for compensation and psychiatric treatment for PTSD were being met with scepticism, resistance, and delays. Perceived stigma, failure to seek help and organisational failures to support help-seeking created high levels of despair that affect families and the community. Insurers are going to extraordinary lengths to avoid payouts, such as spying on victims and invading their privacy using both physical and electronic surveillance. For these police officers, these aggressive tactics exacerbated their mental illness, sometimes resulting in suicide.[111]

In the first half of 2022, there were five suicides by current or former Northern Territory Police officers. A Support and Well-being Services review summary stated that there was no strategy and only limited reporting of data on the mental health and well-being of police officers, and that there was no money for "preventative and responsive" services.[112]

A Beyond Blue survey of 21,000 police and emergency service workers across Australia in 2017-2018 found that employees reported having suicidal thoughts at a rate over two times higher than the general population and were more than three times more likely to have a suicide plan. It also found that "poor workplace practices and culture were found to be damaging to mental health and occupational trauma." One in 2.5 employees was diagnosed with a mental health condition, while this figure is one in five in the general population. Four out of 10 former employees experienced symptoms of PTSD, compared with one in ten current employees, and one in five experienced very high psychological distress. More than half reported they had experienced traumatic events during their work that deeply affected them. Three out of four employees found that the worker's compensation process made them even more unwell.[113]

A Northern Territory Police Association survey in 2022 found that most police officers were unhappy with leadership, understaffing issues, and pay levels, and they were losing faith in the force. 92.6 per cent of officers did not think there were enough police to do what was being asked of them. 87.9 per cent said they were dissatisfied with the current pay freeze. 61 per cent felt that senior managers did not engage with employees at all levels, while 58 per cent said that recruitment and promotions were not based on merit. A further 59 per cent said they did not feel safe to speak up and challenge the way things were done, and 58 per cent said they did not feel recommendations from staff were fairly considered. 58 per cent of staff said they did not feel any action would be taken because of the survey. Northern Territory Police Association president McCue said the results showed the police force was in "complete crisis" and morale is at an all-time low. He mentioned the impact of the Kumanjayi Walker shooting.

Trauma in prison workers

Australian research has revealed that within a sample of prison workers, levels of vicarious trauma increased with every additional hour of exposure to traumatic material. It was noted that vicarious trauma increased with each year of employment. This suggests that prison workers risk developing vicarious trauma throughout their entire careers, with a greater risk of vicarious trauma as their tenure lengthens. There are strong indications that those who work with incarcerated offenders are at a high risk of negative impacts on their physical and mental health.[114] Prison officers exposed to the risks to personal safety arising from interaction with volatile offenders are at an elevated risk of stress and burnout and secondary traumatic stress. This direct exposure to trauma has contributed to numerous negative personal and organisational consequences.[115]

Prison workers vicariously exposed to traumatic material can experience significant alterations in their emotional, physical, psychological, and spiritual lives.[116] The impacts are described as cumulative, pervasive, and insidious. Prison workers may experience emotional numbness and become cynical and pessimistic. This may result in them treating inmates inhumanely. Additionally, prison officers suffering from (vicarious) trauma may be at increased risk of family dysfunction, conflict and divorce, as well as maladaptive means of coping, which may include alcohol and substance abuse.[117]

Factors such as excessive traumatic workload[118] and length of time in one job[119] have increased the risk of developing traumatic responses. Incarcerated offenders are most often victims of trauma themselves; therefore, it is plausible for vicarious trauma to manifest in prison workers following exposure to graphic details of the offenders' crimes, as well as the traumatising events experienced by the offender.[120]

The effects of vicarious trauma often reach far beyond the workplace and into the prison workers' community.[121] Furthermore, prison workers suffering from (vicarious) trauma can have dire consequences for the outcomes of their offender clients, as we have seen in the Dylan Voller case, including a reduced likelihood of rehabilitation and a greater chance of recidivism. This, in turn, has financial, economic, and social impacts on the broader community.[122]

It is worth considering that corrective services staff often deal with offenders who are responsible for inflicting great pain and suffering on their victims, which leaves little space for compassion and empathy.[123] Further research needs to consider how prison management can intervene when signs of secondary stress and trauma first appear or prevent these symptoms from occurring in the first place.

Trauma and vicarious trauma in the Alice Springs community

According to local senior police officers, family dysfunction is the most prevalent cause of rising crime rates in Central Australia. Domestic violence assaults increased by 60% and property crime also by 60% in Alice Springs from August 2020 to August 2021, despite Strikeforce Viper, a specialist team of nineteen officers targeting property crime. Motor vehicle theft rose by 22 per cent. Youths damage at least one stolen vehicle a day, joyriding. On some nights, more than 30 cars are stolen. On some nights, there are 23 home invasions.

According to the *Northern Territory Safe Streets Audit* prepared by the Northern Institute at Charles Darwin University and the Australian Institute of Criminology in 2010, crimes where the offender is Aboriginal, and the victim is non-Aboriginal, are over-reported[124]

Superintendent Deutrom said in an ABC Alice Springs interview on 20 October 2021: "The reality [for] these children [is that] they're lucky if they have their own bed, they wouldn't have their own bedroom. The fridges, if they exist in their households, are not filled with food. The reality is that our prisons are full. Our youth detention centres are full. Our health system is clogged up with alcohol-related and harm issues. Our public housing system is jammed up. There's a great need for accommodation, and police are responsible and have the purview to maintain law and order."[125]

Witnessing this situation and being a victim of it traumatises the community. The outcries can be read on the Facebook page *Action for Alice 2020*.

Outcries for change were getting stronger toward the end of 2022.

Crime is one subject about which everyone has an opinion and on which anyone can claim to be an expert, but hardly anyone takes the time to ponder what is going on here. Hence, the problem is seldom thought through from its very roots.

This was clearly demonstrated again in May 2022, when Alice Springs Town Council attempted to declare the crime crisis an emergency at a special meeting and resolved to call on the Northern Territory government for help, only to discover that a council cannot declare a State of Emergency.

On the same day, the Property Council of Australia released a report to present to the Northern Territory government, seeking a response to worsening youth crime and unacceptable levels of anti-social behaviour in Alice Springs. [126]

In August 2022, Mayor Matt Patterson, on *Australia Overnight*, again called for help from State and Federal governments. Patterson talked about the need to turn back the end of the ban on alcohol in remote communities and to reinstall the cashless debit card.[127]

The Property Council conducted a survey in September 2022 as to why people are leaving the Northern Territory. The results show that crime and anti-social behaviour is the main reason. This severely affects businesses' ability to recruit workers.

What one does not hear mentioned very often is that this is a problem of history[128] and its resulting disadvantage.

The Department of Families, Housing and Communities announced a plan to reform youth detention in September 2022 and called it 'visionary'.[129] It is based partly on the Diagrama model in Spain, which is indeed a visionary model. If appropriately implemented, it could transform the youth detention system from one of the most backward in the world to one of the most innovative. However, the Department has many good policies; the problem is that they are highly under-resourced. The 55-page plan is unclear on how police and courts will be engaged in the model and how the current shortage of staff problems will be approached. Its text includes proposals such as: "Rostering staff with appropriate experience and training to support different cohorts and needs of young people at any given time. Providing overlaps of staff rostering to allow ample time for case management, debriefs on critical incidents, and handovers." This seems to describe standard minimum requirements rather than being 'visionary'. Likewise, the plan does not show how many staff would be considered a full complement, which is best practice in other institutional settings such as hospitals and childcare centres. Moreover, the plan speaks of assessment teams of psychologists, occupational therapists, speech pathology, neuropsychiatry and education, these assessment teams to include members of the family. However, the NT is currently grappling with a skills shortage across all these fields, and the plan does not specify how it will address this problem. Neither are time frames for implementation and evaluation frameworks provided. The detention centre will, against the recommendation of the 2016 Royal Commission, be built next to the Holtze Adult Correctional Facility.

Tourism Central Australia moved a motion in September 2022 urging the government to take immediate action to enforce law and order. They said crime is reaching "crisis levels, and tourists are opting to drive through Alice Springs instead of staying overnight because they fear for their safety." [130]

The same week, NT Police Southern Division Commander Craig Laidler said the statistics were worrying. "Particularly when I know the amount of work police are doing taking people into custody — and we are not seeing it as a deterrent," he said. "We are seeing many new, often young, faces among offenders. [131]

In September 2022, deputy mayor Eli Melky said it was time residents took matters into their own hands. 'People have suggested we find our own security for the town, including a dog squad,' he said. 'I think there is legitimacy in saying that we cannot always rely on government.' Was Melky suggesting vigilante action?

On 28 September 2022, Chief minister Fyles said crime in Alice Springs was 'appalling' and 'unacceptable' and that the government is open to new ideas and initiatives to tackle crime.[132]

In October 2022, the Don Dale correctional centre was highlighted by the United Nations Committee Against

Torture. Change The Record, the Human Rights Law Centre, and National Aboriginal Torres Strait Islander Legal Service made a joint submission to the Committee Against Torture. [133]

In October 2022, Mayor Paterson called for a dog squad trial in Alice Springs led by private security, despite strong objections from Police Minister and Lhere Artepe CEO Graeme Smith. They believe the approach will only shift crime elsewhere in town.[134]

In the same week, spit hoods (like used on Dylan Voller in the viral photo) on children in custody were banned, but new, 'more modern' ones were introduced. Details of the new models were not given.

In November 2022, The Northern Territory government announced reforms to raise the minimum age of criminal responsibility from 10 to 12 years old and overhaul its controversial mandatory sentencing policy for adults. The change falls short of the United Nations Committee on the Rights of the Child's recommendation of a minimum age of 14. In a statement, Attorney-General Paech said that putting 10 and 11-year-olds in contact with the justice system did not deter further reoffending. He did not address the fact that this is also the case for older children and young adults. Nor did he address the fact that the children on our streets are highly transient. He spoke of programs for the very young and their parents. He received many an eye roll on *Action for Alice 2020*, because programs by siloed NGOs and government agencies do not reach the most disadvantaged. A poll by the NT News showed that 76 per cent of respondents are against raising the age, 17 per cent are in favour, and 7 per cent think the age should be higher than 12.

In October of that year, business owners called for a curfew. 91 per cent of Alice Springs agreed with that idea in a poll in the NT News.[135] The question remains: who will police a curfew, and how? Curfew experiments worldwide have shown that they merely move the problem to other locations. The problem in Alice Springs is that people want to 'try' solutions. Trying is not good enough. The problem needs to be deeply analysed and solutions should be evidence-based, not based on the emotions of the moment.

On the 25th of that month, Melky tried to pass a motion in a council meeting to accept private funding for street patrols with dogs. Concerned members of the community forced Melky to withdraw the motion.

Trauma caused by the
law and law enforcement

The Dylan Voller case illustrates the trauma that law and law enforcement cause offenders.

Although many recommendations have been made for specific protection for Aboriginal people under police interrogation, few have been implemented. The Northern Territory police have introduced safeguards for Aboriginal suspects, in legislation and police standing orders. The most extensive effort to provide protection to Aboriginal suspects is the *Anunga Rules*. They are guidelines formulated by the Northern Territory Supreme Court in 1976 for the questioning of Aboriginal suspects. Although they have been copied into police guidelines, they have not been incorporated into legislation. They are in force as precedent.[136]

Volatile situations: The Rolfe Case

Volatile situations, such as the prison experiences of Dylan Voller or the shooting of Kumanjayi Walker in Yuendumu, may be caused by law enforcement workers being as (vicariously) traumatised as the offender.

During the Rolfe trial, a criminologist gave evidence that two of the three shots Rolfe fired at Walker were "excessive, unreasonable and unnecessary".[137] Did Rolfe suffer from symptoms of (vicarious) trauma that caused this (over)reaction? This question did not surface in court during the trial. This is not surprising, because psychological trauma is difficult to prove in court. The question, however, is an interesting one: was it (vicarious) trauma that made Rolfe so trigger-happy? The coronial inquest after the trial found that Rolfe was taking anti-depressants. During the same coronial inquest, text messages by Rolfe were found to be highly racist. [138]

Victim trauma

Reactions to crime vary from emotional and psychological impacts to physical symptoms.[139] Reactions may result in financial loss and tension within the family, which can lead to family breakdown. Being a victim of a crime may result in feelings of powerlessness, which impacts negatively on self-esteem and can lead to isolation and PTSD. Not sufficiently addressing trauma in a community may lead to *chronic post-traumatic stress disorder* in its members.

Australia has ratified the United Nation's Declaration of Basic Principles of Justice for Victims of Crime and Abuse of Power,[140] which describes the right of the victim to respect and recognition. It states that is important that victims are recognized as such and that their suffering as the result of a wrongful act against them is acknowledged. Procedures and communications should be "victim sensitive", and those interacting with victims should act with empathy and understanding. Examples of disrespectful treatment include setting a trial date without consulting the victim first; not providing the victim with privacy during examination; or addressing the victim in a blaming way. It is equally important that indirect victims, such as family members, are treated with respect.

Many victims of crime in Alice Springs felt their suffering was not recognised by the Gunner government, especially after he said: "There is nothing to see here. There is no crime crisis. Victims of crimes were in the wrong place in the wrong time. Crime numbers are going up everywhere. Businesses must protect their businesses sufficiently."[141]

The Declaration describes the protection of the victim. Processes should "minimize the inconvenience for victims", to *"protect their privacy, when necessary, and ensure their safety, as well as that of their families and witnesses on their behalf, from intimidation and retaliation."*

This clause is extremely relevant to the Northern Territory with its high percentage of victims of domestic violence. Victims may be at ongoing risk or may perceive that they are at ongoing risk from the offender and/or the friends and supporters of the offender. Victims may not feel able to report certain crimes if they perceive that their protection cannot be guaranteed. Victims' protection requires risk assessment. The police and correctional services play an important role in these. Victims must be protected against revictimization. Protocols should exist in cases of stalking, domestic violence, and sexual offences.[142]

The risk of recidivism is very high in the Northern Territory, hence robust risk reduction strategies are urgently called for.[143]

Victims must be protected from *secondary victimisation*, which is the harm that can be caused by those who respond to the victim[144] within the criminal justice system, health care settings, the media, social media and the community. In these settings, victims may be blamed or disbelieved. Victims often experience secondary victimisation during the criminal justice process by repeated and insensitive interviewing or having to face the offender. It is also recognised that training and guidelines in institutions that work with victims have the potential to reduce the risk of secondary victimisation.[145]

On social media, victims are often blamed for not hiding their car keys well enough, for leaving bicycles and motorbikes outside, etc., and thus "inviting" victimisation and revictimisation.

Paragraphs 14-17 of the Declaration state that "victims should receive the necessary material, medical, psychological, and social assistance through governmental, voluntary, community-based, and indigenous means. They should be informed of the availability of health and social services and other relevant assistance. Police, justice, health, and social services should receive training to sensitise them to the needs of victims and guidelines to ensure proper and prompt aid. In providing services and assistance to victims, attention should be given to those with special needs because of the nature of the harm inflicted." Early support may prevent complex problems, such as PTSD, depression, substance misuse, loss of employment and debt.

The victim's right to access to justice and fair treatment should be a central obligation for governments. Access to a procedural form of justice and fairness of proceedings implies the equitable application of justice procedures to victims.

Paragraphs 4-6 of the Declaration state that "judicial and administrative mechanisms should be established and strengthened to enable victims to obtain redress through formal or informal procedures that are fair, inexpensive, and accessible. Victims should be informed of their rights in seeking redress. The judicial system should inform victims of their role and the scope, timing, and progress of the proceedings and of the disposition of their cases; it should allow the views and concerns of victims to be presented to the accused. It should avoid delays in the disposition of cases and executing orders or decrees granting awards to victims. Mediation, arbitration and customary justice or indigenous practices should be utilised where appropriate to facilitate conciliation and redress for victims."

An important right of victims is the right to information. Victims should be informed at the earliest stage and throughout the criminal justice process about the victim's role in procedures. They should be provided with information about where they can get further support and compensation. It is essential to ensure that victims understand the information that is given to them, and they should be provided with a contact person with whom to discuss or clarify the information provided.

Procedural justice can be strengthened by training criminal justice system workers on trauma-informed practices and cultural competency, providing interpreting services for victims with limited language proficiency, and providing referral mechanisms that help victims access services, including medical and psychological assistance and social support.

Article 12 of the Declaration specifies that: *"when compensation is not fully available from the offender or other sources, States should endeavour to provide financial compensation to victims who have sustained significant bodily injury or impairment of physical or mental health as a result of serious crimes and the family, in particular dependents of persons who have died or become physically or mentally incapacitated as a result of such victimisation"*.

It is the primary obligation of the offender, not the

State, to redress the impact of crime *vis-à-vis* the victim. However, this does not occur when the offender is not identified or when the offender does not have the necessary funds. The Declaration encourages the establishment of funds for compensation to victims. Efficient and tailored compensation schemes can be cost-effective because they reduce costs associated with the long-term consequences of crime. When the impact of crime is left untreated, this comes at a high price for the individual *and* for society.

Victims of certain kinds of crime are more likely to report the crime than victims of other kinds of crime. In Australia, petty crimes, such as bicycle theft, often remain unreported. Car theft has a high likelihood of being reported because the victim is usually insured. Reasons for not reporting a crime in Alice Springs may include fear of retaliation; shame; a personal relationship between the victim and the offender; lack of trust in the criminal justice system; or for crimes with a relatively small impact, where the victim feels that the crime is not worth the effort of reporting.[146] If we may believe *Action for Alice 2020*, there is a conspicuous lack of trust in the justice system in Alice Springs.

To make victims' voices heard, Victim Impact Statements are read out in the trial. Such statements may aid in the recovery of the victim, make the offender aware of the impact of their crime, thereby contributing to rehabilitation, and may play a role in determining the sentence. The court has no obligation to follow the victim's preference, which may cause further frustration.

In Alice Springs, the general perception of the court is that offenders are "untouchable" and get away with a "slap on the wrist".[147]

NGOs and government organisations do not reach the youth on the street sufficiently

Offenders in Alice Springs may be surrounded by multiple services: a case manager in a NGO; a bed and a case worker at ASYASS; a youth outreach worker at YORET; a domestic violence worker with Tangentyere Council, and a substance misuse worker at DASA; St Joe's College may try to pick them up sometimes; they may be in a diversion program with The Gap Youth Centre; they may have a psychologist at Congress, and have a Territory Families Child Protection Case Worker. Still, weeks can go by in which they are not seen by any of these people because they are often highly transient, and it is difficult to locate them. Young people in foster care are obliged to go to school or be home at a certain hour – but who stops them if they skip school or walk out of the door in the middle of the night? Policymakers do not consider this enough. They do not know that their programs are not reaching the offender. More CCTV cameras and a curfew have proven to be ineffective at reducing crime overall.[148]

(Vicarious) trauma in lawyers and judges

In the early 1990s, Michael Kirby was famously the first to speak about the taboo of burnout, depression and suicide among lawyers and magistrates.[149]

An Australian study in 2008 found that criminal lawyers experience significantly higher levels of subjective distress, vicarious trauma, depression and stress than non-criminal lawyers.[150] This lends weight to the possibility that cases involving disadvantage, violence and vulnerability are more likely to give rise to stress. A more recent study confirms that judicial officers have a stress problem manifesting as non-specific psychological distress, burnout, secondary traumatic stress and alcohol use.[151]

Research also suggests that occupational burnout is a foreseeable consequence of judicial working conditions.[152]

Vicarious trauma features prominently in the academic literature on judicial stress[153] and points to the frequent exposure to violence, abuse and misery, coupled with the requirement to remain stoic. 83.6% of judicial officers report experiencing at least one symptom of secondary traumatic stress, and almost one-third scored in the range for PTSD. 30% reported risky levels of alcohol use, similar to Australian lawyers, and almost double that within the general population.[154]

Kozarov v Victoria[155]

Until very recently, it was difficult to hold workplaces accountable for the results of trauma in their workers because too much onus was placed on workers to prove their mental health condition. The recent *Kozarov* case may lead to a long overdue change. Solicitor Kozarov started a new job in Victoria in 2009. The subject matter of her cases was often extremely volatile. After two years in the job, she became mentally unwell and had to stop working. She was diagnosed with PTSD and argued that the work had made her sick. The workplace denied this. A long legal battle, where the Supreme Court initially found no reasonable foreseeability, ended in a High Court decision with hopeful implications regarding who is responsible when there is a psychiatric, rather than a physical, injury at work. In April 2022, two years after an initial Supreme Court win was overturned at appeal; the High Court found that the employer was responsible for the psychiatric injuries or was negligent. Its vicarious trauma policy established a duty of care, and the employer hadn't acted in accordance with it. Hence, the High Court ordered a substantial damages payout to Kozarov. This case has shifted the onus of proof back onto the employer to provide a safe workplace that looks after the mental health of its workers through appropriate policies and procedures. The case also has implications for police officers, prison officers, youth detention centre officers and social workers.

It is recognised that magistrates' working conditions are markedly more stressful than those of judges. Compared with judges, magistrates are burdened with higher caseloads, more significant time pressure, and both more routinisation and more unpredictability while having few administrative supports, more unrepresented parties, and less prepared counsel.[156]. In criminal matters, they carry the burden of deciding both verdict and sentence, whereas trial judges are responsible only for sentencing, while a jury takes care of the verdict. A combination of these factors translates into higher stress among magistrates.[157] Remote country magistrates may experience additional demands that can cause stress in terms of social isolation, driving time to remote locations, security risks, and complexity of work. Still, there has, to our knowledge, been no empirical investigation of the association between working location and judicial stress in Australia.

To develop responses and interventions to address the stress experienced by judicial officers, a better understanding of the drivers of this stress – and which judicial officers are experiencing the most stress – is required. A national study of judicial stress and well-being and occupational and wellbeing supports for magistrates and other judicial officers in high-volume, summary jurisdictions such as Alice Springs, in the form of judicial education, seems called for. Comparative research with other jurisdictions would seem helpful too.

Having PTSD or other trauma-related disorders is still a taboo to be cleared away in the police force and among prison workers. An Australian study found that criminal lawyers also experienced significantly higher levels of subjective distress, vicarious trauma, depression, and stress than did non-criminal lawyers.[158]

Disability in offenders

Research by the Australian Brain Injury Organisation shows that: "issues relating to non-disclosure, non-diagnosis, lack of sensitivity in assessment tools, lack of cultural relevance and cultural safety in both assessments and responses, and lack of specialised disability knowledge in the criminal justice system all contribute to the continued over-representation of Aboriginal people with disabilities in prison populations."[159] A lack of training in disability identification, lack of time and of cultural staff in prison were identified by the same research group.

Sustainable justice

According to Alexander de Savornin Lohman, the jurist and founder of the Centre for Sustainable Justice in the Netherlands, the purpose of justice is "to create, promote and maintain balanced, healthy and righteous interpersonal relationships." In Australia, the terms "non-adversarial justice" and "solution-focused justice" are used. The intention is the same: justice with a focus on improving inter-humane relations and resolving social issues; justice as a driving force to bring about improvements in our communities.[160]

Traditional justice, especially in the lower court, has come under mounting pressure because it is subject to expectations that cannot be realised: to provide just solutions and to ensure that we live in safe communities by putting an end to criminal behaviour, this being done by handing out punishments. These expectations are based on gut feelings within our communities. There is a substantial gap between what justice can offer and what our communities demand from justice. Moreover, the mystique and awe that still surround the justice system contribute to the fact that there is no balance between the demand and supply of justice.[161]

Justice is placed under further pressure because justice is delivered, as the Australian Chief Judge Dr John

Lowndes put it, 'on the sniff of an oily rag'. [162]

The need to fundamentally rethink the role of justice and the opportunities available to it is becoming increasingly apparent in communities like Alice Springs, where revolving-door justice is observed daily. The past few decades have seen innovations in several countries: for example, the Dutch Mediation Project that works in parallel with courts; the Drug Courts in the USA; New Zealand Restorative Justice, which is incorporated into criminal law; and intercultural law developed in Australia, where judges cooperated with Elders from Aboriginal communities; judge-led mediation in Canada; and 'gerichtliche Mediation' in Germany. In all these new forms of justice, the judge focuses on the future of the parties and on the community. This variety of examples shows that there is a wide range of options available for delivering justice.[163]

The concept of sustainable justice places these developments in a common framework, thereby highlighting the potential of justice as an instrument for improving the welfare of our communities. The sustainability concept raises questions such as: to what extent does the law provide constructive contributions to a sustainable society? Is it still suitable in the modern world for courts to reduce conflicts such as youth crime to legal issues? Sustainable justice focuses on the underlying problems, and the needs that are hidden behind negatively charged statements made by litigants or members of the community.

"The general principle of sustainable judging is to turn bad into good, contributing to social harmony and personal and societal development. This asks for reconsideration of some basic principles of law and justice concerning the function of judicial decision-making and punishment." [164] Sustainable forms of justice require a degree of juridical thinking that we have not been taught in law school.

A public-health issue

In September 1999, the Australian Institute of Criminology ran a round-table seminar on *Public Health Perspectives on Interpersonal Violence*. Crime *is* a public health issue. It shares common causes with ill-health, particularly the trauma resulting from disadvantage and poverty. Fear of crime is itself a cause of anxiety. Community development in education, parental education, and among minorities reduces crime and promotes better health, for example in reducing the effects of alcohol and illicit drugs. Interpersonal violence is widely accepted as a public-health problem rather than a matter for the criminal justice system. At an international level, violence is a focus of the work of the World Health Organisation and the United States Government's Centres for Disease Control and Prevention.

This book points out the importance of having a strong focus on the well-being of populations, along with use of public health data, to aid in the understanding of the underlying problems of crime and identifying solutions. In doing so, public health can make a substantial contribution to crime prevention and can cover a much broader spectrum than can the criminal justice system alone.

Seeing crime as part of the injury/trauma field of public health, with its focus on population-level risk factors, highlights the importance of intensive, intersectoral approaches to preventing and dealing with crime.[165]

Ny Anstalt

In Rafael Rowe's TV series World's Toughest Prisons, the episode Greenland, Prison in the Ice, shows a new state-of-the-art prison.

Ny Antalt is located in Nuuk, the capital of Greenland. The architecture is modern and features clean lines in Corten steel, concrete and glass that look out onto panoramic views. The cubes it consists of are stacked so that prisoners can see beyond the prison walls, and are decorated with nature-inspired designs by an Indigenous artist. This allows prisoners to enjoy the Northern light. The prison, built by the Danish firms Friis & Moltke and Schmidt, Hammer Lassen, operates like a village. Nestled in the Arctic landscape with views of fjords and mountains, it could easily be mistaken for an eccentric modern villa. This humane prison emphasises rehabilitating through positive design. However, it is more than an architectural achievement: it seeks to address and end a human-rights issue that has haunted Greenland for decades. It is designed to relax and disarm. Prison guards are members of Nuuk's community, and although newly arrived prisoners must strip and are frisked, the guards shake hands with every new prisoner and introduce themselves.

Prisoners are locked up in the cell block from 6 pm and in their cells from 9 pm. The daytime is filled with therapy, education, and rehabilitation activities. Prisoners who behave well are allowed to work outside the prison during the day to get used to having a job. The prisoners have "prison phones", mobile phones without a camera or an internet connection. They can call their friends and family with this and can receive calls from them any time. These calls are monitored. The prisoners are allowed to have visits from friends and family and to cook for them.

For exercise, the prisoners shovel snow in the community or on the prison grounds. If they behave well, they are invited to go on hunting trips to stay in touch with their heritage. Seal meat is butchered on the spot and taken back to the prison.

There are few guards on duty at any time. They mainly stay back in the high-tech control room, where the whole complex is visible on monitors. Lights and locks can be controlled from this area. The design itself has been used to manage security at the facility. The complex is designed over three levels which allow the guards to manage the flow of people between different areas and control which prisoners encounter each other. This reduces the possibility of violence. The guards do not carry weapons, which means they can develop better relationships with the prisoners. This is essential to the prisoners' rehabilitation.[166]

Ny Anstalt's running costs are around US$150,000 per prisoner per year. For those with shorter-term sentences, it offers a greater chance of successful rehabilitation. Nuuk is a small community, and eventually, the prisoners must return to that community. For this to be successful and to prevent future crime, this modern prison strives to promote change in each individual offender.[167]

The normality principle & principle of least infringement

Norwegian and Icelandic Correctional Services use the *normality principle*. No one serves their sentence under stricter circumstances than necessary. Offenders are placed in the lowest possible security regime. Prison should be a restriction of liberty but nothing more; that is, no other rights have been removed by the sentencing court. Offenders have all the same rights as other people, and life inside resembles life outside as much as possible. Offenders have the right to study and vote. Sentences are kept as short as possible. On average, they are no more than eight months long, and nearly 90% of sentences are for less than a year. The prison prepares inmates for reintegration by mimicking the outside world. Retributivism and punitive approaches to criminal behaviour are seen as stumbling blocks in the way of progress.[168]

Animals as therapists

Physicians and psychologists worldwide have recommended companion animals for all sorts of conditions, including blindness, deafness, recuperation from surgery, high blood pressure, chemical addiction, and a range of disorders associated with aging.

Animal-assisted therapy has been used as an effective

intervention for the elderly, those who have been physically or sexually abused, and people with chronic mental illness.

Animals are also used in prison settings. Ted Conover[169] found during his time as a correction officer at Sing Sing, that "even more than people on the outside, inmates appreciate pets" (p. 270). Johnson and Chernoff's analysis of poetry written by inmates[170] suggests that "perhaps the scarcity of opportunities to develop relationships with non-inmates and the difficulties inherent in connecting with fellow prisoners are responsible for the striking number of poems about the importance of animals" (p. 161). Robert Stroud, the Birdman of Alcatraz, cared for the birds that came flying onto the prison island. Pennsylvania inmate James Paluch (2004) writes about birds that wait for him, greeting him each morning (p. 23). He defends breaking the facility rule against taking food from the dining hall because "I take it for my babies . . . my bird friends" (p. 27). "Normally, they just swipe up the bread and fly away, but today they stay on the ground and look up at me as if to say 'Thanks'" (p. 200). Johnson and Chernoff observe that "animals as diverse as pigeons and lizards may respond to the prisoners' ministrations and seem to reward their care" (p. 161). The nature of relationships that develop between prison inmates and animals has not been researched in-depth, to our knowledge, but their therapeutic value has been recognised in many studies.

Most of the research regarding animals as therapy has been conducted with populations other than offenders.[171] Most developed seems to be the literature regarding the beneficial effects of animals on the elderly;[172] and around chronic and terminal illnesses.[173] Pets have successfully been introduced into psychiatric populations for whom "there is so much loneliness and rejection in an institution that pets can have a real impact".[174]

At the York Retreat in England, established in 1792 by a Quaker group,[175] farm animals were used to teach the psychiatric patients self-control. In 1867, epileptics hospitalized in Bethel, Germany, were treated with animal therapy. This centre uses pet therapy treatments to this day.[176] In the United States in the early 1940s, at the Army Air Corps Convalescent Hospital in Pawling, New York, men recovering from service-related injuries worked with farm animals as part of a regimen of non-stressful activities. [177]

Clinical research at the University of Maryland that ran from 1977 to 1979 and studied the effects of animals on patients with coronary heart disease found that divorced, single, and widowed men and women died from heart disease at higher rates than those who were married. The scientists examined variables such as neighbourhood, social encounters, the birthplace of parents, life changes, and measures of mood. It was pet ownership that best predicted who lived or died. After documenting the effects on heart disease, Beck and Katcher conducted an experiment designed to compare pet owners talking to a stranger with those interacting with their pets. They found that participants' blood pressure was highest when talking to the researcher and lower when at rest, but lowest when the participants were talking to and petting their animals. And "since that first conclusion, that unlike talking to people, talking to animals reduces stress and blood pressure, the validity of the observation has been confirmed by many other investigators" (p. 81).[178]

By recording the interactions, the researchers could watch people's facial expressions while talking with their animals. Pet owners generally speak to their animals "with softer, higher-pitched voices than normal, their conversation punctuated with simple questions . . . and with their attention fully on the animal to the exclusion of all else" (p. 82).[179]

And although in most social interactions, American men are viewed as engaging in touch less often than women, the same cannot be said about how the sexes relate to their pets. The researchers found that "men and women touched their dogs as frequently and for just as long. . . . There were no significant differences between the sexes" (P 89). Even the mere sight of an animal can reduce tension. In a series of experiments, Kutcher and a research partner had children come into a room with either a lone researcher or the researcher accompanied by a friendly dog. The children's blood pressure was lowest when the dog was present. Fish (present today in medical offices everywhere) were also found to have similar calming effects. The researchers explained their results with a seemingly simple fact: "We relax whenever any neutral visual event draws our attention outward and interrupts our ongoing train of thought." (P 110).

While Beck and Katcher were conducting their first experiments, other researchers were investigating the effects of companion animals in psychiatric treatment. The program at Lima State Hospital for the Criminally Insane (today Oakwood Forensic Center), in Ohio, established in 1975, remained one of the most oft-cited animals-assisted programs and was the first formal program to use a maximum-security population.[180]

The program was started after the unit director was struck by how the usually solitary and unresponsive patients coordinated their efforts to hide and feed an injured wild bird that one of them had come across. After several years, the program was evaluated by comparing patients on a unit with animals to those on one without animals. Both wards had comparable patients and were of equal levels of security. The patients with pets required "half as much medication, had drastically reduced incidents of violence and had no suicide attempts during the year-long comparison. The ward without pets had eight documented suicide attempts during the same year"

(P 232).[181]

Changes in psychology often accompany changes in behaviour. Improvements in both conduct and attendance were noticed after a dog made regular visits to a school for children with severe behavioural handicaps.

Arkow (1998) discusses several behavioural studies that further demonstrate the range of potential treatment effects in psychiatric populations. In one experiment, offenders with chronic mental illness were videotaped answering questions with and without a dog present. Patients spoke more words and responded more quickly when a dog was in the room. In another study, physically ill, depressed outpatients laughed more readily and maintained a sense of humour after becoming pet owners. The unconditional positive regard received from an animal can be of particular significance to prison inmates who have been identified as a population vulnerable to "social isolation that leaves people without the social or family support they need during a . . . crisis."[182] The companionship that develops is also a source of security in an adversarial environment.[183]

With animals, inmates are allowed to interact with a living being with no interest in their past actions or mistakes. Especially for males, who, it has been noted, "have few socially-acceptable outlets for touching and caressing," the mutual affection that a relationship with an animal provides can be therapeutic."[184] For inmates who live lives absent of touch and acceptance, animals can "stimulate a kind of love and caring that is not poisoned or inhibited by the prisoners' experiences with people"[185]

The fact that animals have relaxing and reassuring effects on people is reflected in how animals are increasingly used in everyday work. As airports have become increasingly tension-filled places, the presence of explosive-detecting canines can produce a calming effect, in addition to being more accurate than machines monitored by people. At Los Angeles International Airport, the dogs have been described as cheering people up and providing passengers with a sense of security: "Strolling through a terminal here with Jackson was like being with Julia Roberts on a crowded street. Nearly everyone who noticed her responded with a smile or an outstretched hand, followed by kissing sounds." [186]

The security officers who are partnered with dogs also report feeling more relaxed when on the job.

Given the beneficial physiological and psychosocial effects, it should be no surprise that animals have been incorporated into prison life. Despite their increased development, there are "abundant anecdotal and qualitative assessments but few controlled, empirically based studies" of the programs.[187]

In a review of the literature published by Correctional Services of Canada, animal therapy was found in the United States, Canada, England, Scotland,

Australia, and South Africa. In addition to using a wide variety of animals, these programs also encompass a range of program designs as well. Although dogs are the most common, this recent review reports that animals used in PAPs include wild animals, farm animals, and other domestic animals such as cats.[188]

There are several reasons prisons are increasingly implementing therapy animal programs. Primarily, the programs may be established to benefit a facility's inmates (Lai, 1998). They can also serve as a source of revenue for the prison. An additional benefit comes from the positive community relations fostered (Harkrader, Burke, & Owen, 2004). Inmates are viewed as engaging in positive work and as serving the community. Beyond the correctional benefits for individual offenders and the overall facility, the animals also contribute to a social issue when, for example, the program rescues unwanted pets that would otherwise be destroyed (Lai, 1998).

The great demand for working dogs has created a market where the large blocks of time available to prison inmates makes them ideal candidates to conduct the intensive and time-consuming training required for animals to go on to specialized service work.

One of the forerunners of therapy animal programs was the Purdy Treatment Center for Women, a maximum-security prison in Washington. It was here that a now standard program design was originated—teaching inmates to train dogs— with the help of a former inmate. 189

The arts in prison

The healing properties of the arts and sports have long been recognised in Alice Springs. They cause the town to be resilient in times of hardship. Collaboration between community members in these ields has proven to be highly effective. The Parrtjima light festival, the Anaconda mountain-bike race, the Finke Desert Race, the Beanie Festival, the NT Writers Festival, the Bush Bands Bash, Desert Mob, Desert Song and the Desert Festival are examples of it. The healing properties of both sports and the arts are easily transplanted into prisons and nosirps.

The National Pioneer Women's Hall of Fame, in conjunction with the Alice Springs Correctional Centre, presented *An Exhibition of Prisoner Art and Craft* in 2016.

Culture, care and control are the pillars of the Arrernte Community Boxing Academy. The discipline and focus of boxing provide young people in Alice with a strong support network and a place to manage struggles healthily and positively.

Tourism and its attractions in and around Alice Springs used to be another field where collaboration took place on a large scale. Tourists would come to Alice Springs, no matter what. When there were strikes in the aviation or railway industry, backpackers kept arriving on bicycles on camels and in dusty 4WDs. When I ran Alice's Secret, the smallest backpacker's hostel in Alice, in the 2010s, tourism was booming. There were art galleries everywhere and plenty of tours to choose from.

The decline of tourism and its attached industries began in 2009 when the Australian dollar was exceptionally high, and Asian countries began flying straight into Uluru (Alice used to be the gateway to Uluru). Galleries and other businesses gradually disappeared from the CBD, and many shops were left empty.

Crime and Covid gave tourism the final blow. Our once so vibrant CBD became a no man's land dominated by roller shutters.

Alice Springs is trying hard to get back on its feet. It is vital that modern, science-based solutions be found for the current crime crisis.

A normal life

Consider the case of Mick, described in a PhD thesis on Indigenous desistance from crime written by Kate Sullivan at the Australian National University in 2012: Mick was almost continuously in prison between 18 and 28. He was drug dependent and committed crimes to support his habit. When he was 26, he met his partner, Suzie. Back in prison at 28, Mick "had had enough" and began setting goals. When he turned 30, he "hit rock bottom". He turned to his father for help, and went to a detox centre, a residential rehabilitation program, and a methadone program. Suzie became pregnant. By 31 Mick was "leading a normal life" with one child but no job. His first goal, to stay off the drugs, was achieved. His subsequent goals were to keep out of prison, to stay out of trouble, to get some skills, to get a good job, to get his licence and to buy a car. His ultimate goals were to buy a house and get married. He wanted to be around for his kids. He wanted to experience a "normal life".[190]

Dylan Voller, in an interview with NITV in 2021, said: "I don't want just to be known as the boy in a restraint chair. I want to be known as a young man, a survivor, that broke out of a system like that and continues to fight. My dreams are to have a full-time job and live a normal life. I don't care about being rich. I don't care about being famous. I just want to be stable. Have my mental health, have my own house with my family, have a job, play sports, and continue doing the work that I'm doing, spreading awareness. Broken systems make broken kids, and our youth are our future." [191]

Endnotes

1   Woodburn Hyde, W 1916, 'The prosecution and punishment of animals and lifeless things in the middle ages and modern times', *University of Pennsylvania Law Review and American Law Register*, 64(7):696-730.

2   Olson, T 2009, *The hanging of Mary, a circus elephant*, University of Tennessee Press.

3   See Facebook page *Action for Alice 2020*.

4   Chlanda, R 2020, 'How our most troubled young people are falling through the cracks ... and some possible answers', *Alice Springs News*, 28 November.

5   *Mabo and others v Queensland* (No. 2) (1992) 175 CLR 1

6   *R v Jogee* [2017] AC 387

7   See: *Action for Alice 2020*

8   Pinker, S 2019, *Enlightenment now, the case for reason, science, humanism, and progress*, Kindle Edition edn., Penguin Press.

9   Griffith, M, Levy, N & Timpe, K 2016, *The Routledge Companion to Free Will*, Routledge Philosophy Companions, Taylor and Francis.

10   Forrest, P 2002, 'The Oxford handbook of free will', *Australasian journal of philosophy*, 80(4):542-542.

11   Harris, S 2013, *Free will*, Kindle edn., Free Press.

12   Bourget, D 2014, 'What do philosophers believe?', *Philosophical studies*, 170(3):465-500.

13   https://www.youtube.com/watch?v=9DKhc1pcDFM; https://www.youtube.com/watch?v=TaeJf-Yia3A

14 Fry, S 2019, *The four horsemen, Discussion that sparked an atheist revolution. Foreword by Stephen Fry*, Random House UK.

15 Chair of the Philosophy department at Smith College, visiting professor of Buddhist philosophy at Harvard Divinity School, professor of philosophy at Melbourne University and adjunct professor of philosophy at the Central Institute of Higher Tibetan Studies. Academicinfluence. com has identified him as one of the 50 most influential philosophers in the world over the past decade.

16 Harris, S 2022, *Making sense*, samharris.org

17 *United States v. Grayson*, 438 U.S. 41 (1978).

18 Dennett, D 2014, *Reflections on free will, Stop telling people that they don't have free will,*

https://www.samharris.org/blog/reflections-on-free-will

19 Dennett, D, *The nefarious surgeon, Stop telling people they don't have free will,*

https://bigthink.com/videos/daniel-dennett-on-the-nefarious-neurosurgeon/

20 Vohs, K D & Schooler, J W 2008, 'The value of believing in free will: Encouraging a belief in determinism increases cheating', *Psychological science*, 19(1):49-54. P 53.

21 Baggini, J 2010, 'Dan Dennett and the New Atheism', *Philosophers Magazine*, March.

22 See: Facebook: Action for Alice 2020.

23 Caruso, G 2017, *Public Health and Safety: The Social Determinants of Health and Criminal Behavior*, ResearchLinks Books; Caruso, GD 2014, '(Un)just deserts: The dark side of moral responsibility', *Southwest Philosophy Review*, 30(1):27-38.

24 Pereboom, D 2013, *Optimistic skepticism about free will,* The philosophy of free will: selected contemporary readings,

Oxford University Press.

25 McCay A 2019, *Free will and the law*, Kindle edn., Taylor and Francis.

26 Allsop, James, 2012, 'A life in the law: David Hargraves Hodgson, 10 August 1939', Speech, Farewell Ceremony for the Honourable Justice James Allsop AO Upon the Occasion of His Retirement as a Judge and President of the Court of Appeal of the Supreme Court of New South Wales, 5 June.

27 Hodgson, D 1993, *The mind matters: Conciousness and choice in a quantum world*, Oxford University Press.

28 Hodgson D 2012, *Rationality + Conciousness = Free Will*, Oxford University Press.

29 Deery O 2015, 'Rationality + Consciousness = Free Will, by David Hodgson', *Mind*, 124(493):347-351; Keaton, D 2012, *Hodgson, David. Rationality + consciousness = free will. (Brief article)*, American Library Association Choice, 0009-4978; Levy, N 2013, 'Hodgson, David, Rationality + Consciousness = Free Will', *Australasian journal of philosophy*, 91(1):183-192;

30 Griffith, M, Levy, N & Timpe, K 2016, *The Routledge Companion to Free Will*, Routledge Philosophy Companions, Taylor and Francis. Pp 396-410.

31 Griffith, M, Levy, N & Timpe, K 2016, *The Routledge Companion to Free Will*, Routledge Philosophy Companions, Taylor and Francis. Pp411-426

32 Muller, P E & O'Flaherty, WD 1982, *Karma and Rebirth in Classical Indian Traditions*, University of Hawaii Press, 0031-8221.

33 Vivekananda, S 1964, *The free soul*, 9 edn., vol. The Complete Works of Swami Vivekananda, Advaita Ashrama.

34 Kennett, J & McCay, A 2020, 'Do criminals freely

decide to commit offences? How the courts decide', *The Conversation AU*, October 16.

35 Packer, H 1968, *The limits of criminal sanction*, Stanford University Press.

36 Jones, M 2003, 'Overcoming the myth of free will in criminal law: The true impact of the genetic revolution', *Duke law journal*, 52(5):1031-1053.

37 Cragg, W 1992, *The practice of punishment: Towards a theory of restorative justice* Routledge.

38 Murphy, J 2020, 'An ancient remedy for modern ills: The prerogative of mercy and mandatory sentencing', *Monash University law review*, 46(3):252-284.

39 Mendel, RA 2000, *Less hype, more help: Reducing juvenile crime, what works and what doesn't* American Youth Policy Forum, Washingtom D.C.

40 United Nations, (General Assembly), 1999, International Covenant on Civil and Political Rights Treaty Series 660 (March): 195.

41 Lutham, R & Klippan, L 2016, 'From expected reoffender to trusted neighbor: Why we should rethink prisons.', *The Conversation*, August 14.

42 Holdsworth, SW 1957, *A history of English law*, 2 edn., vol. 8, Methuen.

43 Zacharski, M 2018, 'Mens rea, the Achilles' heel of criminal law', *The European legacy, toward new paradigms*, 23(1-2):47-59.

44 *He Kaw Teh v R* (1985) 157 CLR 523, 582.

45 Barnett, R & Hagel, J 1977, *Assessing the criminal*, Assessing the Criminal: Restitution, Retribution, and the Legal Process Ballinger Pub Co.

46   Van Ness, DW 1993, 'New wine and old wineskins: Four challenges of restorative justice', *Criminal law forum*, 4(2):251-276.

47   Dagger, R 1980, 'Restitution, punishment, and debts to society', in J Hudson & B Galaway (eds), *Victims, offenders, and alternative sanctions,*, Lexington Books.

48   Murphy, J 1988, 'Retributive Hatred: An essay on criminal liability and the emotions 2 ', paper presented to *Liability in law and morals*, Bowling green, Ohio, April 15-17.

49   Murphy, J 1988, 'Retributive Hatred: An essay on criminal liability and the emotions 2 ', paper presented to *Liability in law and morals*, Bowling green, Ohio, April 15-17.

50   Van Ness, DW 1993, 'New wine and old wineskins: Four challenges of restorative justice', *Criminal law forum*, 4(2):251-276.

51   Goldstein, AS 1982, 'Defining the role of the victim in criminal prosecution', *Mississippi law journal*, 52(3):515.

52   Thorpe, N 2020, 'Prison is no place for a child': Australia to discuss raising the age of criminal responsibility', *ABC News*, 26 July.

53   *Convention on the rights of the child* (1989) Treaty no. 27531. *United Nations Treaty Series*, 1577, pp. 3-178.

54   *Equal Opportunity Commission Act* 1986 (Cth).

55   *Minister of State for Immigration and Ethnic Affairs v Teoh* HCA 20, (1995) 183 <u>CLR</u> 273

56   *Family Law Act 1975* (Cth) S43

57   UN General Assembly, International Covenant on Civil and Political Rights, 16 December 1966, United Nations, Treaty Series, vol. 999, p. 171.

58   Pocock, J 2000, *State of denial: The neglect and abuse of*

Indigenous children In The Northern Territory, the Secretariat of National Aboriginal and Islander Child Care SNAICC Inc.,

59   Submitted by Felicity Gerry QC, Rebecca Tisdale, Julian R Murphy, and Julia Kretzenbacher to the Lord Chancellor and Secretary of State for Justice the Rt. Hon Robert Buckland QC to recommend to Her Majesty the Queen.

60   *Grieve v The Queen* [2014] NTCCA 2.

61   Gerry, Felicity et al. 2018, *Petition for Mercy in the Matter of Zak Grieve,* filed 20 July with the Northern Territory Administrator.

62   *NT Criminal Code Act 1983*, Division 2 Presumptions, cl 8; Cl 10; Division 3 Parties to Offences Cl 12 and Cl 13: Part II AA Division 4; Extensions of criminal responsibility: clause 43BG Complicity and common purpose.

63   Krebs, B 2015, 'Mens rea in joint enterprise: a role for endorsement? ', *Cambridge law journal,* 74(3):480-504; Krebs, B 2017, 'Accessory Liability: Persisting in error', *Cambridge law journal,* 76(1):7-11; Krebs, B 2018, 'Joint enterprise, murder and substantial injustice: The first successful appeal post-Jogee', *Journal of criminal law (Hertford),* 82(3):209; Phillips, M 2021, *Accessorial liability after Jogee. Edited by Beatrice Krebs. [Oxford: Hart Publishing, 2019. xiv + 272 pp. Hardback £70.00. ISBN 978-1-50991-889-8.],* Cambridge University Press, Cambridge, UK, 0008-1973.

64   Gerry, Felicity, QC, et al. 2020, 'Petition for Mercy in the Matter of Asher Johnson', Carmelite Chambers, London 30 July.

65   *R v Jogee* [2017] AC 387 ('Jogee').

66   *Ruddock v The Queen* [2016] UKPC 7.

67   Hemming, A 2011, 'In search of a model code

provision for complicity and common purpose in Australia', *University of Tasmania Law Review*, 30(1):53-89.

68 *Chan Wing-Siu v The Queen* [1985] AC 168 ('Chan Wing-Siu').

69 *Clayton v The Queen* (2006) 81 ALJR 439 ('Clayton').

70 Hulley, S 2021, 'Silence, joint enterprise and the legal trap', *Criminology & criminal justice*: 174889582199162.

71 Eades, D 2007, 'Cross examination of Aboriginal children : the Pinkenba case', *Indigenous law bulletin*, 6(25):11-13.

72 Murphy, J 2020, 'An ancient remedy for modern ills: The prerogative of mercy and mandatory sentencing', *Monash University law review*, 46(3):252-284.

73 Gerry et al. 2019, 'Petition for Mercy in the Matter of Zak Grieve' (20 July)

74 Frank, J 1930, *Law and the modern mind*, Transaction Publishers.

75 Priel, D 2020, 'Law is what the judge had for breakfast: A brief history of an unpalatable idea', *Buffalo law review*, 68(3):899.

76 Prinz, J J 2007, *The emotional construction of morals*, Oxford University Press.

77 Danziger, S 2011, 'Extraneous factors in judicial decisions', *Proceedings of the National Academy of Sciences - PNAS*, 108(17):6889-6892.

78 Chen, DL & Loecher, M 2019, 'Mood and the Malleability of Moral Reasoning ', *SSRN*, (September 21).

79 Deadly Connections, Community and Justice Services, Submission 35, in: Australian Law Reform Commission 2021, Review of Judicial Impartiality, Final

Report.

80   ALRC Report 138 December 2021, *Without fear or favour: Judicial impartiality and the law on bias.*

81   Filippi, PD 2018, *Blockchain and the law: The rule of code*, Harvard University Press.

82   https://rm.coe.int/ethical-charter-en-for-publication-4-december-2018/16808f699c

83   https://www.courtinnovation.org/programs/youth-court

84   *Northern Territory Justice Agreement 2021-2027* 2021.

85   https://tfhc.nt.gov.au/__data/assets/pdf_file/0009/1132200/northern-territory-youth-detention-centres-model-of-care.pdf

86   *The Queen v Rolfe (No 5)* [2021] NTSCFC 6

87   Goldflam, R 2011, 'The white elephant in the room : juries, jury arrays and race', *Indigenous law bulletin*, 7(26):35-38.

88   *The Queen v Woods* [2009] NTCCA 2

89   *Juries Act* 1962 (NT)

90   *Racial Discrimination Act* 1975 (Cth)

91   *The Queen v Rolfe* [2010] NTSC 69 (unreported, Mildren ACJ, Blokland and Reeves JJ, 14 December 2010).

92   Northern Territory Law Reform Committee, *Reviews of the Juries Act*, Report 37, 2013.

93   Northern Territory Law Reform Committee, *Two justice systems working together – Report on the Recognition of local Aboriginal law in sentencing and bail*, Report 46, 2020.

94   Northern Territory Law Reform Committee, *Mandatory sentencing and community-based sentencing options*, Final Report 47, 2021.

95   Hiley, G 2019, 'Trail by peers?', paper presented to *JCA Cooloquium 2019*, Darwin, 7-9 June.

96   Anthony, T 2017, 'Blinded by the white: A comparative analysis of jury challenges on racial grounds', *International Journal for Crime, Justice and Social Democracy*, 6(3):25-46.

97   Goldflam, R 2011, 'The white elephant in the room : juries, jury arrays and race', *Indigenous law bulletin*, 7(26):35-38.

98   MacKay, M 2021, 'Remote residents left to represent themselves, as Legal Aid stops accepting bush court files', *ABC News*, 14 April.

99   Jonscher, S & Martin, X 2022, 'NT Police say children as young as eight taking part in Alice Springs crime wave', *ABC News*, 26 June.

100   Maté, G 2004, *When the body says No: The cost of hidden stress*, Vintage; Maté, G 2008, *In the realm of hungry ghosts: Close encounters with addiction*, Knopf .

101   Van de Kolk, B 2014, *The Body keeps the score: Brain, mind, and body in the healing of Trauma*, Viking.

102   Experiences, processes and systems that support, on the one hand, self-destructive beliefs and behaviours and, on the other hand, strength in survival.

103   Bevis, M, Atkinson, J, McCarthy, L & Sweet, M 2020, *Kungas' trauma experiences and effects on behaviour in Central Australia (Research report, 03/2020)*.

104   Averill, Z & Parkinson, A 2022, 'NTPA survey: 80 per cent of police vote against Commissioner Jamie Chalker', *NT News*, August 12: Averill, Z, Parkinson, Amanda, & Roberts Jessica 2022, 'NT Police use spit hoods on children 27 times over four years', *NT News*, 27 July.

105   Averill, Z & Parkinson, A 2022, 'NTPA

survey: 80 per cent of police vote against Commissioner Jamie Chalker', *NT News*, August 12.: Averill, Z, Parkinson, Amanda, & Roberts Jessica 2022, 'NT Police use spit hoods on children 27 times over four years', *NT News*, 27 July.

106   Monks, H, Mandzufas, J., and Cross, D. 2022, *The impact of poverty on the developing child: a narrative view*, Institute for Social Science Research, The University of Queensland,

107   Bower, C 2018, *Nine out of ten young people in detention found to have severe neuro-disability*, Telethon Kids Institute, https://www.telethonkids.org.au/news--events/news-and-events-nav/2018/february/young-people-in-detention-neuro-disability/

108   Web Page: <Australian Neurolaw Database> Accessed 21 November 2021.

109   Halloran, M 2004, 'Cultural maintenance and trauma in indigenous Australia', *E law : Murdoch University electronic journal of law*, 11(4):1-12.

110   https://www.youtube.com/watch?v=FVxjuTkWQiE

111   ABCTV 2016, *Four Corners*, 1 August.

112   Wood, D 2022, 'No defined strategy to deal with mental health': NTPFES well-being review delayed, as two more police officers take their lives', *NT Independent*, 13 June.

113   Wood, D 2021, 'No defined strategy to deal with mental health': NTPFES well-being review delayed, as two more police officers take their lives', *NT Independent*, June 13.

114   Armstrong, Gs & Griffin, ML 2004, 'Does the job matter? Comparing correlates of stress among

treatment and correctional staff in prisons', *Journal of Criminal Justice*, 32(6):577-592; Johnson, NS 2016, *Secondary traumatic stress, compassion fatigue, and burnout: How working in correctional settings affects mental health providers [Doctoral Dissertation]*, Antioch University; Lambert, EG, Hogan, NL, Griffin, Ml & Kelley, T 2015, 'The correctional staff burnout literature. ', *Criminal Justice Studies*, 28(4):397-443; Munger, T, Savage, T & Panosky, DM 2015, 'When caring for perpetrators becomes a sentence: Recognizing vicarious trauma.', *Journal of Correctional Health Care*, 21(4):365-374.

115   Finn, P 1998, 'Correctional officer stress: A cause for concern and additional help', *Federal Probation*, 62(2):65-74; Johnson, NS 2016, *Secondary traumatic stress, compassion fatigue, and burnout: How working in correctional settings affects mental health providers [Doctoral Dissertation]*, Antioch University; Thomas, B 2012, *Predictors of Vicarious Trauma and Secondary Trauma Among Correctional Officers [Unpublished dissertation]*. , Philadelphia College of Osteopathic Medicine.

116   McCann, il & Pearlman, LA 1990, 'Vicarious traumatization: A framework for understanding the psychological effects of working with victims', *Journal of Traumatic Stress*, 3(1):131-149.

117   Campbell, J & Bishop, A 2019, 'The impact of caseload and tenure on the development of vicarious trauma in Australian corrective services employees ', *Psychotherapy and Counselling Journal of Australia*, (12).

118   Cunningham, M 2003, 'Impact of trauma work on social work clinicians: Empirical findings', *Social Work*, 48(4):451-459.

119   Lewis, KR, Lewis, LS & Garby, TM 2013, 'Surviving the trenches: The personal impact of the job on probation officers', *American Journal of Criminal Justice*, 38(1):67-84.

120   Berg, MT, Stewart, EA, Schreck, CJ & Simons, RL 2012, 'The victim–offender overlap in context: Examining the role of neighborhood street culture', *Criminology*, 50(2):359-390; Jennings, WG, Zgoba, KM, Maschi, T & Reingle, JM 2014, 'An empirical assessment of the overlap between sexual victimization and sex offending', *International journal of offender therapy and comparative criminology*, 58(12):1466-1480.

121   Meffert, SM, Henn-Haase, C, Metzler, TJ, Qian, M, Best, S, Hirschfeld, A & Marmar, CR 2014, 'Prospective study of police officer spouse/partners: A new pathway to secondary trauma and relationship violence?', *PLOS ONE*, 9(7):1-8.

122   Morash, M, Kashy, DA, Smith, SW & Cobbina, J 2016, 'The connection of probation/parole officer actions to women offenders' recidivism', *Criminal Justice and Behavior*, 43(4):506-524.

123   Nelson, M, Herlihy, B & Oescher, J 2002, 'A survey of counselor attitudes towards sex offenders', *Journal of Mental Health Counseling*, 24(1):51-67.

124   Morgan, A, Williams, E, Renshaw, L & Funk, J 2010, *Northern Territory Safe Streets Audit*.

125   Brash, S & Haskin, E 2021, 'Family dysfunction key to rising crime rates in Central Australia, say police', *ABC Alice Springs*, 20 October.

126   Smith, C & Sumpton, D 2022, 'Alice Springs Town Council passes motion declaring crime crisis an 'emergency'', *NT News*, 18 May.

127   https://omny.fm/shows/mike-williams-overnight/matt-patterson-re turns?fbclid=IwAR1W1RKlp39hFkoGr_ fobUAy0ueWmkZ4ZZikRTReqk7SZMyEjs5lhpYScT0

128   Eric Turner in a private conversation.

129   https://tfhc.nt.gov.au/__data/assets/pdf_file/0009/1132200/northern-territory-youth-detention-centres-model-of-care.pdf

130   Brash, S & Haskin, E 2021, 'Family dysfunction key to rising crime rates in Central Australia, say police', *ABC Alice Springs*, 20 October.

131   Brash, S & Haskin, E 2021, 'Family dysfunction key to rising crime rates in Central Australia, say police', *ABC Alice Springs*, 20 October.

132   https://www.mix1049.com.au/360-with-katie-woolf/latest-from-katie/114454-crime-in-alice-springs-appalling-and-unacceptable-says-chief-minister?

133   Parkinson, A 2022, 'on Dale facing potential United Nation's Committee Against Torture investigation', *NT News*, 7 October; Averill, Z & Parkinson, A 2022, 'NTPA survey: 80 per cent of police vote against Commissioner Jamie Chalker', *NT News*, August 12; Averill, Z, Parkinson, Amanda, & Roberts Jessica 2022, 'NT Police use spit hoods on children 27 times over four years', *NT News*, 27 July.

134   ABC News, Alice Springs Facebook page 2022, 13 October.

135   Smith, C & Sumpton, D 2022, 'Alice Springs Town Council passes motion declaring crime crisis an 'emergency'', *NT News*, 18 May.

136   *R v Anunga* (1976) 11 ALR 412.

137   *The Queen v Rolfe* (No 3) [2021] NTSCFC 6.

138   Jonscher, S 2022, ''Blatantly racist' and 'disgraceful' texts between Zachary Rolfe and colleagues read out at Kumanjayi Walker inquest.', *ABC News*, 15 September.

139   Wedlock, E & Tapley, J 2016, *What works in supporting victims of crime: A rapid evidence assessment.*

140   UN *General Assembly, Declaration of Basic Principles of Justice for Victims of Crime and Abuse of Power:* resolution / adopted by the General Assembly, 29 November 1985, A/RES/40/34.

141   See *Action for Alice 2020*, February-April 2022, comments.

142   Kropp, R & Hart, S 2000, 'The spousal assault risk assessment (SARA) guide: Reliability and validity in adult male offenders', *Law and Human Behavior*, 24:101-118.

143   Bonta, J, Blais, J & Wilson, H 2014, 'A theoretically informed meta-analysis of the risk for general and violent recidivism for mentally disordered offenders', *Aggression and Violent Behavior*, 19:278-287.

144   Campbell, R & Sheela, R 1999, 'Secondary victimization of rape victims: Insight of mental health professionals who treat victims', *Violence and Victims*, 14:261-275.

145   UN *General Assembly, Declaration of Basic Principles of Justice for Victims of Crime and Abuse of Power:* resolution / adopted by the General Assembly, 29 November 1985, A/RES/40/34.

146   Action for Alice 2020, Facebook page analysis by the author.

147   Action for Alice 2020, Facebook page February-April 2022.

148   Chlanda, R 2020, 'How our most troubled young people are falling through the cracks … and some possible answers', *Alice Springs News*, 28 November.

149   Kirby, M 1995, 'Judicial stress: An

unmentionable topic', *Australian Bar Review*, 13:101-115; Kirby, M 1997, 'Judicial stress – an update', *Australian Law Journal* 71(774).

Vrklevski, LP & Franklin, J 2008, 'Vicarious trauma: The impact on solicitors of exposure to traumatic material', *Traumatology (Tallahassee, Fla.)*, 14(1):106-118.

151   Schrever, C 2019, 'Australia's first research measuring judicial stress: What does it mean for judicial officers and the courts?', *Judicial officers bulletin*, 31(5):41-43.

152   Miller, MK, Greene, EL, Dietrich, H, Chamberlain, J & Singer, JA 2008, 'How emotion affects the trial process', *Judicature*, 92(2):56; Miller, MK, Greene, EL, Dietrich, H, Chamberlain, J & Singer, JA 2008, 'How emotion affects the trial process', *Judicature*, 92(2):56; Hagen, T & Bogaerts, S 2014, 'Work Pressure and Sickness Absenteeism Among Judges', *Psychiatry, psychology, and law*, 21(1):92-111.

153   James, LC & Richardson, S 2013, 'Medical Communication', *Medical writing (Leeds)*, 22(1):65-66.

154   Schrever, C 2019, 'Australia's first research measuring judicial stress: What does it mean for judicial officers and the courts?', *Judicial officers bulletin*, 31(5):41-43.

155   *Kozarov v Victoria* [2022] HCA 12.

156   Anleu, SR & Mack, K 2017, 'Impartiality and emotion in judicial work', *Judicial officers bulletin*, 29(3):21-24.

157   Kirby, M 1995, 'Judicial stress: An unmentionable topic', *Australian Bar Review*, 13:101-115.

158   Vrklevski, LP & Franklin, J 2008, 'Vicarious trauma: The impact on solicitors of exposure to traumatic material', *Traumatology (Tallahassee, Fla.)*, 14(1):106-118.

159   Synapse, AsBIO 2021, *Assessing the disability*

185

needs of Indigenous prisoners. P7.

160   de Savornin Lohman, AF 2011a, *Explanatory notes for sustainable justice,* Centre for Sustainable Justice.

161   de Savornin Lohman, AF 2011a, *Explanatory notes for sustainable justice,* Centre for Sustainable Justice;

162   Twelfth AIJA Oration in Judicial Administration The People's Court, 2002, 'Into the Future', delivered by Ian L Gray, Chief Magistrate of Victoria at The Banco Court, Supreme Court of Queensland George Street, Brisbane, 22 June.

163   de Savornin Lohman, AF 2011a, *Explanatory notes for sustainable justice,* Centre for Sustainable Justice; de Savornin Lohman, AF 2011b, 'Working document on sustainable justice ', paper presented to *Werkdocument Duurzame Rechtspraak,* Montaigne Center for Judicial Administration and Conflict Resolution, Utrecht, the Netherlands, 2 December.

164   Charter of Sustainable Justice 2015.

165   McDonald, D 2000, 'Violence as a public health issue', *Australian Institute of Crimonology, Trends and issues in crime and criminal justice,* 163 (July).

166   Sarah Lazarus, Humane prison to bring Greenland's most dangerous criminals home, CNN, March 17, 2018. Web page: < https://edition.cnn.com/2018/03/16/europe/humane-prison-greenland/index.html> Accessed on 7 August 2021.

167   Netflix, 2020, The world most Dangerous prisons, Sries 5, prison in the snow.

168   Caruso, G 2017, *Public Health and Safety: The Social Determinants of Health and Criminal Behavior,* ResearchLinks Books.

169   Conover, T, Newjack: *Guarding Sing Sing,* New

York: Random House, 2000.

170   Johnson, R, and Chernoff N, 2002, 'Opening a Vein: Inmate Poetry and the Prison Experience', The Prison Journal 2002 82:2, 141-167.

171   Beck, A & Katcher A 1996, *Between pets and people: The importance of animal companionship*, West Lafayette, IN: Purdue University Press; Moneymaker, J & Strimple, E *1991,* 'Animals and inmates: A sharing companionship behind bars,' *Journal of Offender Rehabilitation, 16, 133-152.*

172   (e.g., Baun & McCabe, 2000; Perelle & Granville, 1993; Siegel, 1990)

173   (e.g., Batson, McCabe, Baun, & Wilson, 1998; Becker, 2002) and AIDS patients (e.g., Gorczyca, Fine, & Spain, 2000).

174   Lee, D. 1987, 'Companion animals in institutions. In P. Arkow (Ed.), The loving bond: Companion animals in the helping professions' Saratoga, CA: R & E. Pp. 223-246. P 232.

175   Beck, A & Katcher A 1996, *Between pets and people: The importance of animal companionship*, West Lafayette, IN: Purdue University Press; Graham, B 2000, *Creature comfort: Animals that heal.* Amherst, NY: Prometheus Books; Lai, J 1998, *Pet facilitated therapy in correctional institutions.* Paper prepared for

Correctional Services of Canada by Office of the Deputy Commissioner for Women.

176   Beck, A & Katcher A 1996, *Between pets and people: The importance of animal companionship*, West Lafayette, IN: Purdue University Press.

177   P. Arkow (Ed.), The loving bond: Companion animals in the helping professions' Saratoga, CA: R & E. Pp. 223-246; Beck, A & Katcher A 1996, *Between pets and people: The*

importance of animal companionship, West Lafayette, IN: Purdue University Press.

178   Beck, A & Katcher A 1996, *Between pets and people: The importance of animal companionship,* West Lafayette, IN: Purdue University Press.

179   Beck, A & Katcher A 1996, *Between pets and people: The importance of animal companionship,* West Lafayette, IN: Purdue University Press.

180   Graham, B 2000, *Creature comfort: Animals that heal.* Amherst, NY: Prometheus Books; Lai, J 1998, *Pet facilitated therapy in correctional institutions.* Paper prepared for Correctional Services of Canada by Office of the Deputy Commissioner for Women; Moneymaker, J & Strimple, E *1991,* 'Animals and inmates: A sharing companionship behind bars,' *Journal of Offender Rehabilitation, 16, 133-152;* Lee, D. 1987, 'Companion animals in institutions. In P. Arkow (Ed.), The loving bond: Companion animals in the helping professions' Saratoga, CA: R & E. Pp. 223-246. P 232.

181   Lee, D. 1987, 'Companion animals in institutions. In P. Arkow (Ed.), The loving bond: Companion animals in the helping professions' Saratoga, CA: R & E. Pp. 223-246. P 232.

182   Hart, L 2000, 'Psychosocial benefits of animal companionship.' In A. Fine (Ed.), Handbook on animal-assisted therapy: Theoretical foundations and guidelines for practice (pp. 59-78). San Diego, CA: Academic Press. P 60.

183   Arkow (Ed.), The loving bond: Companion animals in the helping professions' Saratoga, CA: R & E. Pp. 223-246; Lee, D. 1987, 'Companion animals in institutions. In P. Arkow (Ed.), The loving bond: Companion animals in the helping professions' Saratoga, CA: R & E. Pp. 223-246. P 232.

184   Arkow (Ed.), The loving bond: Companion animals in the helping professions' Saratoga, CA: R & E. Pp. 223-246. P 2.

185   Beck, A & Katcher A 1996, *Between pets and people: The importance of animal companionship,* West Lafayette, IN: Purdue University Press. P 153.

186   Sterngold, J, 2002, 'In Los Angeles, a traveler's best friend'. *The New York Times, March 21, p. A24.*

187   Lai, J 1998, *Pet facilitated therapy in correctional institutions.* Paper prepared for

Correctional Services of Canada by Office of the Deputy Commissioner for Women. P 4.

188   Lai, J 1998, *Pet facilitated therapy in correctional institutions.* Paper prepared for

Correctional Services of Canada by Office of the Deputy Commissioner for Women. P 4.

189   Arkow (Ed.), The loving bond: Companion animals in the helping professions' Saratoga, CA: R & E. Pp. 223-246; Graham, B 2000, *Creature comfort: Animals that heal.* Amherst, NY: Prometheus Books; Lai, J 1998, *Pet facilitated therapy in correctional institutions.* Paper prepared for Correctional Services of Canada by Office of the Deputy Commissioner for Women; Moneymaker, J & Strimple, E *1991,* 'Animals and inmates: A sharing companionship behind bars,' *Journal of Offender Rehabilitation, 16, 133-152;* Lee, D. 1987, 'Companion animals in institutions. In P. Arkow (Ed.), The loving bond: Companion animals in the helping professions' Saratoga, CA: R & E. Pp. 223-246.

190   Sullivan, K 2012, *Motivating and maintaining desistance from crime: Male Aboriginal serial offender's experience of "going good",* Doctorate of Philosophy thesis, Australian National

University. Pp 221-226.

191   NITV 2021, *'I don't want to just be known as the boy in a restraint chair' - Dylan Voller*, 10 November.

Chapter Two – How we think about crime

This chapter presents the reader with an overview of bizarre practices in courts throughout the centuries. It then looks at three iconic cases in the Northern Territory. Finally, it presents the reader with a thought experiment regarding blameworthiness.

The punishment of lifeless things, plants and animals

Ancient Greece

In ancient Greece, municipalities had a *Prytaneum*, an administrative centre. Here, throughout classical antiquity, animals and inanimate things were subjected to legal trials. These legal processes may have originated in agricultural festivals where an axe was put on trial as the slayer of an ox, in a highly complex ritual.

The athlete Theagenes used to go to his bronze statue on the island of Thasos and whip it as a way of punishing opponents in athletic competitions. The statue, tilted off-balance by the whipping, fell onto Theagenes and killed him. The statue was prosecuted for murder by Theagenes' sons. The Thasians found the statue guilty and cast it into the sea, beyond their borders.[1].

The Prytaneum was the Town Hall of every Greek town, as much as the Lower Court is in contemporary Alice Springs. It represented the values and unity of the community. One of the important functions of the Prytaneum was as a location to hold murder trials. Many Greek writers mention these trials. "If a murderer was unknown or could not be found, he was nevertheless tried; also lifeless things, such as stones, beams, pieces of iron, etc., which had caused the death of a man by falling upon him, were tried here, as well as animals which had similarly been the cause of death.".[2]

The Athenian statesman and orator Demosthenes said in his oration Κατα Αριστοκρατους (Against Aristocrates (of Sparta)): "If a stone or a piece of wood or iron or anything similar falls and strikes a man, and the person who threw the thing is unknown, but the thing which killed the man is known and in the hands of the judges, it is tried at the Prytaneum. If it is not right that inanimate and senseless things when under such a charge, be left untried, it is surely impious that a man who is possibly innocent but who, even if guilty, is at all events a being, should be adjudged without a hearing and be given to his accusers."[3]

Plato gives the law in full. He exempts its applicability to thunderbolts or "other fatal darts from gods" and makes no distinction between "men falling upon a thing or the thing falling upon him."[4] Plato also refers to animals subject to trial in the Prytaneum: "And if a beast of burden or other animal cause the death of anyone, except in case of anything of that kind happening in the public contests, the kinsmen of the deceased shall prosecute the slayer for murder, and the wardens of the country, such, and so many as the kinsmen appoint, shall try the cause, and let the beast, when condemned, be slain by them and cast beyond the borders."[5]

To understand the issues raised by cases like this, we must take into account the Greek view of murder. The second case (and probably the third) was merely an amplification of the first; if the human murderer could not be found, the thing or animal that had been the agent in the slaying, if it could be found, had to be tried. Not only had a crime been committed; the community had been defiled. Some person or thing was to blame and must be punished to expunge the pollution.

A boy was killed by running into the path of a javelin that had been hurled by a youth practising javelin-throwing in the gymnasium. The boy's father accused the youth of accidental homicide. The question to be decided was, who was to blame: the boy, the youth, or the javelin? If it was either of the first two, the case would be referred to the court of the Palladium, where cases of unpremeditated murder were tried: if it was the javelin, the case would be assigned to the Prytaneum.[6]

Ancient Persia

The ancient Persians treated animals as responsible beings. "In the religious laws of the Vendidad, if a mad dog was not muzzled and, without barking, wounded a man or sheep, it was decreed that it be punished for the wounding as if it had tried to commit murder with premeditation; this punishment took the form of a progressive mutilation corresponding with the number of persons or beasts bitten, beginning with the loss of the ears and ending with the amputation of the tail. Insanity could not be pleaded for the dog in exculpation of his deed." [7]

In the Bible

The book of *Exodus*[8] recounts how the Hebrews put on trial an ox that gored a human to death. The ox was to be stoned, and its flesh could not be eaten. The owner was acquitted unless it was shown that the ox had been in the habit of goring and had not been restrained; in this case, both ox and owner were put to death.[9]

Middle Ages – Europe

In medieval Europe, insects and rodents and cocks were brought before the court to face charges. "All kinds of animals were condemned and put to death. The list of prisoners comprises a miscellaneous crew, including asses, beetles, bloodsuckers, bulls, caterpillars, cockchafers, cocks, cows, dogs, dolphins, eels, field mice, flies, goats, grasshoppers, horses, locusts, mice, moles, rats, serpents, sheep, slugs, snails, swine, termites, turtledoves, weevils, wolves, worms and nondescript vermin."[10]

We have records from the ninth century showing that domestic animals, such as pigs and dogs, were tried in the criminal courts like men and, if found guilty, were put to death, while wild animals of the noxious sort, such as rats and locusts were tried in the ecclesiastical courts. Their punishment was either death or excommunication and banishment by formal decree.[11]

The legal annals of the ecclesiastical court of Autun in France in 1522 record a trial that was won by the jurist Bartholomew Chassenee. A group of rats were brought to trial for having eaten and destroyed local barley crops, but the rats failed to appear on the day of the trial.

Their advocate Chassenee pleaded that the summons had been too local and of too individual a character and that not some but all the rats of the diocese should be summoned. In consequence, the bishop summoned every rat to appear on a certain day; but still no rats appeared. Chassenee argued that because the rats were spread over many villages, their migration required more time. Delay in the proceedings was granted, but still... no rats! This time their absence was excused by their advocate "on the ground that a summons implied full protection to the parties summoned while coming and going; but that his clients, though anxious to appear, were afraid of their natural enemies the cats, which belonged to the plaintiffs. He therefore demanded that the plaintiffs be bonded under penalty to keep their cats from frightening the rats. This plea seemed to the court to be valid, but the plaintiffs demurred, and in consequence the period for the appearance of the rats was adjourned sine die and judgment was given by default." (Woodburn Hyde 1916, p. 707 University of Pennsylvania Law Review).

In Savignysur-Etang, in Bourgogne, France, in 1457, a sow, together with her six pigs, was charged for murdering and partly devouring an infant. The sow was found guilty and sentenced to death by hanging, though her piglets were pardoned, because of their youth and innocence and the fact that their mother had set them a bad example, and most importantly, because proof of their complicity could not be found. (Woodburn Hyde 1916, p. 707 University of Pennsylvania Law Review).

Act 4, Scene 1 of Shakespeare's *Merchant of Venice*, contains the following lines:
> "*Thy currish spirit*
> *Govern'd a wolf, who, hang'd for humnan slaughter*
> *Even from the gallows did his fell soul fleet.*"

Men found guilty of? the crime of bestiality, *offensa cujus nominatio crimen est*, were put to death with the animal. At Montpellier in France, in 1565,, a man and a mule were burnt alive for this offence; as the mule objected, its feet were first cut off. This type of punishment was also inflicted in the US. In the Cotton Mather records of June 6, 1662, in New Haven, Connecticut, a man by the name of Potter was hanged for this crime together with a cow, two heifers, three sheep, and two sows. The legislation that made this possible was based on the Mosaic law.[12] (Woodburn Hyde 1916, pp. 709, University of Pennsylvania Law Review).

The football fans of Darlington, in the north-west of England, are reported to chant "Who hung the monkey?" when their team is playing Hartlepool United (which is also known as the "Monkeyhangers"). This refers to the local legend that during the Napoleonic Wars, a monkey dressed in a French army uniform – the only survivor from a shipwreck – was washed up onto the beach at Hartlepool, (The monkey had presumably been a ship's pet). Lacking the knowledge to distinguish a monkey from a Frenchman, the local inhabitants held a trial. The monkey proved unable to provide satisfactory answers in its defence, was found guilty of being a French spy, and was sentenced to death and hanged on the beach.

Outside Europe

In Eastern Bengal, if a man was killed by a tiger, his family was socially disgraced until the offending tiger was killed and eaten. If it could not be found, the punishment was carried out vicariously by the slaying of another tiger. This practice was still in place when Woodburn wrote his book *The Persecution of Animals and Lifeless Things* in 1916.

Among the Bogos of Northern Abyssinia, an ox or any domestic animal which had caused the death of a man had to be be slain. The Malagasy of Madagascar never killed a crocodile except in retaliation. The Dyaks of Borneo never attacked an alligator unless it had destroyed one of their tribe. In this case revenge was "the sacred duty of the victim's relatives, and the man-eating alligator is supposed to be pursued by a righteous Nemesis; when one is caught, it must be the guilty one, for the fates would not permit an innocent one to suffer." As recorded by Woodburn, the contemporary code of people in Malacca required that a buffalo or head of cattle that gored a man to death should itself be killed; the owner was not held responsible.

Among the Mangbetu of Central Africa (now the Democratic Republic of the Congo), animals were punished for various offences.

In East Africa a dog was publicly scourged for entering a mosque, and among the Maori of New Zealand pigs were put to death for trampling a sacred place. These practices were still in place when Woodburn wrote his book *The Persecution of Animals and Lifeless Things* in 1916.

Such practices continued well into the 20th century: in Tennessee, also in 1916, an elephant called Mary was tried for murder and hanged from a railway crane.

Blameworthiness; a thought experiment

This history of bizarre practices, which is, in fact, about blameworthiness, concludes with a thought experiment about blameworthiness.

Imagine you are resting in a clay pan under a tree on a warm spring day. Suddenly, a heavy branch breaks off from the tree, falls, and hits you on the head. You need stitches and are sore for weeks. Who deserves the blame for this incident?

Now imagine you are resting under the same tree on a warm spring day. Suddenly, you are attacked by a dingo. You need stitches, and are traumatised and not well for quite some time.

This problem is different in a few interesting ways, but these do not include blameworthiness or free will on the part of a self-aware, autonomous "solid self" in the form of the dingo.

Now imagine you are attacked by a ten-year-old child with a baseball bat. You need stitches and are not well for quite some time.

This problem is different in a few interesting ways once again. Is one of them that it includes the blameworthiness or a free will by a a self-aware, autonomous "solid self" in the form of the child?

Now imagine you are attacked by a twelve-year-old child. Twelve is (or will be) the age of criminal responsibility in Australia. A solid self endowed with free will and blameworthiness has miraculously emerged. Where in the mind, in the brain or in the body of the child did this happen, exactly? Or does the child suddenly have a 'soul' or 'spirit' that carries this responsibility?

Now imagine that it was a mentally disabled grown man with a baseball bat who attacked you. An able-bodied, angry grown man....

Where in this sequence does a solid self endowed with free will and blameworthiness come in, and how?

The punishment of humans

Bizarre practices of law enforcement and by courts are not restricted to inanimate things, trees and animals. Museums all over Europe bear witness to the cruel creativity of humans when it comes to ways of torturing their own kind.

The medieval Iron Maiden was an iron coffin in which inward-facing rows of spikes pointed at the victim, who was slowly pierced from all directions as the coffin was shut.

The rack was the torture tool of the Spanish Inquisition. The victim's arms and legs were tied with ropes to rollers at each end of a wooden frame. As the cranks of the rollers were turned, the ropes tightened, and the victim's limbs were stretched, causing excruciating pain.

The thumbscrew consisted of a vice and two metal plates between which a victim's thumb was placed. The vice was then tightened, and the thumb slowly crushed.

The Spanish Boot was a device for torturing a victim's lower legs. The legs were placed into a pair of tightly fitting iron boots. Wooden wedges were then inserted between the boot and the victim's skin. Mallets were then used to drive the wedges in, first causing abrasions and lesions and, ultimately, breaking bones. Some versions featured inward-pointing spikes, nails or blades to worsen the effect.

The Breaking Wheel was a wagon wheel with spokes onto which the victim was tied so that their limbs were woven between the spokes. The torturer then took a hammer and smashed different parts of the limbs. Once the victim had died, the wheel was raised onto a shaft for the public to see. The victim could also be tied to the outside of the wheel with their feet secured to the ground. The wheel would be turned until the victim's body broke in two.

In rat torture, the victim was bound to a table or rack with a rat placed onto their chest. A bucket was placed over the rat, and a fire was lit on the top of the bucket. The rat tried to escape but couldn't burrow through the steel bucket, so would burrow into the victim's body instead.

We shake our heads in disbelief when we visit such exhibits. We have become so much more civilised!

The author of this book predicts that at some point in the future we will equally shake our heads over the current law enforcement and court practices of the Northern Territory. The exhibition will show the causing of severe disadvantage by an uncaring and greedy coloniser and then, when the damage is optimal, the trialling of the victims by judges in costumes that impersonate the coloniser, and the punishment of the victims through isolation, deprivation of basic needs such as daylight, clothing and toilet paper, and humiliation until the victims try to kill themselves.

Endnotes

1   Woodburn Hyde, W 1916, 'The prosecution and punishment of animals and lifeless things in the middle ages and modern times', *University of Pennsylvania Law Review and American Law Register*, 64(7):696-730. P 702.

2   Woodburn Hyde, W 1916, 'The prosecution and punishment of animals and lifeless things in the middle ages and modern times', *University of Pennsylvania Law Review and American Law Register*, 64(7):696-730. P 171.

3   Demosthenes, Oration 23, Against Aristocrates 423; 76.

4   Plato, Laws IX, 873 E-874.

5   Plato, laws, IX, 873 E-874 A.

6   Woodburn Hyde, W 1916, 'The prosecution and punishment of animals and lifeless things in the middle ages and modern times', *University of Pennsylvania Law Review and American Law Register*, 64(7):696-730. Woodburn Hyde 1916, p. 173 American Journal of Philology. P 173.

7   Woodburn Hyde, 1916, *University of Pennsylvania Law Review* P 700.

8   Exodus, XXI.

9   Woodburn Hyde, 1916, *University of Pennsylvania Law Review* P 700.

10   Woodburn Hyde, W 1916, 'The prosecution and punishment of animals and lifeless things in the middle ages and modern times', *University of Pennsylvania Law Review and American Law Register*, 64(7):696-730.

11   Such sentences followed the Hebrew mandate of Exodus, XXI.

12   Exodus XXII, 19; Leviticus XX, 15-16.

The thirty-one problems and three iconic cases

The widely-publicised Dylan Voller case illustrates how a problem develops into revolving-door justice and counterproductive prisons that are absurd, traumatising, vicariously traumatising, and absurdly expensive.

The Zak Grieve case illustrates how the combination of mandatory sentencing and the laws of complicity put young and vulnerable offenders *and* the public at risk. The still-unfolding Zak Rolfe case, and the Dylan Voller case, illustrate how trauma in offenders, victims, and law enforcement causes volatile situations that put the whole community at risk. The Dylan Voller case and the case of Mick (see Literature Review) show that most prisoners want "a normal life" and would, therefore, benefit from the *normality principle*.

The problems that we must overcome

The literature review revealed thirty-one problems that must be addressed to begin solving the problem of youth crime in Alice Springs. The problems can be divided into three broad groups:
- How we think about crime;
- Problems within the law; and
- Trauma-related problems.

How we think about crime

1. Opinions that are not based on science: emotions, feelings, and folklore
2. Perceptions of 'them'; the sense that the problem is someone else's but our own
3. The hunger for revenge and punishment
4. Strong beliefs in a "solid self" with free will, despite the scientific evidence against it
5. A belief in quick fixes implemented by people who do not understand the problem
6. Signalling: Naming & shaming on social media – prison architecture

Problems within the law

7. Awe of the concept of *mens rea* in criminal law
8. The division between criminal law and civil law
9. The age of criminal responsibility
10. The laws of complicity
11. Silence and gratuitous concurrence in legal proceedings
12. Mandatory sentencing
13. The impact of irrelevant factors on judicial decisions
14. Revolving-door justice
15. All-white juries
16. The closure of Bush Courts

17. The steady defunding of community-based mediation services
18. The lack of diversion out bush

Trauma-related problems

19. Offenders' intergenerational trauma
20. The adverse childhood experiences of offenders
21. The current life traumas of offenders
22. Trauma and vicarious trauma in the Alice Springs community
23. Traumas that the law and law enforcement cause to offenders and workers
24. Victim trauma
25. Organisations that do not sufficiently reach youth on the street
26. Siloing of NGOs and other agencies
27. (Vicarious) trauma in lawyers, judges, police officers and prison workers
28. Offenders' disabilities
29. The waxing and waning of political approaches to the problem
30. Tokenism, identity politics and the infantilisation of Aboriginal people
31. Housing and homelessness

Some of these problems are mentioned in the current documents of hope: *Northern Territory Aboriginal Justice Agreement*[1] and the *Northern Territory Youth Detention Centres Model of Care*,[2] but most are not.

The Zak Grieve Case

The Zak Grieve case[3] illustrates how the combination of mandatory sentencing and the laws of complicity cause unequal justice and put young offenders at risk.

Zak Grieve was eighteen years old when he found himself involved in a serious crime where four men planned and carried out the killing of a man in 2011. The body was taken to a campsite outside Katherine, where it was found the next morning. Grieve had been involved in the planning but was at home asleep when the murder was committed. He was convicted of murder and sentenced to the mandatory minimum sentence of life imprisonment with a non-parole period of twenty years; the heaviest of all of those convicted, while he had been the only one of the four to abandon the murder plan.[4] This was caused by a problem within the law, the combination of the laws of complicity and mandatory sentencing. This complex area of law will be explained further in the chapter "Problems within the law".

The Dylan Voller Case

Dylan Voller, a Ngarrenjerri man, was born in 1997. He is a perfect example of one of the young people that roam the streets of Alice Springs, although he was luckier than many because he had a home to go back to. He grew up in Alice Springs, where his behavioural problems soon became apparent. He broke the arm of another child in preschool and was expelled from five schools due to his issues and his refusal to take Ritalin because it made him nauseous.

Dylan's mother tried to get help for her son's behavioural issues on numerous occasions. When the boy broke her window, at age eleven, she was told that if she reported the incident to the police, Dylan would get the help he needed. Nothing could have been further from the truth. Once in custody, Dylan did not receive any significant mental health interventions; instead he was the subject of a long list of further traumatising transgressions that shocked the whole nation when they were revealed in the Four Corners episode *Australia's Shame.* [5]

The following timeline is constructed from Voller's testimony before the Royal Commission. Where other sources have been used, this is indicated.

In October 2010, thirteen-year-old Dylan was held up by his neck against a wall and thrown into a cell in the behavioural management unit at Don Dale Youth Detention Centre. The officer was charged but found not guilty of assault. He was a casual employee, and his contract was not renewed.

In December of that same year, Dylan was being held in isolation after threatening self-harm. He was grabbed by the neck, thrown onto a mattress, and forcibly stripped naked. The officer involved was found not guilty of aggravated assault.

In April 2011, Dylan was on the phone while in prison. When he refused to hand the phone over, a guard took it off him, kneed him and knocked him to the ground. The officer was found not guilty of assault. His casual contract was not renewed but he was later re-employed at the Alice Springs Youth Detention Centre, despite objections from the Professional Standards Command.

In October of that year, Dylan was being held in isolation after threatening self-harm. Three officers entered the room, one of them grabbed him by the neck, stripped him naked and left him crying in his hands on the floor.

In August 2014, an angry guard threw a pear at Dylan and attempted to block the security camera by throwing wet toilet paper at it. He then told Dylan he planned to harm him on the outside.

That same month, Dylan was one of the six children who were tear-gassed in the Don Dale isolation unit after another child caused problems. The boys had been held in isolation in the Behaviour Management Unit. In 2021, following a class action, the six children who were gassed and 1200 other ill-treated children received compensation for the tear-gassing incident.

During 2014, Dylan was involved in more than 200 prison incidents of self-harm, assault on staff and others (some requiring hospitalisation) since he was jailed for aggravated robbery and endangering a police officer.

In March 2015, Dylan was transferred to the Alice Springs adult prison and strapped into a restraining chair for almost two hours. The use of mechanical restraints on children was legalised in the Northern Territory in 2016.

In July 2016, footage of Dylan shackled to the restraining chair and wearing a spit hood was featured on the ABC TV program "Four Corners" episode *Australia's Shame*.

In December of that year, Dylan gave evidence at the Royal Commission into the Protection and Detention of Children in the Northern Territory.

Dylan was released early from prison in February 2017[6] and began campaigning immediately for improved conditions for youth in detention.[7] In the same year, Dylan's confidential files were found at the Alice Springs rubbish tip.[8]

In 2019, the now 21-year-old Dylan pleaded guilty to staging a bomb hoax at the Commonwealth Games marathon in Gold Coast.[9]

In February 2020, Dylan was sentenced to a 10-month prison sentence over an incident in which he jumped onto railway tracks, exposed his penis and assaulted a transit guard in Western Australia. A warrant for his arrest was issued in NSW on 19 June 2020 in relation to an armed robbery in Moama, New South Wales in May 2019.[10]

In September 2021, The High Court found that media outlets were responsible for Facebook comments in a defamation case that was pursued by Dylan Voller. The defamation case centres on comments made by third parties on Facebook in response to news articles. The High Court ruled that media outlets were considered the publishers of the comments and were therefore responsible for any defamatory content.[11]

Although Voller has apologised for his behaviour in a letter and has thanked the community for supporting him, he was told by his sentencing judge that he had to "stop blaming others" for his misfortunes. Moreover, a Northern Territory Supreme Court judge has questioned his culpability for his "onerous" treatment in jail, arguing that Voller's own behaviour may have provoked the incidents he says caused him trauma.[12] Former Federal MP Natasha Griggs said after the Royal Commission hearings that: "the public should stop treating Voller like a martyr".

Voller is now a married man with children and is doing his best to get the help he needs. Drugs remain a problem for him. He has indicated that the youth workers at Bush Mob in Alice Springs were a great help for him. The fact that he was charged with violence against his partner in April 2022 indicates that he is still struggling. The fact that he is now a national icon does not make things easier for him.

In June 2022 he was found in the possession of marijuana. He acted aggressively when the police entered the room that he was in. Dylan held a pair of scissors to his neck and said: "Come on, shoot me."[13]

The 2016 Royal Commission into the Protection and Detention of Children in the Northern Territory was created because of the exposure of the treatment of Dylan Voller to investigate how children were treated by the welfare system and in detention centres in the Northern Territory. It released its concluding report in 2017.

It was noted on the first day of the Commission's hearings that there had already been many reports, reviews, and inquiries into the matters the Commission was asked to investigate and there had been little improvement. The Commission was determined not to be 'just another inquiry' that fails to lead to positive and long-lasting change for the community and the children and young people of the Northern Territory. It was to find out whether, in the treatment of children in youth detention centres in the Northern Territory, the law was broken and rules were not followed, and whether policies, procedures and systems were in place to prevent children from being treated badly.

The report found "shocking and systemic failures" over many years that were known yet ignored. It found that youth detention centres were not fit for accommodating, let alone for rehabilitating children and young people. Children were subject to verbal abuse, physical control, and humiliation, being denied water, food, and the use of toilets. Children were dared or bribed to carry out degrading and humiliating acts or to commit acts of violence against each other. Prison staff restrained children using force to their head and neck areas. The use of 'ground stabilising' tactics meant that children were thrown to the ground and sat on. Isolation was used inappropriately, punitively, and inconsistently with the Youth Justice Act[14] and caused very likely lasting trauma. The report recommended the closing Don Dale's Youth Detention Centre; raising the age of criminal responsibility to 12, and only allowing children under 14 years of age to be detained for serious crimes; a paradigm shift in youth justice to increase diversion and therapeutic approaches. It also recommended developing a new model of bail and secure detention accommodation and increasing engagement with Aboriginal Organisations. Six years after the recommendations, only the last shows any signs of being implemented. At the time of this writing (2022), solicitor John Lawrence is standing every Friday in front of the Don Dale facility (which is in the former condemned Berrimah adult high security prison) in protest of the treatment of his young clients who have severe mental health issues and who are locked up in a cage-like cell for 22 hours a day.

The Zachary Rolfe Case

The *Rolfe* case[15] is a good example of how volatile situations can become in the Northern Territory. In 2019 in Yuendumu, 19-year-old Kumanjayi Walker, a disabled Aboriginal repeat offender, was shot three times by Constable Zachary Rolfe while resisting arrest, and died shortly afterwards.

Walker had escaped from CAAPU[16] to attend the funeral of a family member in Yuendumu. His ankle bracelet was found at the fence of CAAPU, and police were looking for him. Several came close, but Walker escaped into the bush. During another attempt to arrest him, Walker wielded an axe.

During his arrest on the day of his death in Yuendumu, Walker attacked Rolfe with a pair of scissors, causing a small puncture of the skin on Rolfe's shoulder. Rolfe shot Walker once immediately after the puncture. This shot was not in question before the court. It was the two shots in Walker's back during a struggle with Rolfe's colleague that caused the murder charge. They were fired while Walker was on the floor struggling with Constable Eberl, still holding the pair of scissors. Walker did not die at the scene but some time later at the police station. Medical staff had left the community the previous day because of violence.

Two days later, based on his bodycam footage, Rolfe

was charged with murder. In 2021, he was found not guilty by an all-white jury. The case was heavily publicised and continues to divide the communities of Alice Springs and Yuendumu. Many answers to the question of why Rolfe was so trigger-happy have been considered, including in an inquest by the coroner after the trial, but trauma was not one of them.

To an observer of Rolfe's bodycam footage, it seems that both offender and arresting officer were equally highly escalated and therefore, de-escalation of the situation was not possible. Rolfe had watched footage of the previous attempt to arrest Walker a few days earlier, during which Walker yielded an axe, more than thirty times on the day before the shooting.

Walker's family and the community of Yuendumu have asked for change. They want police without uniforms and guns in the community. They want Australia to see their pain. They had not been given a chance to say goodbye to Walker. They were led to believe that he was transported to a hospital, while he died on the floor of the locked police station while his family and friends were waiting outside. They were not given any information while waiting there for many hours.

The coronial inquest that was held after the trial revealed text messages by Rolfe to colleagues and friends that showed significant racist sentiments.

An expert report filed at the inquest concluded

that "the death of Kumanjayi Walker was the result of brutal, structural, racial violence perpetrated by the NT government through its police and health agents."[17]

What would have happened at the trial if these issues had been in evidence? What would have happened if the jury had not been all white? What would have happened if it had been shown that Rolfe himself suffered from the results of trauma, and that this had made him trigger-happy? The coronial inquest did find that he was in treatment for mental health issues.

The Rolfe case is an excellent example of the feeble nature of blameworthiness and the volatility of situations that are so unique to the Northern Territory.

Endnotes

1   https://justice.nt.gov.au/attorney-general-and-justice/northern-territory-aboriginal-justice-agreement/the-agreement

2   https://tfhc.nt.gov.au/__data/assets/pdf_file/0009/1132200/northern-territory-youth-detention-centres-model-of-care.pdf

3   Transcript of Proceedings, *R v Grieve* (Supreme Court of the Northern Territory, 21136195, 7 December 2012) 1188-1189; *Grieve v The Queen* [2014] NTCCA 2

4   Gerry, Felicity et al. 2018, *Petition for Mercy in the Matter of Zak Grieve*, filed 20 July with the Northern Territory Administrator.

5   ABC Television, 2016, *Four Corners*, 26 July. https://www.abc.net.au/4corners/australias-shame-promo/7649462.

6   Bardon, J 2017, 'Dylan Voller, former Don Dale youth detainee, granted early release from prison', *ABC News*, 2 February.

7   Aikman, A 2017, 'Dylan Voller leads protest at juvenile justice royal commission', *The Australian*, 13 March.

8   Shubert, S 2017, 'Dylan Voller's confidential files among those dumped at Alice Springs tip shop', *ABC News*, 5 July.

9   Forbes, T 2019, 'Dylan Voller pleads guilty to making Commonwealth Games marathon bomb hoax', *ABC News*, 22 May.

10 Jensen, I 2020, 'Dylan Voller still wanted over moama armed robbery", *Reverine Herald*, 19 June.

11 Byrne, E 2021, 'High Court finds that media outlets are responsible for Facebook comments in a defamation case that was pursued by Dylan Voller', *ABC News*, 8 September.

12 Hickey, P 2020, 'WA magistrate tells Dylan Voller to stop blaming others for offending after sentencing him to 10 months in prison for rail station offences", *The West Australian*, 2 February.

13 Young, R 2022, 'Don Dale 'survivor' Dylan Voller busted with weed at lawyer's office following scissor incident', *NT News*, 1 June.

14 *Youth Justice Act* (2005) NT.

15 *R v Rolfe* [2021] HCA 38.

16 Central Australian Aboriginal Alcohol Programs Unit.

17 Walls, J 2022a, 'Kumanjayi Walker inquest hears Yuendumu elders concerned to discipline kids for fear of intervention, 'tribal payback", *NT News*, 19 September: Walls, J 2022b, 'Yuendumu shooting death 'a result of brutal, structural, racial violence by NT Police', court hears', *NT News*, 21 September.

Chapter three - The white elephant

Problems within the law

This chapter discusses various problems within the law. The concept of *mens rea* and free will and the law is looked at in a local context, as well as: the division between criminal law and civil law; complicity and mandatory sentencing; the age of criminal responsibility; silence and gratuitous concurrence; irrelevant factors in judicial decisions; revolving-door justice; all-white juries; legal aid; defunding of mediation services; and lack of diversion in remote communities.

Mens rea and free will

Mens rea is one of the two pillars that our criminal law is based on. It is for this reason that it evokes an awe that is not necessarily healthy or useful. I do not suggest doing away with the concept, but I do recommend doing away with the awe. A healthy dose of scepticism is called for.

Social media algorithms, artificial intelligence, and our own genetics and environments are factors that influence us without us necessarily being aware of this. It raises the question: are offenders responsible for their actions? Free-will sceptics argue that no-one is truly responsible for any crime, no matter how serious. I suggest that the formative social environments that influence us leave no room for free will.

This view is not held by the courts, nor by the public. The criminal justice system presumes that an offender is free to decide whether to engage in criminal behaviour – or not. The courts acknowledge that there are exceptions. Those who were very young, acted upon an impulse of automatism, were sleepwalking or were mentally ill when the incident occurred should not be held responsible for their offences. These cases are seen as lacking free will and the ability to reason. The court caters for the doubt about whether these cases are sufficiently rational to be tried at all, to be fit for a person to stand trial. However, the law sees most defendants as able to participate in a trial. Still, it recognises that others cannot because their condition may deprive them of the free will needed to instruct their lawyers, present their version of events, or follow court proceedings.

With the exception of the work of David Hodgson,

Australian legal jurisprudence has not dealt with the questions concerning the origins of human behaviour. When one reviews case law in which courts attempt to create exceptions to punishment, courts debate the defences (insanity, duress, coercion). Still, they do not analyse why these defences differ from other modes of behaviour. While the policy goals for punishment are debated, they have always shown a strong preference for free will as the solid basis for their underlying philosophy.

I propose a new understanding of the law's various frameworks for holding offenders, especially vulnerable offenders, responsible, or doing away with them altogether, while retaining some legal mechanisms for incarceration for the purpose of healing and rehabilitation. This view may be seen as revolutionary concerning prescriptions for the legal system in a way that compatibilism and libertarianism are not.

The connection between trauma in the body and brain, because of disadvantage, and mens rea is seldom mentioned. The consequence of free-will scepticism is that mens rea becomes the Achilles heel of criminal law. Mens Rea defences are automatism, duress, mistake, lawful correction, mental illness, necessity, and self-defence. Note that **trauma** is not on this list. This is a problem. Someone who behaves in an anti-social manner as the result of trauma in the brain may be acting automatically because of that trauma. They may be acting under duress of that trauma, but such reasoning is not likely to be accepted in courts. Someone who is traumatised is not insane or mentally ill. Hence, the full weight of criminal law comes down on the young and vulnerable, traumatising them further and setting them up for further catastrophe and reoffending.

This is why Michael Zacharski in *Mens rea, the Achilles' heel of criminal law* asks: "How is it possible that contemporary jurisprudence has not developed a more dependable legal means of recognising a defendant's state of mind?

The division between criminal law and civil law

The concept of Anglo-American criminal law has evolved over a thousand years, responding to new knowledge about the origins of human behaviour and to power struggles between church and state. In the Anglo-Saxon period, it considered crime as a tort (essentially, something that causes loss or harm).

The remedy was compensatory. And although the Roman tradition of the Law of the Twelve Tables speaks of intent as opposed to negligence, it too treats crime as a tort. As the law and society matured, criminal conduct became a concern of society, not of individuals. The King's Courts in in England in the 12th century, under Henry II, described the crimes of homicide, mayhem, robbery, arson, and rape. Compensatory remedies for these crimes ended, and punishment emerged as a new remedy for criminal conduct. [1]

As a result, in communities visited by crime, a problem arose: the invisibility of the victims.

The offender takes centre stage in the criminal law system. Only in a civil case before the court would the victim take centre stage. Since the offender generally lacks money or property, it is not worth suing them. Hence, the victim's voice remains mostly unheard.

It seems desirable to maintain criminal law as it provides an effective method of vindicating the rights of secondary victims, restrains retributive emotions in the community, and enforces public values. In Alice Springs, victim/offender reconciliation could be added to the offender's sentence, and take place as part of the therapy of the offender that is recommended in the Conclusion of this book to lessen the feelings of victimhood, anger, resentment, and hatred that are expressed on social media pages such as *Action for Alice 2020*.

Mandatory sentencing

Let us return to the Zac Grieve case. I recap what it is about:

Four people, Grieve, Malyschko, Halfpenny and Buttery, planned the killing of a man in 2011. The body was transported to a campsite outside Katherine, where it was found the following day. Halfpenny pleaded guilty to murder and testified that Grieve, Malyschko and Buttery had all physically participated. On this basis, the Crown asked the jury to accept that Grieve was physically involved in the crime. This was despite the evidence of both Grieve and Malyschko that Grieve had not been present but had gone home because he "could not do it". CCTV footage of his vehicle confirmed this. Grieve was at home asleep when the murder was committed, but he was convicted of murder and sentenced to the mandatory minimum sentence of life imprisonment with a non-parole period of 20 years. This was the heaviest sentence of all those convicted, while he had been the only one of the four to abandon the murder plan.[2]

The Northern Territory legislation[3] describes one form of accessorial liability for minor offences and another for more serious offences. The liability for minor offences is on the table to be discussed and changed in the Northern Territory as this book in in preparation.

However, for more serious offences (which are not up for debate and change), the legislation requires reasonable steps to withdraw. [4] The question in the Grieve case was: did Grieve withdraw from the murder plan sufficiently? The criteria for withdrawal and reasonable steps are not precise enough in the legislation. This lack of certainty is a considerable risk to equal justice. [5]

During the trial where Zac Grieve was found guilty of murder, Justice Mildren said:

> "I take no pleasure in this outcome. It is the fault of mandatory minimum sentencing provisions which inevitably bring about injustice." "Legislation of this kind is unprincipled and morally insensible; it cannot encompass the factual and moral distinctions between crimes essential to a just and rational sentencing policy." (quoting Professor Norval Morris) "However, the prerogative of mercy which rests with the Crown can still be enlivened. ... I recommend to the Administrator that after you have served a minimum of 12 years of that sentence ... you be released on parole."[6]

Mandatory minimum sentences reduce judges to instruments of injustice. New Zealand has passed the Three Strikes Legislation Repeal Act 2022, which repeals the mandatory sentencing regime commonly known as the Three Strikes Law. The Northern Territory Law Reform Committee has recommended the abolition of mandatory minimum sentences, mandatory minimum parole periods and mandatory life sentences for murder. Hopefully this is the beginning of the end of brutality in sentencing by governments far divorced from the reality of vulnerability in criminal justice systems."[7]

Not only serious crimes like murder attract mandatory sentencing. In 2000, Wurramarrba, a 15-year-old boy from Groote Eylandt, was sentenced to a mandatory 28 days' detention for stealing some pencils. Wurramarrba was found hanged in his Darwin cell, causing national outrage. The background of the boy as described in the coroner's report[8] reminds us of the kids on the streets of Alice Springs:

[Although he] was raised a close-knit Aboriginal community, with widespread family and clan ties, he was a lonely, neglected boy. He was an orphan. His mother died of natural causes in 1986 when he was not quite 2 years old. His father was killed in 1995, knocked down by a motor vehicle in Darwin. The evidence does not permit me any solid appreciation of what role the Deceased's father had played in his upbringing till then, but the indications are: not much. [7].

Mr Mamarika, a family member, gave this account of the boy's upbringing:

"Well he was look after by his grandmother when he was young, since his mother pass away, and his grandmother pass him to his auntie but his auntie pass away. So he was floating around the Community, and see he was looking around for a new family but couldn't find any new family because family ..... auntie and tell him to find families. So he find this other family, outside family. So he was staying at Umbakumba and Angurugu. He was staying at Angurugu with is father's family, and when he went back to Umbakumba he was staying there with another family, you know.[..]. Well down there he was trouble like mess, messing up the ......here." [2]

Mr Mamarika was aware that the boy was a cannabis smoker and a petrol sniffer. At the time of his death, Mr Mamarika was engaged, at the request of Don Dale staff, in finding a family with whom the boy could live after his release. Mr Mamarika knew that the boy did not want to return to Groote Eylandt because he was greatly attached to his grandmother, who was in Darwin to receive kidney dialysis treatment. The boy preferred to live with her and wanted to help care for her – she is wheelchair-bound – but the placement was seen as impracticable. [9]

Ms Hazel Lalara made the following statement to police:

"Yes, I helped brought that little boy up when his mother died, so I was a full grandmother acting like a full grandmother to him and when his other grandmother was sick she went out and lived in Darwin and I have brought these children up, look after them and then his father die when his mother died, in a car accident in Darwin, happened in Parap. [10].

This may give the impression that Ms Lalara became the principal caregiver, but that impression is misleading. The boy also stayed with others: an auntie (unnamed because she had died in, it seems, in 1999), one Lucy Bara, one Marianne Wurramarrba, of Angurugu (his aunt), one Mike Wurramarrba, of Umbakumba (his uncle), and others. [12].

Nobody had stood *in loco parentis* to the boy for some years, at least since his father was killed when the boy was nearly eleven. During the next few years, the boy lived in at least four communities, and also at the Don Dale Centre and the Wildman Wilderness Camp, being cared for, from time to time, by what seems to have been at least six households, probably more. [15]. As far as is known, during the boy's lifetime, the Child Welfare authorities did not investigate his circumstances or report them. [17].

"Angurugu and Umbakumba are settlements on Groote Eylandt in the Gulf of Carpentaria. Their populations and predominantly Aboriginal. They are "dry areas" under the Liquor Act. Housing and other material goods are sparse. Unemployment rates are high. Social problems such as petrol sniffing, alcohol abuse, and domestic violence are rife. School attendance is low. Third-world health problems are common. Young Aboriginal boys, adolescents and men from Umbakumba and Angurugu descended upon Alyangula and commit crimes there. From Umbakumba it is too far to walk: a vehicle must be stolen for the trip. Angurugu is within walking distance; however, a car will be stolen for that trip too, either from Angurugu or from the mining complex or the airport car park. On arrival, they aim to break into the two licensed clubs. Alcohol, cigarettes and crisps are quickly stolen, and then the thieves scatter, drinking as they go, and looking for a vehicle to drive home. If they run out of liquor, they may enter a house or two in search of more. Eventually, a car or cars are taken, and the offenders drive back to Angurugu or Umbakumba, drinking as they go.

When they arrive there they drive the car wildly around the community. Some of the original offenders will leave the vehicle and other previously uninvolved young males from the community will get in. The driving tends to go on until the car heads out onto bush tracks or until it crashes or runs out of fuel. [27] This was the background of Wurramarrba. This is the background of many of the offenders in Alice Springs.

Wurramarrba left a note that said: "my Land"; "crys about"; "Families"; "my fauther and"; "Too of my aunties"; "sorry"; "I'm sorry". "I didn't want too die becaues I was too young. But now I'm growing up and I'll come soon, meet my people in heaven. My land be there anytime." [182]

Our governments can repeal and replace ineffective laws with evidence-based legislation. As noted, the Northern Territory government is currently reviewing its mandatory sentencing laws. Cases like those of Grieve and Wurramarrba may convince the government that the current sentencing policy is ineffective, expensive, and inhuman. There are two questions the government should be looking at regarding mandatory sentencing: firstly, is there evidence showing that mandatory sentencing reduces crimes and reoffending? Secondly, what are the costs, both financially and socially, of mandatory sentencing?[9]

In October 2022, the government introduced much-publicised reforms to pare back mandatory sentencing after a report by the Law Reform Committee the previous year recommending such reforms. Mandatory sentencing will remain for murder, sexual offences and assaulting police and emergency workers. For other offences, judges will have the option to give offenders one of two forms of correction order: an enforced correction order, where offenders will be sentenced to engage in community work and government programs; or, for more serious offending, an enforced intensive correction order, which includes intensive supervision, curfews, electronic monitoring and participation in behaviour and other training programs.

A last word from Mildren J:

"Prescribed minimum mandatory sentencing provisions are the very antibook of just sentences. If a court thinks that a proper just sentence is the prescribed minimum or more, the minimum prescribed penalty is unnecessary. It therefore follows that the sole purpose of a prescribed minimum mandatory sentencing regime is to require sentencers to impose heavier sentences than would be proper according to the justice of the case." [10]

Complicity

Accessories to a crime, as Zac Grieve was, are found in the context of gangs and crowd violence, but also in the context of crimes that are planned in small groups. The laws around accessory liability or complicity are therefore highly relevant to youth crime in Alice Springs. Recently, there have been several decisions in the common-law jurisdiction which deal with the liability of accessories in the context of the conduct element and the fault element. They ask the question of whether there was an intention by the accessory to participate in the main offence; and of whether the accessory could have foreseen that the main offender would commit the crime.

Let us look again at the Zac Grieve case. This was the case of "the mother who paid for an ex-lover's murder; the son who organised the hit; the accomplice who turned against his mates; and the man who wasn't there." [11] Four people were charged. Three accused went to trial: Buttery (the mum), Malyschko (the son), Grieve (the man who wasn't there), one co-offender turned Crown witness (Halfpenny). The mother was sentenced to eight years, with four years' no-parole; the son was sentenced to life, with eighteen years' no-parole; the co-offender turned Crown witness was sentenced to life with twenty years' no-parole; Zak Grieve was sentenced to life with twenty years' no-parole. Grieve was deemed to have had the intention to participate in the main offence and to have been able to foresee that the main offender would commit the crime. He was therefore seen as an accessory to the murder.

The common-law prerogative of mercy had to be exercised for Zak Grieve to remove the "pains, penalties and punishments" associated with the conviction, although it did not remove the conviction itself.[12] The prerogative of mercy is a lengthy, painful, and expensive process. Where to start to change the laws around complicity is a question easily asked, but complex to answer. As no domestic law seems free of perils, it seems that answers must be sought at an international level. Article 7 of the *European Convention on Human Rights* seems a good place to start if we want young offenders like Grieve to receive sentences that further their rehabilitation and allow them to leave prison as productive members of the community.

The age of criminal responsibility

The Northern Territory began seeking to raise the age of criminal responsibility from 10 to 12 in October 2022.

In 2019, the United Nations Committee on the

Rights of the Child recommended 14 years as the minimum age, based on child development studies which found that children under fourteen often lack impulse control and have a low capacity to understand consequences. The earlier a child enters the justice system, the more likely they will re-offend.

Young people in custody should receive a standard of education comparable to anyone else in the education system. In many cases, incarcerated youth have higher educational needs.

It's a step in the right direction, but the question remains: what we are going to do with offenders between seven and 12 years old who are on our streets (and those in Darwin, Katherine, and Tennant Creek)? They often do not have sufficiently functional families or communities to go back to. Based on hundreds of conversations in my community, I therefore suggest replacing youth detention and prison sentences for those under 25 with "Nosirps" for de-escalation, learning and healing: a place where all services for offenders' complex needs are amalgamated under one roof. This is to combat the notorious problem of the siloing of NGOs that now offer valuable services but do not reach transient kids sufficiently.

Only after we have helped heal this generation of children and young adults can we begin increasing the age of criminal responsibility in a truly meaningful way.

Prison guards should not be around vulnerable

children and young adults with complex needs: they have training in security, not an education in treating trauma. Keeping the premises locked to keep the community safe can be done with minimal intermingling of staff with offenders. The quarters of such security staff can and should be at the periphery of the premises, as in the Ny Anstalt facility in Nuuk, Greenland.

Instead, the people who interact with the young offenders in custody should be specialists such as one-on-one mentors, doctors, psychiatrists, psychologists, therapists, Aboriginal Elders and teachers, as well as family members.

When a young person is placed in custody, it is the responsibility of the state that this person is cared for adequately and that the best interest of the child is always paramount.

Raising the age needs political will, a will that is lacking amongst those that live in Alice Springs due to the youth of offenders who commit serious crimes. The obvious solution is a facility with a hard shell (making it impossible to get out) but a soft centre, where children and young adults feel safe enough to heal and explore their dreams and talents under the leadership of trusted one-on-one mentors. This kind of hard shell/soft centre resembles a lychee fruit. Let us call it the *Lychee Model*. Many people, from real estate agents to restaurant owners, have suggested such a model during my endless talks over the past two years. It is one that many people come up with when they give serious thought to the problem. I generally spoke with people for an hour to an hour and a half, often over lunch. When the first emotional responses of anger and sadness had subsided, this is what most people came up with, irrespective of their cultural background. Many, Aboriginal and non-Aboriginal, agreed that Aboriginal leadership within such a Nosirp would be a prerequisite.

Silence and gratuitous concurrence in proceedings

A secondary problem caused by the laws of complicity is that offenders remain silent or engage in gratuitous concurrence during police interviews. 'Gratuitous concurrence' means that they will say "yes" or appear to agree with a proposition when they have no understanding of what has been said. Typical crimes by young people in groups are break-ins to find car keys, alcohol and tobacco, and car theft followed by joyriding. When there is a chase and police catch one of the offenders, this person must assist the police in finding the others to establish who is complicit in the crime. There is a problem with this. Offenders are likely to have low literacy and numeracy and a limited understanding of English. These significant linguistic and social disadvantages may result in gratuitous concurrence or remaining silent.[13]

Difficulties in communication and comprehension are very real. Many don't understand how questions are asked, especially direct questions. This can easily lead to misunderstanding and incorrect answers being given.[14]

The *Anunga Rules* are supposed to protect Aboriginal offenders during police interrogations. However, these rules do not protect the alleged offender against the trappings of silence or gratuitous concurrence. The so-called "wall of silence" put up by peers in a joint enterprise is a risk to successful police investigations and criminal trials because of the laws around complicity.

Cultural narratives of the young people who roam our streets include distrust of the police and a 'no-snitching' culture (and the image of themselves as manipulative "professional criminals". The primary concerns of young suspects are the legal risks of talking and the protection of their peers. So when the role of the law and law enforcement generates silence, this becomes a dangerous trap, as silence may be interpreted as guilt, and this pushes offenders towards being charged. Silence, just like speech, can be subject to misinterpretation, and in the context of offenders' interviews, the police may interpret silence as guilt, thereby using it against them. The void created by young people's silence provides a vacuum for the police and prosecution to run with their own narrative instead of the real narrative.[15]

The interpretation of silence as guilt ignores the vulnerability that people feel when faced with the power of the police and the criminal justice system. Recent research shows that fear of racism and being called an animal, or even fear of death, push young offenders into remaining silent.[16] The killing of Kumanyaji Walker in Yuendumu, the Rolfe trial, and the release of racist text messages by Rolfe during the Coronial Inquest after the trial, hammer home the legitimacy of these fears.

Research involving twenty 'active street offenders' found that some feared that they would shift from 'complainants into suspects' by talking themselves 'into a hole', being caught lying, and 'drawing attention to their own misdeeds' in their conversations with police.[17]

The impact of irrelevant factors on judicial decisions

How judges and magistrates are influenced by irrelevant factors is described by Schauer in *What the judge had for breakfast* (2009). Recent work in cognitive science provides strong evidence for a link between emotion and moral judgment. Judges and magistrates in Alice Springs process heavy caseloads of vulnerable offenders and victims, and are constantly witnessing tragedy.

The occupational health and wellbeing of judicial officers is a matter of public safety. In Australia, judicial stress was first described in a lecture by Justice Kirby in 1995 as an unmentionable topic.[18] In 1997 he raised the topic again and noted that he hoped there was now more recognition of the deep malaise within our legal institutions.[19] It took the suicides of two magistrates in Victoria, in 2017 and 2018, for the issue to become a subject of interest.

There has, to my knowledge, been no empirical investigation of the association between working location and judicial stress in Australia. To develop responses and interventions to address the stress experienced by remote judicial officers, a better understanding is needed of the drivers of this stress, and of which judicial officers are experiencing the most stress. It would be beneficial to have a national study of judicial stress and wellbeing, along with occupational and wellbeing supports in the form of judicial education for magistrates and other judicial officers in high-volume summary jurisdictions such as Alice Springs.

There are indications that an unexpected solution for this problem is nearing: a great equalizer in the form of decentralised justice or blockchain justice. De Filippi, in *Blockchain and the Law: The Rule of Code*, describes how blockchain may improve the criminal justice system using a distributed-ledger architecture. Criminal charges may be shared and tracked in a ledger accessible by law enforcement, prosecution, courts, probation, defense attorneys, and corrections organisations. When charges were added or dropped by law enforcement, prosecution, or courts, that information would be posted to the ledger, with the expected result being a faster, more efficient administration of justice. In later stages the judge may become largely obsolete, and unbiased justice would result. England and Wales are already moving towards this system, and the European Commission has adopted the *'Ethical Principles Relating to the Use of Artificial Intelligence (AI) in Judicial Systems'*. [20]

Revolving-door justice

The Centre for Sustainable Justice explains on its website (www.sustainablejustice.org) how one of the biggest obstacles to sustainable justice is the adversarial nature of the courts. This becomes crystal clear when one visits Alice Springs' local court and looks at the crimes addressed there. It seems apparent that we must move from an adversarial model to a cooperative model, one where the paramount factors are sustainability, the social ecology, and the quality of interpersonal relationships in our community. This would need the engagement of the judicial powers in improving the social ecology and the provision of a framework for developing a judicial system which is of greater help to our community as a whole. [21]

The introduction of mediation and Alternative Dispute Resolution, the development of Drug Courts, Problem-Solving Courts, Therapeutic Jurisprudence, Restorative Justice, and the increased focus on integrated conflict resolution, are all signs that the impact of global sustainability has reached the judicial system in Australia. This shift has introduced a new focus in court justice, towards a better future: the improvement of the relationships between parties involved in litigation, and the resolution of crime-related problems in our communities. This shift started in the 1980s and will eventually work through into the whole legal system. In the Northern Territory, it seems long overdue.

"The sustainable justice perspective unlocks a vision of the justice system and forms an inspiring guiding principle for future courts. The principles of sustainable justice and social responsible justice will revamp the justice system and give it a new allure and it opens new perspectives for transparency in the administration of justice."[22]

A white elephant

The Zachary Rolfe Case in 2022 hammered home the need for more Aboriginal people on juries. One of the biggest hurdles to better Aboriginal representation on juries is the fact that there are only two jury districts in the Northern Territory: Darwin and Alice Springs, while more than three-quarters of Aboriginal people live in more remote areas. If we want to allow further representation from Indigenous communities – and this is something we should want – then jury districts should be widened. This is not a simple task. [23]

The Electoral Roll can and should be used to obtain a list of suitable jurors. Large sections of the community are currently excluded: not only Aboriginal people, but also migrants. In 2021, more than 24,000 people were missing from the electoral roll. The jury list could also be expanded by adding to the Electoral Roll names taken from Centrelink and MVR databases. An extra 17,000 people could be identified this way. For juries to function as they should, and for Aboriginal people to gain confidence in the judicial system, juries in the Northern Territory must be representative of the population of the Northern Territory.[24]

The Sixth Amendment of the US Constitution stipulated that court trials must be held with the help of an impartial jury.

This has resulted in the doctrine that juries must be drawn from a representative cross-section of the community. The Northern Territory should develop a similar doctrine, despite the hurdles presented. Since jury duty is part of being a citizen, there should be ongoing efforts to encourage Aboriginal people to get onto the Electoral Roll. Barriers to participation on juries by Aboriginal people should be removed.

One of these barriers is that many Aboriginal people are deemed not proficient enough in English to perform jury service. Another barrier is the ineffective service of juror summonses.[25] Despite their complex nature and the very real problem of the tyranny of distance in the Northern Territory, these obstacles must be addressed sooner rather than later.

Legal Aid pulling out of bush courts in the Northern Territory

Bush courts handled critical legal work. This work is now under serious threat, despite the recently signed Aboriginal Justice Agreement. The Northern Territory Legal Aid Commission stopped taking new clients in remote communities from April 2022, when remote circuit courts were suspended due to Covid-19.

Defendants must represent themselves if the North Australian Aboriginal Justice Agency (NAAJA) cannot. Bush courts are due to return, but when they do, and NAAJA has a conflict of interest, such as already representing a victim, witness, or defendant, they are obliged to refer people to another legal service. This would normally be Legal Aid.

This denial of legal rights means that the fundamental human right to legal representation is breached.

The steady defunding of community-based mediation services

Mediators play an essential role in helping defuse conflicts in the community. There are now concerns that the Northern Territory could become the only jurisdiction in Australia without a community mediation service, after the Community Justice Centre was defunded in the Territory budget for 2022. Mediators and social workers say that the Centre's role is significant in preventing family and community disputes from escalating to the courts. The Centre also helps Territorians gain skills to resolve conflicts peacefully.

The lack of diversion out bush

Arresting offenders does not address the boredom orthe disadvantage that lead offenders to offend. Arrests alone will not reduce crime. Unless we respond to the root causes of why offenders take to our streets, crime is here to stay. The lack of diversion programs in remote communities because there are no remote providers is of great concern.[26]

Endnotes

1   Bennett, E 2016b, 'Neuroscience and Criminal Law: Have We Been Getting It Wrong for Centuries and Where Do We Go from Here? ', *Fordham Law Review*, 85(2 (3)).

2   Gerry, Felicity et al. 2018, *Petition for Mercy in the Matter of Zak Grieve*, filed 20 July with the Northern Territory Administrator.

3   *NT Criminal Code Act 1983*, Division 2 Presumptions, cl 8; Cl 10; Division 3 Parties to Offences Cl 12 and Cl 13: Part II AA Division 4; Extensions of criminal responsibility: clause 43BG Complicity and common purpose.

4   Krebs, B 2015, 'Mens rea in joint enterprise: a role for endorsement? ', *Cambridge law journal*, 74(3):480-504; Krebs, B 2017, 'Accessory Liability: Persisting in error', *Cambridge law journal*, 76(1):7-11; Krebs, B 2018, 'Joint enterprise, murder and substantial injustice: The first successful appeal post-Jogee', *Journal of criminal law (Hertford)*, 82(3):209; Phillips, M 2021, *Accessorial liability after Jogee. Edited by Beatrice Krebs. [Oxford: Hart Publishing, 2019. xiv + 272 pp. Hardback £70.00. ISBN 978-1-50991-889-8.]*, Cambridge University Press, Cambridge, UK, 0008-1973.

5   Gerry, Felicity, QC, et al. 2020, 'Petition for Mercy in the Matter of Asher Johnson', Carmelite Chambers, London 30 July.

6   Transcript of Proceedings, *R v Zak Grieve* (Supreme Court of the Northern Territory, 21136195, Mildren J, 9 Janu-

ary 2013).

7   On-line Seminar 21 September 2022, J Gerry, R Goldflam, T Anthony and L Bartels, Mandatory sentencing in Australia – a question of legitimacy.

8   Findings in the death of Johnno Johnson Wurramarba [2001] NTMC 84; Coroner's Court, Darwin: D0019/2000; 19 December 2001.

9   A.G. Fyles at CLANT 2017

10   Trenerry v Bradley (1997) 6 NTLR 175

11   Steven Schubert.

12   R v Foster [1985] QB 115

13   Visser, S 2020 b, 'Is the CDP "work for the dole" program in remote communities legally and ethically defensible?'. submitted to.

14   Australian Law Reform Commission, The Recognition of Aboriginal Customary Laws (ALRC 31) 1986, Part V.

15   Hulley, S 2021, 'Silence, joint enterprise and the legal trap', *Criminology & criminal justice*:174889582199162.

16   Lee, Jr S and Robinson, M A 2019, '"That's my number one fear in life. It's the police": Examining young black men's Exposures to trauma and loss resulting from police violence and police killings', *Journal of black psychology*, 45(3):143-184

17   Rosenfeld, R, Jacobs, BA & Wright, R 2003, 'Snitching and the code of the street', *British journal of criminology*, 43(2):291-309. P 298.

18 Kirby, M 1995, 'Judicial stress: An unmention-able topic', *Australian Bar Review*, 13:101-115.

19 Kirby, M 1997, 'Judicial stress – an update', *Australian Law Journal* 71(774).

20 Filippi, PD 2018, *Blockchain and the law: The rule of code*, Harvard University Press.

21 de Savornin Lohman, A F 2011a, *Explanatory notes for sustainable justice*, Centre for Sustainable Justice, https://papers.ssrn.com/sol3/papers.cfm?abstract_id=2210037.

de Savornin Lohman, AF 2011b, 'Working document on sustainable justice ', paper presented to *Werkdocument Duurzame Rechtspraak*, Montaigne Center for Judicial Administration and Conflict Resolution, Utrecht, the Netherlands, 2 December.

22 de Savornin Lohman, AF 2011b, 'Working document on sustainable justice ', paper presented to *Werkdocument Duurzame Rechtspraak*, Montaigne Center for Judicial Administration and Conflict Resolution, Utrecht, the Netherlands, 2 December.

23 Goldflam, R 2011, 'The white elephant in the room : juries, jury arrays and race', *Indigenous law bulletin*, 7(26):35-38.

24 Goldflam, R 2011, 'The white elephant in the room : juries, jury arrays and race', *Indigenous law bulletin*, 7(26):35-38.

25 Goldflam, R 2011, 'The white elephant in the room : juries, jury arrays and race', *Indigenous law bulletin*,

7(26):35-38.

26   See: Jonscher, S 2022, "Blatantly racist' and 'disgraceful' texts between Zachary Rolfe and colleagues read out at Kumanjayi Walker inquest.', *ABC News*, 15 September; Jonscher, S & Martin, X 2022, 'NT Police say children as young as eight taking part in Alice Springs crime wave', *ABC News*, 26 June.

Chapter four – Trauma

"The Indigenous kids I work with are powerless and voiceless. They are currently legally represented by the North Australian Aboriginal Justice Agency, or the NT Legal Aid Commission, as it was with all the abused children who appeared in Four Corners' Australia's Shame program. For just under ten years, NAAJA has chosen to pursue a policy of not opposing, resisting or even publicly criticising the inhumane carceral policies of the previous NT Country Liberal Party government or the current NT Labor government.

The German anti-Nazi and martyr, pastor Paul Bonhoeffer said that "Silence in the face of evil is itself evil. Not to speak is to speak. Not to act is to act". NAAJA's policy of not publicly criticising and thereby collaborating has been a catastrophic failure and disgrace. The purpose and philosophy of the Close Don Dale NOW! movement is action. This will include direct action and civil disobedience. They say change happens when ordinary people do extraordinary things. It seems it has to be this way."

John Lawrence, The NT Independent, June 29, 2022.

In this chapter, we look at the harm caused by (juvenile) detention; trauma and neurolaw; offenders' intergenerational trauma; adverse childhood experiences in offenders; the fact that NGOs and government organisations do not sufficiently reach the offenders; the siloing of NGOs and other organisations; victim trauma; vicarious and other trauma in lawyers, police officers and prison workers; disability in offenders; the waxing and waning of political approaches to the problem; sustainable justice; and crime as a public-health issue.Alice Springs has always been a divided town. The latest great division was caused by the Zach Rolfe murder trial, where an all-white jury decided that the killer of a disabled young black man should walk free. Rolfe's lawyers successfully omitted damning evidence, of racism and a violent past, that came to light in the coronial inquest that followed.

A Facebook page titled *I support Zach Rolfe*[1] reports news and opinions that are pro-Rolfe; the page *Justice for Walker*[2] does the same in favour of the victim. Division in Alice Springs is along the usual lines of political left and political right, and along racial lines. Our shared stories lie in the arts and sports, where collaboration is successfully achieved, and in the shared trauma that is described below.

Offender trauma and neurolaw

In the previous chapters, we have seen that factors beyond our conscious control (genetic, social, environmental) shape our behaviour.

Trauma changes the brain, and the law is slowly catching up with this fact. However, the Australian Neurolaw database contains only one case where trauma in a young Aboriginal offender is considered.

The case *R v Hawkins* in 2015 concerned the sentencing of an offender for burglary, going equipped for theft, attempting to take a motor vehicle dishonestly and without the consent of its owner, theft, and possession of stolen property.

The offender said at first that he did not remember the offence – but later pleaded guilty. The judge made the following findings, based on the pre-sentence report and a report from the Court Alcohol and Drug Assessment Service: the offender was Aboriginal and 21 years old at the time of the offence. He had been in a foster home. He started drinking alcohol and smoking cannabis at a very young age, and using other drugs during his teenage years. He had a significant criminal history; he had been found guilty of 68 offences and was found to be at medium-high risk of reoffending.

In the sentencing consideration, the judge noted that "He is still a relatively young man, and neuroscience shows that the male brain is not fully mature and developed until the mid-twenties". By referring to two other judgements, the court found that even after the age of 18, the youth of the offender should still be taken into consideration. The judge continued: "This is, of course, more so when the youthful offender is a first offender, but even later, particularly with the slow development of maturity, especially in young men, rehabilitation is usually more important than general deterrence."

While the judge admitted that the offender's long criminal behaviour indicated a limited opportunity for rehabilitation, he pointed out that the rate at which the brain matures should also be taken into consideration. The court, therefore, after considering the offender's disadvantaged childhood that led him into drugs and crime, ordered a total sentence of two years and eight months, with a non-parole period of one year and 10 months.[3]

In this case, Neurolaw was clearly being practised.

More often than not, offenders *suffer from the same symptoms as victims* do. Offenders are often victims themselves, and their offending behaviour stems from trauma. When we look at the trauma that offenders may be carrying, we must first look at cultural trauma, a form of trauma from which most other forms of trauma spring.

Cultural trauma

It is safe to say that most offenders in Alice Springs are the victims of cultural trauma.

Culture suppresses anxieties, self-consciousness, and the awareness of mortality.[4] It provides a sense of meaning and value.[5] Existence would be anxiety-ridden without that meaning and value.[6] Engaging in cultural rituals, practices, and activities maintains one's worldview. Conflict over competing cultural priorities arises from unequal power and status between the members of a community. The dominant culture suppresses the minority's cultural practices, motivated by the need to assert the significance of its own cultural worldviews.[7]

Constant suppression of cultural practices brutally disrupts a culture, making it highly vulnerable to trauma. Hence, cultural trauma is a condition in which cultural knowledge and practices have been weakened so that they fail to give meaning and value.[8]

The results of cultural trauma are that members experience high anxiety levels, which leads to unhelpful coping strategies and forms of collective helplessness. These unhelpful coping mechanisms may become the norm, thereby increasing the likelihood that cultural trauma and its effects are carried into the next generation.[9]

The above observations provide us with an acute understanding of the situation of offenders in Alice

Springs. The dominant European culture since settlement suppressed the cultural practices and knowledge of Aboriginal people.[10]

For Aboriginal Australians, settlement meant forceful land dispossession, theft and rape of women, slavery, and the introduction of diseases. Missionary zeal made them convert to Western religion and reject their own spiritual beliefs. Settlement also meant that British law displaced indigenous customary law.[11] In the recent past, the White Australia Policy and forced removal of children further destabilised Aboriginal social structures, cultural practices and cultural transmissions.[12]

Legislative interference in the Native Title Act; confusing half-support for Aboriginal reconciliation; ambiguous reactions to the findings of the Stolen Generation report into the forced removal of children;[13] the dismantling of ATSIC, which was deemed to be too preoccupied with symbolic issues; and a reluctance to mainstream Aboriginal services – all these have undermined the pursuit of indigenous cultural autonomy and encouraged a culture of dependency.[14] Taken as a whole, this can be described, according to Human Rights and Equal Opportunity Commission, as cultural genocide.

This is the cause of massive cultural trauma. This is the reason why our young people offend. This cannot be seen simply as a criminal issue; it must be seen as a public-health issue.

Interventions into cultural knowledge and practices lead to PTSD. This, in turn, causes the sky-high rates of imprisonment we see in the Northern Territory. It also causes infant mortality, suicide, substance abuse, medical conditions and lower life expectancies.[15] Aboriginal people show incredibly high levels of hopelessness, helplessness, disorientation, irritability and insomnia,[16] and are four to five times more likely to die from the consequences of a mental disorder than the non-Aboriginal population.[17]

Reliance on welfare income, income management, and nonsensical CDP "work for the dole" activities only exacerbates the perception of dependence and feelings of helplessness.

Of all approaches, the most promising and rewarding seem to be those that reinvigorate the Aboriginal culture and ways of life. Anecdotal evidence seems to support the idea that reconstruction of Aboriginal cultural meaning and relevance may help in addressing the problems of Aboriginal people.[18]

Examples of programs in the Northern Territory that address cultural trauma are the *Aboriginal Empowerment Program*, which focused on family well-being; also, the Belyuen Health Centre showed that significant improvements in health outcomes of Aboriginal people were achieved by taking into consideration Aboriginal social kin relationships and responsibilities, methods of time-keeping, gender issues, and the use of traditional healers and language.[19]

The *Strong Women, Strong Babies, Strong Culture Program* led to improvements in the health and well-being of pregnant women. This program consisted of taking participants out bush to collect bushfood to increase exercise, and traditional pregnancy practices, such as the smoking ceremony. The program significantly decreased the rates of low birth weights and pre-term births amongst participants.[20]

The effects of cultural trauma often involve law-related factors such as drug and alcohol problems and domestic violence. Therefore, cultural recovery is also relevant in the context of Aboriginal Australians' experience of the law.[21] Cultural recognition has, after all, played out in the courts in Australia, most notably in the acknowledgment of Indigenous land rights in the *Mabo case* and in the *Native Title Act*. These have opened a narrow but hopeful path towards a Treaty, sovereignty, self-government, and restitution for past injustices.

Australian jurisdictions have begun, but soon ended, restorative justice practices that recognised the importance of Aboriginal culture in procedural justice before the law. They were called the Nunga, Koori and Murri courts. The outcomes of using these courts were not reported well enough because of a lack of policy and funding.

The dominant culture often finds that Aboriginal Australians do not deserve to be treated any differently than other Australians, due to the Australian values of egalitarianism with a "fair go" for all "Aussie battlers". There is a perception that Aboriginal people have "to get over it and move on". It is not difficult to understand that such an attitude is partly responsible for the resistance by the majority culture in Australia towards Aboriginal cultural reinvigoration and, therefore, is a hurdle we must overcome if we are to resolve the problem of crime in Alice Springs.

Cultural trauma causes inter-generational and personal trauma

Cultural trauma causes personal trauma as a response to the shattering events that caused the cultural trauma. It is so persistent and overwhelming that it leaves the person unable to cope. This type of trauma is passed down from generation to generation. It may be passed on through methods of parenting, modes of behaviour, domestic violence, the use of harmful substances and/or mental health issues. These issues are the *result* of trauma and the *cause* of *new* trauma, in one vicious cycle.

Secondary exposure to trauma occurs when children witness the past traumatic experiences of their family and community members who speak of massacres, dispossession, slavery, rape, and violence that took place in the past. Without first addressing the healing needs of communities and their members, other interventions are likely to have limited impact. It seems critical that healing programs have a vital element of restoring, reaffirming, and renewing cultural identity, connection to country and participation in community.

If done well, sustainable justice can play a significant part in this.

Parental incarceration

It is not known how many children have parents in prison. There is no process for identifying them, no oversight, no support for them, and no government department responsible for them. They are not considered by the justice system. There are no processes or protocols in the police force, courts or prisons related to them. This lack of policy may well be a significant contributor to (re)offending by children and young people, as expected outcomes – such as stigma, homelessness, instability, stress, and poverty – suggest.

A Victorian parliamentary inquiry in 2022 into the children of imprisoned parents found that parental incarceration is likely to interrupt childhood developmentand have detrimental impacts on the emotional, and social wellbeing, and the mental and physical health, of the child. This can lead to intergenerational trauma and incarceration.[22]

Adverse childhood experiences

Life on the streets in groups that form gangs is in itself extremely traumatising and re-traumatising. The links to violent experiences inherent in gang membership may correlate strongly with PTSD, anxiety, and paranoia. There is little research into this as yet, but a small study found that "as compared to non-gang prisoners, street gang prisoners have higher levels of exposure to violence, symptoms of paranoia, PTSD, anxiety, and forced control of their behaviour in prison."[23] Clearly, mental health in gang-like groups deserves more research. Gang members may undermine other members' mental health, or persons with existing mental health problems may be attracted to gang membership. Judicial responses, policies, and intervention strategies need to identify and address the mental-health needs of these gang members and prisoners who come from such a background, if successful rehabilitation is to be achieved.

Victim Trauma

Post-traumatic street disorder

American research has identified gang-impacted communities as populations susceptible to PTSD or "post-traumatic street disorder"[24], a term coined by researchers. Residents of these communities are exposed to ongoing acts of crime that impact their mental well-being and increase their chances of suffering from PTSD symptoms. Such residents experience traumatic moments in their own neighbourhoods that leave them feeling unsafe and mentally scarred.

Residents in gang-impacted communities may experience symptoms like hypervigilance, nervousness, nightmares, and overall anxiety. Some may become numb to the constant violence. All these reactions can be observed among the inhabitants of Alice Springs.

Social media offers new platforms on which victims can express themselves. Potential victims and victims maintain a Facebook page on which they exchange experiences. Below are some posts from *Action for Alice 2020* by victims of crime in Alice Springs (the posts have not been edited and may contain racist comments, swearing and other inappropriate language as well as spelling and other mistakes):

14 April 2022

Well after a combined 18 years we are done, like a lot of families we will no longer be subjected to the crap that is going on throughout the NT. We will be leaving great jobs and friends selling up and walking away, for the sake of our mental health, we both wish to be able to enjoy social events knowing our house won't be broken into or our car stolen we won't be spat at, abused or call a white C*** because we won't give smokes or money. We love Central Australia- but have come to hate what Alice Springs has become. Counting down the days ....

14 April 2022

Just had 2 persons try to access our home @ Stuart Hwy Braitling... we were threatened with violence...called police.. they responded quickly... why do we have to put up with this behavior ... we live in fear of these little s....ts ...after 40 years had enough ... we are out of here...

13 April 2022

After nearly 50 years if providing a 24-Hour Emergency callout service, this service will cease
effectively as of 14'h April 2022. The overall demand for this service has become overwhelming and is affecting our day-to-day operations with exhausted staff which in turn is affecting their work/life balance and the operation of the company as a whole. Our focus will now be on project-based construction and quality workmanship rather than fixing vandalism after hours. This social problem has now been thrust upon our business making day to day operations increasingly difficult so we will now focus on building this town rather than patching it up. Our normal repair service will still be active during normal working hours. Key clients such as Shopping Centres, Hotels, building owners will be given direct phone numbers to enable their businesses to be secure and function as usual. We apologise whole heartedly for this decision as it is a necessity in

Alice Springs with the current challenges it faces. Neeta Glass.

11 April 2022
My father who is disabled was assaulted earlier today after a boy aged roughly 10-11 years old asked him for a smoke and my father said "No your to young" in which this child called my father a "fat C**t" and threw a full large can of red bull at his back and proceeded to abuse him.

11 April 2022
We were also a long term family of Alice. Sadly we had to make the decision (not one that came easy for many reasons) but after my kids were petrified to go to yeperenye to get basics from the supermarket and Coles being no better unfortunately. My kids started to see a standard of behaviour as "the norm". It is NOT. It's not ok and it's not normal. We'd get home and lock ourselves in our own yard and house and dare not leave after dark. We'd hide car keys and be thankful if the cars were still there in the morning. So we asked why were we so there. With mixed emotions we made the move! We don't think twice about our safety.
My kids have discovered a level of freedom I simply could not offer in Alice. We walk after dark. I feel the most relaxed I have in years. Alice was a unique place and we'll be forever grateful for what it gave us and the people become family but sadly the past 5years had us feeling there was no way back for Alice.

11 April 2022
We left town. Moved our family away after loving Alice for years. We knew we lived with fear. We knew we lived assessing every situation and making adjustments all the time to keep us and our property safe. Like getting dropped off and picked up from the movies/dinner out instead of leaving our car parked in town; waking multiple times a night when the dogs bark and being on high alert; having house sitters instead of

leaving house empty; not walking anywhere after dark; getting my husband to buy alcohol as I was so afraid of getting bailed up in the Woolies car park while putting alcohol in the car. All these things and more that any Alice resident can relate to and normalises. So here we are in our new town. Sleeping through the night and feeling quite safe wherever we go, at whatever time of day or night. I feel like the biggest invisible weight has lifted. I didn't know how heavy it was til it wasn't there any more. We miss the beautiful Alice. We miss our friends. But we won't move back and it makes me sad to think that beautiful Alice is losing people who love it because of the crime.

11 April 2022 2:50am.
East Side Club, Alarm blaring. Thought it was a fire. walked down street, two hooded people slip out of the Bush Balm medicine house (Purple House)
As i try sleep i hear the argument and the speeding away of a car, then a epic crash. loud screams. A car slows past me to sus me out, clearly their escort car, calling me out, waiting for someone. threats aside. I'm born here, to say I'm use to it.... is not healthy.
Matter of fact, I just cannot imagine what our mental health must be like with just so much crime.

10 April 2022
Go to Coles to buy some crap. Come out to the Carpark and 10 or so 10 to 15yr old boys and I'll say boys because men don't behave that way. Leaning on the car I politely said hey fellas I need to get in the car. Fuck u cunt was the response. So I fired back with a few words myself. They swore at me in language so I swore back in language. They then threatened to take me back to santa Teresa and bash me I said that's fine I'll take you to my family at papunya and let them cut you. They hit the car window and tried to run. I may be old and slow but I can still give a good hip and shoulder and dropped one on his arse. He

got up and was apologetic and said he just wants to go home. I asked him where his family was and his response was that they went back bush and left him in town. So a 14/15yr old kid from bush left in town by his family to fend from himself. I asked his name to which I new some of his family and ones who are in town, put him.in the car dropped him off at Lara. He said sorry again and thanked me for taking him to extended families.

My question to TF, the GUNNA flogs why aren't you helping these kids, either get them away from family who do not care about them and place them with family who will or fuckin provide a service with people of cultural knowledge to help support these kids. We are losing another generation and a generation of kids who have no respect for anyone but more importantly no respect for themselves.

Just to add I didn't hurt the young fella and never would hurt a kid, but to hear his story and to have it confirmed by his extended family is heart breaking. Lots of these kids have no role models no one to guide them. I know plenty of people who can and would make a difference but typically funding always goes to fucktards with no idea on how to help. End of rant.[25]

11 April 2022

Darwin getting all the love... we've been screaming out for years and all problems supposedly solved by a street sweep for government to spend one night with guards in Alice. This is so out of control and yet we have to abide.

My home was nearly entered by 4 scum with a crow bar, stole our belongings and got a smack on the knuckles.

This behaviour is fuck'd.

If you come to my door again I will hunt to harm as I'm fuck'n done living under your rule of your land... if it's your land show some fuck'n respect for it, you fuck'n animals the rubbish and damage you cause is not respect for your land it's total disrespect . You have not been shown what is right and wrong but believe me you are so wrong and nothing good will come of this.

We want to live peacefully with you as the custodians of this land but this behaviour will not work.

I know that my family came here to support as much as possible but because of the behaviour are now here defending human rights and want to leave and have been trying. Myself and children have suffered greatly to be here (an extent you would never understand) but it has been to help in some way for you.

If you read this we are no different we bleed the same and need the same. If life is difficult you are in the most abiding town to help you so please If life is absolutely shit please ask for help. No-one wants you to hurt anymore even though that feels out of reach.

We love this town and we love you so please stop trying to stop us helping you.

Be honest, be wise and be you, under all that harm you've suffered as I can say as a White folk I've suffered hugely too, but can't hide behind my race to act out and let's be honest I've been an asshole over time and been treated like one too.

Let's face this together as soon as possible as many of us are genuinely here to do.

Alice Springs taxi driver Toni Ryland suffered over $25,000 in damage in September 2022 when her vehicle was stolen and found to be a total write-off, and was paid no compensation by Victims of Crime because they do not compensate for business losses.

A few months earlier, business owner Lavinia Fischer-Dvorsky had to close her business Guitar and Vocal Classes because of excessive damage.

Business owners who are insured are getting no

compensation from Victims of Crime, nor is there any emotional support available.

A female Indian restaurant owner said: "When I came to Alice Springs a couple of years ago, I felt very safe. I could walk alone late at night without fearing being robbed or hurt. But unfortunately, it has changed in the past two years. I don't feel safe going out alone in the evenings. There is the fear of someone throwing stones at the car and of being attacked, especially by kids. Even driving in town, one never knows when those kids would just come in front of your car with their bikes. Being a business owner, it has affected us a lot. We have these kids walk into our restaurant and steal soft drinks from the fridge. When they were stopped, they threw glass bottles back at us, which is so scary, so we feel helpless and asked the staff not to run after them as we didn't want anyone to get hurt at our place. At home at night, I check on the cameras to see that no one is around the house to steal. Since I have put alarms in the house, I feel like an animal locked in a cage. So, to sum it up, Alice is not safe anymore."

Trauma in prison workers

Prison guards in Alice Springs walked off the job in July 2022 following similar industrial action in Darwin. United Workers Union NT's Secretary Erina Early said: "The levels of overcrowding and short staffing are at a crisis point, and it's a disaster waiting to happen. Correctional officers have a dangerous job even under ideal circumstances, but now the extra pressures force skilled and dedicated workers to leave the industry."

There was also industrial action in both Darwin and Alice Springs in May 2022. Corrections Commissioner Matthew Varley said in June 2022 that an increase in the number of prisoners caused stress, attrition, and excessive overtime work. Union figures suggest a lack of 48 corrections officers in Alice Springs. Union delegate and corrections officer Phil Tilbrook believed the department was "dysfunctional".[26]

Corrections officers are often faced with allegations of abuse and misconduct, which are sometimes found to be false, with charges dropped.[27] Those guards are left with stress-related trauma. Guards must constantly be aware of their actions and protect the rights of the offenders above their own needs and safety, even when offenders show violent behaviours. Stress in prison officers causes anxiety, depression, PTSD and panic disorder.

To ensure they have access to justice, there needs to be a serious overhaul of the role of security. There should be minimum contact between the offender and the guard. State-of-the-art camera technologies should be in place to record all situations without lapses so that a comprehensive picture is recorded of situations leading up to violent incidents. Staff training focused on trauma and deflecting conflict should be a priority, and access to mental health support and clinical supervision should reduce burnout and the stigma of mental health issues. Even with this kind of training in place, guards should not be around offenders. They should guard the perimeters of the facility. Offender violence should be dealt with as it is in hospitals, not as it is in prisons, because crime in Alice Springs is a public-health issue, not a criminal-law issue.

(Vicarious) trauma in lawyers and magistrates

Lawyers experience very high levels of vicarious trauma and trauma. Even without prior trauma, contact with legal processes is stressful. Hence, lawyers work with highly stressed people. They encounter people, victims and offenders whose lives have been shaped and severely harmed by traumatic events.

However, reflective practice skills are completely absent in the law curriculum. In the current bachelor's degree of a lawyer there is no unit about trauma in clients, nor is there one in self-care. Sustainability was a unit that could be chosen before the bachelor's degree became a three-year-long course instead of a four-year-long one. It did not cover sustainable justice practices. The postgraduate Diploma of Practical Legal Training (PLT) contains one unit of self-care, which is part of a one-morning session. The master's degree does not include any such units. Hence, lawyers, especially those who come to work in Alice Springs, are utterly unprepared for what awaits them. The workplace may provide trauma training. Such training generally does not last longer than a couple of days. The workload is heavy, and lawyers are often expected to perform beyond the call of duty.

Burnout in the legal profession is often caused by a lack of boundaries between work and personal life. More than any other profession, the legal culture results in practitioners working in high-pressure environments with excessive hours, resulting in burnout and mental health issues, including depression and anxiety. A recent study of 200 legal professionals across Australia and New Zealand revealed that 85% of employees suffer from anxiety or know of a colleague who does, while 80% suffer from depression or know of a colleague who does.[28]

Trauma and magistrates

There are no specific studies about the mental well-being of the magistrates in the courts of Alice Springs, but a few days of observation in the lower court hammers home the sheer absurdity of the situation. While wearing the wig and the gown, closely resembling the coloniser, magistrates face an endless row of disadvantaged, traumatised, disempowered people of colour and send these people to places where they become even more disadvantaged, traumatised, and disempowered. One can only imagine what this does to a person.

Traditionalists argue that wearing the wig and gown imbues court proceedings with a certain sense of respect and gravitas, promoting formality and maintaining order. But opponents say that this form of apparel causes lawyers to appear out-of-touch with ordinary people and can make people feel intimidated or inferior in court. Others find it outright comical. A 2003 survey of 360 members of the public conducted by the **Law Institute of Victoria** found that 54% believed that wigs and robes should still be worn in court. There are no studies I could find that looked into what it feels like to resemble the brutal coloniser, in dress and hairstyle.

In his 2017 Tristan Jepson Memorial Foundation Sydney Lecture, David Heilpern[29] shared his challenges and insights regarding vicarious trauma, PTSD, fatigue, the inability to recognise problems and reluctance to seek help. He raised six core issues that need to be addressed to "lift the judicial veil" on the serious mental health issues affecting judicial officers: modern technology; decision fatigue; viewing emotion as bad, intellect as good; security threats; the loneliness of the job; and the need for more research on mental health issues and the judiciary, along with remedies.[30]

He mentions that, in the same year, there was a Law Report titled *Is practising criminal law bad for your mental health?*" on ABC Radio National. Peter McGrath SC, a vastly experienced criminal barrister, spoke of a particularly distressing sexual assault case:

...during the trial, I can remember different stages, at one stage the officer in charge was giving evidence before the jury and just burst out crying in the witness box and couldn't go on and we had to adjourn. At another time, the judge's associate, and she was a very experienced woman who had seen a lot of trials, she was unable to come into court, we had to adjourn because she was very affected. At one point the court officer, who was a crusty old fellow who had been in so many cases and heard it all, he was ... we couldn't start the call one morning and where was he, he was in the corner of the anteroom and he was just sitting on his chair and weeping and shaking his head and saying, "Those poor boys, those poor boys." And I was thinking, God, who's next?

"Someone is missing from his description. The judge. What was he or she feeling? How was the judge dealing with all this evidence that he or she would need to rule on? "We ought to stop talking of judicial stress and start calling it for what it is — anxiety, panic attack, insomnia,
traumatic response, depression, PTSD, substance use disorder and the like."

"According to the most recent research, 33% of solicitors and 20% of barristers suffer from disability and distress due to depression. They tend not to seek help and often self-medicate with alcohol. Given that judicial officers are almost exclusively drawn from the ranks of the profession, it would be a reasonable conclusion that a significant number of judicial officers suffer from debilitating mental health issues during their time on the bench. There is a veil based on assumptions regarding judicial officers. The sooner that veil is lifted, the sooner judicial officers can admit to difficulties, access help and better serve the community."

"For country magistrates, the sheer volume of traumatic work is hard for those outside the criminal justice system to comprehend. We are also coroners, and I will often spend my lunch time running through gruesome evidence and reading suicide notes. Responses to trauma for judicial officers are often cumulative and exponential. Modern technology has made the trauma much more "in your face". Real violence is now captured on CCTV, smart phones, in-car-videos and DVEC's."

In the lower court, there is no jury, and thus the magistrates alone must determine guilt or innocence, based on the evidence of the victim and the defendant. That means they must assess the truthfulness of the witnesses carefully. This involves, "getting inside the head" of both. This requires a determined focus and concentration, and this level of absorption makes vicarious trauma unsurprising. They cannot just listen dispassionately to the evidence; they have to digest and ruminate on each morsel and judge the people before them. "This is a level of intimacy, for want of a better word, that perhaps fills the sponge more rapidly than one would expect."

The relationship between decision fatigue and vicarious trauma is entirely unresearched. There is a good chance that each exponentially affects the other.

Throughout their education, their practice and their role as judicial officers, magistrates are taught to suppress their emotions in a quest for apparent objectivity. It is perhaps time to recognise that the expression of emotion is not the opposite of administering justice. Judicial officers are humans, not automatons, and suppressing emotion every day is a recipe for fragile mental health.

One great fear among judicial officers is that if they have a mental health issue, they could lose their appointment. They must be physically and mentally fit to exercise the functions of a judicial office efficiently.

Security threats are inherently traumatic experiences, and many judicial officers experience a significant number of these over the years. These threats pose a real danger to the mental health of judicial officers for obvious reasons, and it is challenging to separate hyper-vigilance from realistic precautions.

The job can feel exceptionally lonely, despite the

collegiate nature of the bench. There are limits on social life. Many judicial officers work in single courts and are away from loved ones for days or weeks. This way of life offers little opportunity for informal talk therapy or debriefing that can empty the sponge.

Clearly, there needs to be more research into mental-health issues and the judiciary in Australia. The particular focus should be on the following issues:

- What are the current rates of vicarious trauma/PTSD in Australian judicial officers?
- When does the issue become more acute?
- Is there a relationship between judicial officers sitting alone and in country courts and increased levels of PTSD?
- What percentage of disciplinary matters involving judicial officers have an underlying mental health issue? For lawyers, it is reportedly 80%.
- Is there evidence to support the hypothesis that an annual "mental health" check-up for judicial officers would be of assistance?
- Does it help to opt out of certain types of cases for a time?
- What are the most effective methods of increasing resilience — mentoring, education, buddying, debriefing, supervision?[31]

Trauma among the police

The Kumanjayi Walker shooting, the trial that followed and the coronial inquest that followed the trial has hammered home the need to look at trauma in police officers. Was Rolfe motivated by racism, was he used to using excessive force, or was he traumatised? The coronial inquest revealed that he was being medicated for depression.

Police officers often face traumatic situations and witness the trauma of others. As a result, they are known to have elevated rates of PTSD, depression, and suicidal thoughts and actions. Due to the work culture, this subject has been quite taboo. In August 2016, A Four Corners exposé titled *Insult to Injury* revealed how police officers' claims for compensation and psychiatric treatment for PTSD were being met with scepticism, resistance and delays. Perceived stigma, failure to seek help and organisational failures to support help-seeking created high levels of despair that affect families and the community. Insurers are going to extraordinary lengths to avoid making payouts, such as spying on victims and invading their privacy, using both physical and electronic surveillance. For these police officers, the aggressive tactics exacerbated their mental illness, sometimes resulting in suicide.[32]

In the first half of 2022, there were five suicides by current or former Northern Territory Police officers. A

Support and Well-being Services review summary stated that there was no strategy for the mental health and well-being of police officers, and only limited data reporting on it, and that there was no money for "preventative and responsive" services.[33]

A Beyond Blue survey in 2017-2018 of 21,000 police and emergency service workers across Australia found that employees reported having suicidal thoughts at a rate over two times higher than the general population and were more than three times as likely to have a suicide plan. It also found that "poor workplace practices and culture were found to be damaging to mental health and occupational trauma." One in 2.5 employees was diagnosed with a mental health condition, compared with one in five in the general population. Four out of 10 former employees experienced symptoms of PTSD, compared with one in 10 current employees, and one in five experienced very high psychological distress. More than half of employees reported that they had experienced traumatic events during their work that deeply affected them. Three out of four employees found that the worker's compensation process made them even more unwell.[34]

A Northern Territory Police Association survey in 2022 found that most police officers were unhappy with leadership, understaffing issues, and pay levels, and that they were losing faith in the force. 92.6% of officers did not think there were enough police to do what was being asked of them. 87.9% said they were dissatisfied with the current pay freeze. 61% felt that senior managers did not engage with employees at all levels, while 58% said that recruitment and promotions were not based on merit. 59% said that they did not feel safe to speak up and challenge the way things were done, and 58% said they did not feel recommendations from staff were fairly considered. 58% said they did not feel any action would be taken because of the survey. Northern Territory Police Association president McCue said the results showed the police force was in "complete crisis" and morale is at an all-time low. He mentioned the impact of the Kumanjayi Walker shooting.

When we look at our shared story of trauma: the harm caused by (juvenile) detention; trauma and neurolaw; offenders' intergenerational trauma; adverse childhood experiences in offenders; victim trauma; vicarious and other trauma in lawyers, police officers and prison workers; and trauma-induced disability in offenders – we also see that NGOs and government organisations do not sufficiently reach the offenders.

Anyone who has worked for NGOs and other organisations in Alice Springs knows how hopelessly siloed they often are. They often do not reach the most vulnerable and transient.

This, in combination with the waxing and waning

of political approaches to the problem, makes that sustainable solutions have not been found.

There is only one answer to this problem: substantial investment in sustainable justice. This means seeing crime in Alice Springs as a public-health issue that needs public-health responses, under one roof, in an establishment that is the opposite of a prison. I have referred to this as a "Nosirp" until we find a better word for it. Sustainable solutions are expensive. It is impossible to know how expensive such an establishment would be. But we should measure its projected cost against the total cost of crime in Alice Springs, as I have calculated.

The Ny Anstalt facility in Nuuk, Greenland, built between 2013-2017, cost AUS$52,381,385 to build and costs AUS$231,869 per prisoner per year to run.

It is very simple: if we do not make a similar investment in the futures of the children in our wider community, and the futures of our police, lawyers, magistrates, judges, and prison workers and their families...crime in Alice Springs is here to stay.

In light of the enormity of the problem described above, putting a small private army with dogs on the streets, as recently suggested in the council, seems a very questionable, short-term solution. In my view, it should be avoided at any cost.

Endnotes

1   https://www.facebook.com/profile.
php?id=100069550777541

2   https://www.facebook.com/standwithyuendumu/

3   *R v Hawkins* [2015] ACTSC 333

4   Greenberg, J, Solomon, S & Pyszczynski, T 1997, *Terror management theory of self-esteem and cultural worldviews: Empirical assessments and conceptual refinements*, Advances in experimental social psychology, 29 Academic Press, Inc; Yalom, ID 1980, *Existential Psychotherapy*, Basic Books.

5   Jonas, E, Schimel, J, Greenberg, J & Pyszczynski, T 2002, 'The Scrooge Effect: Evidence that mortality salience increases prosocial attitudes and behavior', *Personality and Social Psychology Bulletin*, 28.

6   Greenberg, J, Solomon, S & Pyszczynski, T 1997, *Terror management theory of self-esteem and cultural worldviews: Empirical assessments and conceptual refinements*, Advances in experimental social psychology, 29 Academic Press, Inc.

7   Becker, E 1971, *The birth and death of meaning*, Free Press.

8   Halloran, M 2004, 'Cultural maintenance and trauma in indigenous Australia', *E law : Murdoch University electronic journal of law*, 11(4):1-12.

9   Halloran, M 2004, 'Cultural maintenance and trauma in indigenous Australia', *E law : Murdoch University electronic journal of law*, 11(4):1-12.

10 Trudgen, R 2000, *Why warriors lie down and die*, Aboriginal Resource and Development Services.

11 Chisholm, R & Nettheim, G 1997, *Understanding law*, 5 edn., Butterworths.

12 Atkinson, J 2002, *Trauma trails, recreating song lines: The transgenerational effects of trauma in Indigenous Australia* Spinifex Press.

13 Manne, R 2001, *In denial: The stolen generations and the Right*, Schwartz publishing.

14 Nadler, A 2002, 'Intergroup helping as power relations: Maintaining or challenging social dominance between groups through helping ', *Journal of Social Issues*, 59(487).

15 ABS 2003, *The health and welfare of Australia's Aboriginal and Torres Strait Islander peoples (4704.0)*, AGP Canberra: Hogg, RS 1994, 'Variability in behavioural risk factors Hunter, E 1995, 'Freedom's just another word: Aboriginal youth and mental health', *Australian and New Zealand Journal of Psychiatry* 28; Perkins, JJ, Sanson-Fisher, RW, Blunden, S & Lunnay, D 1994, 'The prevalence of drug use in urban Aboriginal communities ', *Addiction*, 89; Swann, P & Raphael, B 1995, *Ways Forward National Consultancy Report on Aboriginal and Torres Strait Islander Mental Health*, AGP Service.

16 Eckermann, A 1992, *Binan Goonj: Bridging cultures in Aboriginal health*, University of New England Press; Koolmatie, J & Williams, R 2000, 'Unresolved grief and the removal of Indigenous Australian children ', *Australian Psychologist*, 35.

17 ABS 2003, *The health and welfare of Australia's Aboriginal and Torres Strait Islander peoples (4704.0)*, AGP Canberra.

18 Halloran, M 2004, 'Cultural maintenance and trauma in indigenous Australia', *E law : Murdoch University electronic journal of law*, 11(4):1-12.

19 Coombs, HC, Brandl, MM & Snowdon, WE 1983, *A certain heritage* A certain heritage ANU Press.

20 Fejo, L, Rae, C & Report, C 1996, *Strong Women, Strong Babies, Strong culture* AGP Service.

21 Halloran, M 2004, 'Cultural maintenance and trauma in indigenous Australia', *E law : Murdoch University electronic journal of law*, 11(4):1-12.

22 Inquiry into children affected by parental incarceration 2022, Parliament of Victoria, Legislative Council, Legal and Social Issues Committee.

23 Wood, J & Dennard, S 2017, 'Membership: links to violence exposure, paranoia, PTSD, anxiety, and forced control of behavior in prison', *Psychiatry*, 80(1):30-41.

24 Reeves, J 2021, Post Traumatic Streets Disorder: A battle within. Kindle Edition.

25 https://www.facebook.com/Action-for-Alice-2020

26 Walls, J & Averill, Z 2022, 'Prison guards on strike after chronic understaffing leads to 'racking and stacking' of inmates', *NT News*, July 18.

27 Meldrum-Hanna, C & Worthington 2016, 'CCTV footage shows repeated victimisation of Dylan Voller in NT youth detention Centres', *ABC News*, 25 july.

28 Chow, DF 2021, *Preventative measures to stop burnout in the legal profession*, 7 September, Australian Lawyers

alliance.

29 Adjunct Professor at Southern Cross University and former Magistrate of the NSW Local Court 1999–2020.

30 Heilpern D 2017, speech presented at the Tristan Jepson Memorial Foundation, 25 October.

31 Heilpern D 2017, speech presented at the Tristan Jepson Memorial Foundation, 25 October

32 ABCTV 2016, *Four Corners*, 1 August.

33 Wood, D 2022, 'No defined strategy to deal with mental health': NTPFES well-being review delayed, as two more police officers take their lives', *NT Independent*, 13 June.

34 Wood, D 2021, 'No defined strategy to deal with mental health': NTPFES well-being review delayed, as two more police officers take their lives', *NT Independent*, June 13.

Chapter five

Toward sustainable justice

This chapter results from countless private conversations with community members of all cultural backgrounds and ages, over several years.

It is a chapter in which the hopes and imagination of the community of Alice Springs have no limits.

Street-connected children and street-ism

For "street-ism" I used part of the definition by UNICEF (1995) (not the part referring to children who are under eighteen years old, because we are using the upper age limit of 25), which describes two categories of children and young people as subject to street-ism.

On the one hand, there are roaming children and

young people for whom the street is their source of income. On the other hand, there are children and young people for whom the street is their normal place of residence. They are not adequately protected by adults, and they do not have a permanent home.

The Northern Territory has one of the highest rates of youth homelessness in Australia, with over 3,500 young people being homeless on any given night, according to Anglicare.

Not all our street-connected young people are homeless, and not all young people and children who are homeless end up living in the open or on the streets. Many end up sleeping in places that are out of sight: on the floors of friends or strangers; in the bush; in the riverbed; or in temporary accommodation. Not all young people and children who can be described as 'street-connected children' are necessarily homeless. They may spend time on the street, but they may go back to their family or parents when they need a place to sleep. We can use the term 'street-connected children' to describe children who depend on the streets to live, either on their own, or with other children or family members; and who have a strong connection to public spaces – parking lots, streets, industrial areas, parks – and for whom the street plays a vital role in their everyday lives and identities. This wider group includes young people and children who are not homeless but regularly accompany other children or family members in the streets.

In other words, 'street-connected children' are children who depend on the streets for their survival – whether they are homeless, have support networks on the streets, or have a combination of these factors.

Every single child and young person has their own unique story. Poverty, disadvantage, displacement due to conflicts or family breakdown, parental illness or death, parental imprisonment or neglect, violence, and abuse of children at home or within communities – all these drive young people to the streets. Discrimination, lack of access to justice, and a lack of legal status (due to a lack of birth registration) all contribute to homelessness among young people. Dealing with each child as an individual, with their own backstory and identity, is key to understanding their situation. It is difficult to say how many street-connected young people and children there are in Alice Springs, because street-connected children are a dynamic, transient, and mobile population which requires specific methodologies to identify, ones that are different from standard household surveys or censuses.

Estimates or counts that are done at a fixed point in time can be misleading, depending on when the counts take place; the numbers of children in the streets can fluctuate with seasonal change, or if the government removes street-connected children and young people in advance of events, political meetings, or celebrations.

The children are often invisible. While researchers can take a snapshot of the ones currently on the streets, they don't capture the children who are indoors on that day or at that moment. Moreover, as street-connected children and young people experience high levels of stigma, they often are suspicious of attempts to count them, fearing negative consequences as a result of of being counted. So they prefer to remain below the radar. Notwithstanding these challenges, it is crucial to establish reliable numbers of street-connected children and understand the realities of their lives.

Organisations working with street-connected children need accurate data to design their programs better. Donors need data to ensure that their health, education and justice funding also reaches street-connected children. Governments need accurate data on street-connected children to devote the resources required to fulfil their obligations to these children under the Child Rights Convention. I attempted to count the street-connected children and young adults in Alice Springs in 2022. By my estimates there are 100 to 150. The *Alice Springs News* estimated the number to be between 150 and 200 in 2018, and 100 in 2021.

While young people should not be forcibly removed from the only home they know and placed elsewhere for "their own good", neither is it acceptable to leave children exposed to danger with no protection or recourse to justice.

Many street-connected children are harmed daily by adults, including government officials, the police, other children, and their own families. They are also denied access to education and healthcare.

Young people who are already vulnerable due to not having any ID, not having an adult being able to advocate for them, or not having appropriate shelter, can be vulnerable to abuse. Children are often robbed, beaten, or otherwise targeted. Street-connected young people and children are vulnerable to exploitation by abusers who may sexually assault them, forcibly recruit them into criminal activities, traffic them or send them out into the street to beg and steal. For many street-connected children and young people, street-connected gangs act as surrogate families which protect them from violence or harassment by outsiders and offer support. However, they also draw the children into violent criminal activities and drug use.

While the perception that all street-connected children and young adults being addicted to drugs is inaccurate, many engage in substance abuse to cope with homelessness, trauma, illness, hunger, stigmatisation, and discrimination. Long-term use at an age when children and young people are still physically and mentally developing can cause long-term problems in adulthood.

Although many street-connected children and young people show incredible resilience in the face of unspeakable hardships, their sense of well-being is generally low.

Street-connected children and young people often suffer from depression, anxiety, and trauma, which may lead to substance abuse and suicide attempts.

Most crimes in Alice Springs are committed by these children and young people. They are the ones that end up incarcerated at one stage or another.

The children and young people on the streets of Alice Springs often do not know or experience parental care. Many residents of Alice Springs believe that this is just the type of care they need. They need one-on-one care (at least), *plus* any other care for their health and well-being. Remember: one person can make *the* difference.

Perceptions of 'them'; the feeling that the problem is someone else's and not our own

The fact that almost all offenders on the streets of Alice Springs are Aboriginal should not mislead us into believing that there is a relationship between race and crime. Aboriginality is, of course, not an indicator of criminality; rather, the indicator is trauma because of disadvantage. Race is a dubious concept, and not an empirical one. We need to see crime as *our* problem: a problem of the people of Alice Springs. *We* must solve it, assisted by our local government using the Bonnemaison model discussed above, by NGOs, private organisations, the council, and individuals.

It takes a village

The meme "it takes a village to raise a child" has become a cliché. This makes it no less true. Less well-known is the continuation of what is supposedly this African proverb: *"The child who is not embraced by the village will burn it down to feel its warmth."* This is precisely what is happening in Alice Springs: its children are burning down the town to feel its warmth. It is a loud and clear cry for help. The problem will not be solved before *we* own it, and until *we* listen.

The infantilisation of Aboriginal people

Alice Springs-based social worker and counsellor Kalikamurti Suich writes:

"Between 1910 and 1970, between 10 and 33 per cent of Aboriginal and Torres Strait Islander children were forcibly removed from their families. The policies of child removal that became known as the Stolen Generations left a legacy of trauma and loss that continues to forcefully affect communities, families, and individuals today. The removal policy was one of assimilation. Assimilation assumed black inferiority and white superiority. People of Aboriginal and Torres Strait Islander people and white parentage were particularly vulnerable to removal. Children taken from their parents were taught to reject their Aboriginal heritage and were forced to adopt white culture. Their names were changed. They were forbidden to speak their language. They were placed in institutions where abuse and neglect were common. The 1997 *Bringing Them Home Report* concluded that the policies of child removal breached fundamental human rights. In 2008, Prime Minister Rudd made a National Apology to the Stolen Generations."

Initiatives by Australian governments have reinforced this paternalism consistently since 1967, when a referendum was followed by changes in the Constitution requiring Aboriginal people to be included in the census. The altered powers in the Constitution allowed the Federal parliament to make special laws with reference to Aboriginal people, who had previously been excluded from Federal law under Section 51. The measure was seen as encompassing Aboriginal Australians in a non-discriminatory regime, but what actually happened was that the government obtained the power to expand the Commonwealth's role in Aboriginal Affairs.

The 2007 Northern Territory Intervention, announced by the Howard government, suspended the

Racial Discrimination Act, enacted the Northern Territory National Emergency Response Bill and rolled the army into remote communities. It quarantined welfare payments, banned alcohol and pornography, imposed compulsory health checks on children, and forced the Commonwealth's acquisition of township leases on Aboriginal-owned land.

This strongly undermined Indigenous sovereignty. The Intervention and its supporters signalled that Aboriginality was inherently violent and abusive. Aboriginal adults were all tarred with the same brush: as failing to be protectors and carers for their children, as victims of abuse themselves, and/or as complicit in the abuse. This stigma resulted in lasting psychological damage for many.

A work-for-the-dole Program (CDP), introduced Trojan horse-style along with the other new regulations, was discriminatory and a form of modern-day slavery. It caused even more loss of autonomy.

Reforms of income-management welfare linked Centrelink payments to a 'Basics Card' that had to be used to buy 'essentials' such as food, rent and clothing. The card was only accepted in certain shops in the Northern Territory, which caused lines, embarrassment, and stigma at checkout counters. The government was signalling that recipients were not capable of managing their money and that they were solely responsible for problems within their communities.

In 2008, the Rudd Government, the Aboriginal and Torres Strait Islander Social Justice Commission and peak Indigenous health bodies signed a Statement of Intent to 'work together to achieve equality in health status and life expectancy between Aboriginal and Torres Strait Islander peoples and non-Indigenous Australians by the year 2030'.

The Federal government would report annually on the progress of the targets. Despite the annual budget of $3.5 billion, the results were deeply disappointing.

The Close the Gap goal of 'statistical equality' is problematic because of its 'predominantly individualistic focus, which fails to account for an imbalanced distribution of power and a limited degree of control exercised by Aboriginal and Torres Strait Islander Australians (both individually and collectively) over their own circumstances'.

Closing the Gap framed Aboriginal people once again as being in need of measurement, monitoring and rectification. The initiative failed to address the inequality of power distribution in Australia. To achieve real progress towards equality and sustainable justice, radical change is needed to 'deliver control over the Indigenous affairs agenda into the hands of Indigenous Australians'.

With this history in mind, it does not take a skilled observer to see what is and has been unfolding in Alice Springs. There is blatant Apartheid, open for all to see. This Apartheid causes trauma, not only in the inflicted but also in the inflictors. The social landscape described above is the social landscape in which this book is being written. There is no comfortable ground to stand on. The more one reads about the problem, the more hurdles one finds that have to be overcome to solve the problem of (youth) crime in Alice Springs. This may suggest that the problem is insoluble. So we may have to turn the question around. To understand what drives those who roam our streets, we must deeply listen to them. They say and signal: "Don't white people have problems of their own to solve? Why come here to solve our problems with your organisations, your programs, your white Toyotas? Let us solve our own problems in a way that we see fit, and in a way that is different from your way."

Whenever white people decide to take on the role of solving problems for Aboriginal people, or to rejig the system that keeps Aboriginal people stuck generation after generation in disadvantage, they are assuming a position of power: the power to decide what is right or good for Aboriginal people. They are signalling to Aboriginal people: we know what is best for you. This is the reason why nothing changes. People have come up with all sorts of ideas to 'close the gap'. But the gap will not close if the only people doing the changing are Aboriginal. White people must change too. Whenever white people position themselves as interventionists, this is how Aboriginal people will see them.

So what can white people do? Like war reporters, white people can bear witness to the harms done by the cultural genocide that has taken place over two centuries. We would know very little about cultural genocide in other countries if the people who witnessed such atrocities had not borne witness, then later taken a stand and said to the world, "Yes I saw that happen. I saw that done to those people." We must observe, and record what is being observed. This is one of the goals of this book. What is currently observable is the enormous difference between the advantaged and the disadvantaged, the haves and the have-nots. When there is a problem in the community that we now share, we need to behave more like observers and listeners rather than preachers and problem-solvers. We need to take a step back and ensure that Aboriginal voices are heard above our own, because if their voices are not heard, others will talk over them. Until this happens it will be impossible to find a genuine solution to the problem of crime.

If we turn things around and see things through a different lens, instead of asking "what hurdles do we have to overcome to solve the problem of youth crime", we might rephrase the question as follows: "What hurdles must we overcome to solve the problem of white society not sharing its power with Aboriginal people?" And then we must be still and listen. What we hear when we listen is that Aboriginal children and young people do not think of youth crime as the problem: they are hungry, and they want Christmas presents too. So they take some of what we have. From their perspective, we have taken so much more from their people already. They are taking back the power they have lost.

Colonisation is still happening. This is a truth that is often difficult for non-Aboriginal people to swallow. The idea of decolonisation requires a deep understanding of privilege. The latter can be quite shocking to non-Aboriginal people: "I am a good person; how can I be identified as one of the people who hold such power over marginalised people?" Deep listening allows what I call 'Aboriginalisation' – the voices of Aboriginal people being heard. Decolonisation is what non-Aboriginal people need to do; this would allow space for Aboriginalisation, in a process of collaboration that will take many years from a period of public truth-telling.

Bearing in mind the often uncomfortable truth of the need for decolonisation, this book still tries to shine a light on the phenomenon of crime in Alice Springs from as many directions as possible, and by attempting to ask the right questions.

The young people on our streets are there because for them, the street is the best option. They find the companionship, friendship, and protection they need in the group they hang out with. They provide for their physical and psychological needs by committing crimes together. Prison, no matter how awful, is often a better alternative too. At least in prison there are meals and a mattress.

Community ideas

The lychee model and the principle of least infringement

Crime in Alice Springs is a public-health issue rather than a criminal-law issue. To solve the problem, we therefore need to adopt a public-health approach instead of a criminal-law approach.

We have learned from the Covid pandemic that it is

possible to keep people inside boundaries while exercising the *least infringement* principle. The boundaries must be hard, like the skin of a lychee, to keep the community safe. Inside the secure boundary, the approach should be soft as the flesh of a lychee, and tailored to the needs of the individuals and the groups within – in the same way as in the therapeutic communities that Alice Springs already has, at DASA and CAAPU, where culturally appropriate treatment for drug and alcohol addiction is provided.

The Nosirp

There are overseas examples where these principles are already being practised by the criminal justice and law enforcement systems. Ny Anstalt in Nuuk, Greenland, is one of them. This book proposes a similar approach for Alice Springs: an establishment that provides justice without retribution for offenders between 10 and 25 years old. Let us call it a 'Nosirp' instead of a 'prison', because it would be the opposite of a prison: it would heal instead of traumatising. The perimeters would be hard and secured by tough measures. However, the people who provided security within this kind of system would have hardly any contact with the residents. Inside, a soft approach, following the normality principle and the least infringement principle, would help offenders to de-escalate, heal, and obtain education and/or employment.

How exactly this could be done is not part of this book. A think-tank is needed. Aboriginal voices should be heard. However, the following working method, described in the publication *It's about time* by the Central Australian Aboriginal Congress in Alice Springs, seems a good place to start

https://www.caac.org.au/news/new-publication-its-about-time/

Other organisations in Alice Springs have initiated important research into trauma and Aboriginal people, and their insights could be incorporated into the Nosirp's therapeutic programs. Examples are the *Uti Kulintjaku* and the *Uti Kulintjaku Watiku* projects of the NPY Women's Council.

A critical study was conducted in the women's prison of Alice Springs in 2020. Its report provided an opportunity for Aboriginal women who are clients of the *Kunga Stopping Violence Program* in the Alice Springs Correctional Centre to contribute to a deeper understanding of the life events that led to their incarceration. The research explored the lives of twelve Aboriginal women who had been incarcerated for violent offences. Analysis of their life stories leading up to their incarceration demonstrated the critical need for services that can effectively respond to the trauma in women's lives and prevent future incarceration. It identified the interventions, services, and supports that can divert women into programs to prevent incarceration, highlighted the need for a coordinated response, and identified reforms to meet the needs of Aboriginal women experiencing complex trauma. The methodology used was *Dadirri*, a traditional process of deep listening while being fully present and aware.

The power of architecture to affect human behaviour

Design can be a meaningful intervention. In Scandinavian countries, beauty is seen as a healing agent. The Ny Anstalt facility, according to the architects, is a statement about the power of architecture to affect human behaviour and "mimics the rhythm and structure of everyday life."

Positioned between a landscape of mountains and the Nuuk Kangerlua fjord, Ny Anstalt was designed to blend seamlessly with its surroundings and create a connection to nature for inmates to appreciate. "Respect and dignity are at the heart of the design, reflected to the point between people and institution, as well as in the relationship between the building and the unique natural setting that surrounds it." "The contrast between beauty and roughness was a guiding theme in the design." The architects focussed on openness, light, views, security and flexibility, and incorporated local, native culture into the design process. "Each residential block is divided into a series of private 12-square-metre rooms, with bar-less windows providing views over the building's concrete wall towards the sea and surrounding landscape. A panoramic window spans the length of the common area, framing breathtaking fjord views, while in the chapel, tall narrow windows between timber-fin walls look out over the mountains. The interior walls and the concrete perimeter wall are decorated by Greenlandic Indigenous artists."

The principles followed by the architects of Ny Anstalt would fit perfectly in the Red Centre's desert landscape. Such a building should stand on its own and *not be* on the grounds of the existing prison. In building such a humane space, we would not have to raise the age of criminal responsibility immediately. Raising the age is, of course, necessary, but we are currently dealing with extremely young offenders in Alice Springs, and they have nowhere to go. Only when this generation of vulnerable young people has undergone sufficient healing and recovery does raising the age make sense. The same counts for the laws of complicity and mandatory sentencing. As the Nosirp would be non-punitive and healing, most problems within the law should fall away, at least for those aged between 10 and 25. The Nosirp should be so effective that voluntary admission would be possible and even desired.

Police officers, magistrates, lawyers, and prison workers would feel less stressed and traumatised if they knew that the young offenders they were dealing with would be well cared-for after being arrested. After arrest, the offender should be immediately delivered into the hands of culturally safe experts, and their (mental) health should be assessed immediately. De-escalation and treatment by culturally safe trauma experts should begin immediately.

It should not matter whether the offender was on remand or serving their sentence.

The concepts practised in the Nosirp should be explained to the public by a special information centre: a Centre for Sustainable Justice in Alice Springs. Such a centre could attract visitors to Alice Springs from interstate and abroad.

I have already set up a Centre with this name in connection with the publication of this book.

There are many points of entry into incarceration at which a decision not to detain but to use an alternative, such as the Nosirp, could be made. The most obvious point is the initial encounter with the police and the "discretion of the constable" on whether or not to detain. Often a young Aboriginal person enters custody as one of a group. The laws of complicity put them at risk immediately. Special training of police and the presence of Aboriginal advisors could lead to an informed decision to not detain, but to use the Nosirp option instead.

The next point of entry is the charge sergeant at the police station. At Menindee police station, the local headmaster arranged for Aboriginal Aunties to sit with this Sergeant. This reduced the charge rate by 40%. Alice Springs could make this a practice after special training of charge sergeants.

At the next point, the bail hearing, an offender is still presumed innocent. The main reasons for denying bail are the likelihood of failing to appear before the court or the risk to public safety. The failure-to-appear reason is often used against Aboriginal offenders because of the lack of a fixed address, or incapacity due to lack of education or disability. The answer to this problem is the Nosirp, which could provide a fixed address pending the court appearance, along with assistance with court proceedings, paperwork and actually escorting the offender to court.

The Nosirp could also be used for those on remand if bail was refused. Magistrates would feel much better about refusing bail if they knew the offender would be adequately cared for. S.5 of the *Sentencing Act* requires the sentencing officer to co nsider every alternative to incarceration.

If a guilty verdict was reached, the Nosirp could be the alternative to prison. It would be likely to reduce reoffending because it would provide effective intervention and assistance to those who had offended b ecause of trauma, disadvantage, poverty, or disability.

One-on-one parent figures would ensure that the Nosirper was cared for appropriately.

Lastly, the Nosirp could provide certificated VET provider-run training and work on-site to improve rehabilitation. In Ny Anstalt, some offenders go to work in the community and come "home" in the evening to eat and sleep.

The proposal

Centre for Sustainable Justice in town

The Centre for Sustainable Justice Australia researches and informs. It forms a bridge between the Nosirp and the community. SuzanneVisser has set up such a centre:

www.sustainablejusticeaustralia.com

The Nosirp

Thinking about where and how the Nosirp should be ran is the next step in the process beyond this book. The following keywords shouild be kept in mind:

Key words:
Justice without retribution
Lychee model (hard on the outside; soft on the inside)
Public Health model
Principle of least infringement
Normality principle
Aboriginal led and run
Community involvement

The Sustainable Justice Charter revisited

A Nosirp and Centre for Sustainable Justice, as described above, should improve social harmony, quality of life, and transparency, through the integration of the values of social sustainability into justice, as the Sustainable Justice Charter suggests.

The Sustainable Justice Charter should be the framework for how the Nosirp worked.

Social harmony, well-being, and the general feeling of safety within the community would be improved because the children and young people would be cared for. Personal and societal development, within a framework of human rights and principles securing legal uniformity and equality, would be promoted.

The justice system would be able to intervene effectively and would act in pursuit of the sustainability of society and its members.

Social sustainability and its interconnectedness with ideas like love, empathy and compassion would be practised.

A criticism of the existing justice system – that it does not appropriately and effectively meet community needs – would be lessened.

The main goal of sustainable justice – to increase the quality of life by improving the quality of relationships and social networks – would be promoted by practising and teaching mature inter-humane relationships, mutual respect, empathy and understanding, and the ability to transform negative emotions into creativity and constructive behaviour. The values of social sustainability would complement judicial values and contribute to the effectiveness of the judicial system.

Conflicts a nd c riminal a cts would become opportunities to restore and improve social harmony.

Individual cases would be seen as vehicles to reduce the individual and societal burden of the problems that are causing crime and are a result of crime.

Judicial power is given by society to the justice system on the assumption that this benefits society. Judicial officers using judicial power would be actual agents of societal change who could act as catalysts for a better society.

True prestige, independence, and their positions as ultimate decision-makers would confer upon judges and magistrates a charisma that enabled them to accomplish outcomes that others could not achieve. This would give them a pivotal position for attaining socially sustainable outcomes.

Socially sustainable outcomes would be achieved by using minimal but effective doses of power. A well-chosen and well-directed corrective impulse of power could restore and heal the harmony that has disturbed the community.

By removing punishment and replacing it with de-escalation, healing, education, and employment, bad would be turned into good, contributing to social harmony and personal and societal development.

Awareness of one's actions supports social sustainability. Education in this principle would have to be part of the therapy inside the Nosirp, because, from the perspective of social sustainability, people should not escape that awareness but rather accept their actions and learn from the process.

Community well-being and the sustainable interests of the parties would be served if the judge actively confirmed the parties' awareness of their actions, encouraged mutual respect, and enhanced mature behaviour and the parties' capacity to deal with their problems constructively, focusing on the best sustainable future for all, including the community. Other stakeholders and social-service providers would have to be involved in offender-victim reconciliation to achieve socially sustainable outcomes. Restorative practices could be applied in the Nosirp which brought the parties and other stakeholders together in a collaborative process that aimed to restore harmony in the affected social networks.

Sustainable "punishment" in the form of a hard shell would aim to bring or restore harmony in socially valuable networks, including those of victims, offenders, and their relatives. Implementing the normality principle inside would help offenders to become valuable members of society; therapy would stimulate and support them in developing constructive pro-social behaviour and reducing unhealthy and anti-social behaviours.

Social isolation should not be part of life inside because this would break down social networks, which often causes severe, sometimes lifelong and irreparable harm to relatives of offenders who are innocent. Treatments that harm socially valuable networks should be avoided whenever possible. The family should be able to visit and have a meal with the offender and stay overnight in a guest unit on the premises.

Social sustainability does not reject the principles of retribution and deterrence if the results of applying these principles support the values of social sustainability for the community and those involved. The difficulties that ex-prisoners and people with a criminal record experience in getting socially accepted again contribute to their return to criminal behaviour.

Highly trained judicial officers should use therapeutic techniques and assist other stakeholders in bringing about constructive behavioural change in the offenders. In this way, they would use their judicial power as a catalyst to build a socially sustainable society. This is called 'smart sentencing'.

The contribution of the justice system to the quality of life and social sustainability of the community should be clear, transparent, and measurable from material, social, and psychological perspectives.. A system for measurement with solid parameters should be developed concerning the structure of the justice system and the contribution of individual judicial officers.

Social sustainability should provide valuable guiding principles to the justice system, encouraging it to change to contribute to social harmony more effectively. Conflicts about material interests and criminal behaviour should be used to foster the improvement of relationships and social networks, realising the best sustainable future for everybody involved. This could be realised by enhancing the responsibility and accountability of those involved, improving their capacity to manage conflicts and problems in socially constructive ways. This way of working avoids the legalisation of conflicts and adversarial attitudes.

A starting point should be an indissoluble interconnectedness between law and interpersonal respect. This will result in less victimisation and less escalation of conflict, and ultimately, less offending.

A justice system based on social sustainability principles would become a role model for guiding people in the best ways to manage conflicts and other challenges constructively without harming others.

Bi-partisan cooperation

Politicising the issue of crime in Alice Springs is only worsening the problem. Robust bipartisan will and cooperation are needed. A comprehensive long-term solution that is not subject to waxing and waning support must be found relatively quickly. We should be hard *and* soft on crime, using the lychee model. We should cease doing what we are doing, because what we are doing has led to the situation we are in. Was it Einstein who said....?

Healing through caring

Like the loyal companions they are, animals have led us through this book. The American elephant Mary in the title was later joined by the Ancient Greek 'beasts of burden', the Ancient Persian dogs and sheep, the Biblical oxen, the medieval European rats, cats, asses, beetles, bloodsuckers, bulls, caterpillars, cockchafers, cocks, cows, dogs, dolphins, eels, field mice, flies, goats, grasshoppers, horses, locusts, mice, moles, serpents, sheep, slugs, snails, swine, termites, turtledoves, weevils, wolves, and worms; the Shakespearean wolf, the Connecticut cows, heifers, sheep, and sows; the Bengal tiger, the African crocodiles and buffalos, the Indonesian alligators, the New Zealand pigs, the Australian yellow rabbit and finally, the white elephants in the room when it comes to the Northern Territory justice system....

Like the loyal companions they are, animals will help us conclude this book by exploring the healing qualities of animals for those who lack not only care, but also the opportunity *to* care.

Horses

Many studies have emphasised the positive impact of working with horses on mental and physical health. In

2013, in the Netherlands, twenty-three children and adolescents with psychosocial problems participated in a study on the effectiveness of using horses in therapies and coaching. The study explicitly linked positive psychology and the use of horses. It shows that using horses in interventions results in a significant increase in well-being and the use of personal strengths. Individual goals were set for each participant. Development was observed in 78% of cases, of which 44% achieved their goals completely, or above expectations. [1]

Pups in Prison

Closer to home, in a unique program that started in 2020 at the Southern Queensland Correctional Centre, dogs live with prisoners in jail as they are being trained as companion animals. It is the only course of its kind in the Australian prison system. It is bringing happiness, personal satisfaction and future job potential, as offenders serve their sentences. The offenders follow the Certificate III course in Companion Animal Services as part of the Pups in Prison program run by Assistance Dogs Australia (ADA). Once the offenders are released, there are opportunities for them in animal-related workplaces. Pups in Prison has trained Australia's only two fully accredited court facility dogs to support witnesses giving evidence, many of whom are children or victims of sexual assault.

The prison also has the only dedicated correctional facility dog in Australia. Stella lives in the community but goes to the jail every day, working with psychologists to support prisoners at risk. "Stella helps them emotionally regulate and really helps people trust and open up and deal with some of their difficulties," ADA Queensland client services manager Jane Kefford said. "She comes to play with her Pups in Prison friends too, so she's enjoying a good life." The Pups in Prison program not only gives inmates opportunities; it also provides a much-needed service for people with a disability in the community, such as sufferers from PTSD.

Furmentality

Closer to home, the Alice Springs-based psychiatrist Verushka Krigovsky (everyone calls her Verushka) has a comfort dog in her counselling room to make her patients feel comfortable. She is part of the Furmentality group, an organisation formed around pets and mental health. She says: "I love animals – ALL animals – so much so that I am a vegan. I am a psychiatrist working in Alice Springs with outreach to some of the most remote aboriginal communities in Australia. No matter our age, we all experience mental anguish at some time in our lives, with some of us suffering ongoing mental illness. Research has shown, and I have seen first-hand, the powerful positive effects animals have on our lives; – from teaching us compassion, care, and responsibility to staving off loneliness, improving depression and decreasing anxiety, as well as being a 'ready-made family'. With Furmentality, I hope to highlight these positives with the aim of hospitals and health organisations incorporating animals into their general management plans. My camp dog, Lana Banana, the 'pin-up girl' of our organisation [...], visits patients on the wards and outpatient clinics. She delights everyone she meets and is a big hit with Aboriginal patients, especially when they hear she's from the Finke community. I couldn't ask for a better co-therapist." [2]

While Mary the elephant opened this research, let Lana Banana close it. Woof!

See you at Sustainable Justice Australia (a room in my home for the time being).

www.sustainablejusticeaustralia.com
info@sustainablejusticeaustralia.com

Endnotes

1   Tramper, E 2013, Leiden University.

2   https://www.furmentality.life/FurWeb/

Afterword

While this book was in preparation for going to press, Minister Kate Worden[1],stated, incredibly, in an ABC *Four Corners* episode,[2] that the youth detention system *has already been reformed*. The work has been done, in her view. A new youth justice facility is being built to replace the notorious Don Dale facility. According to Worden, this new facility will be focused on rehabilitation. Most of the 227 recommendations of the Royal Commission of 2016 have not been implemented, but this was a conscious decision, according to Worden.

Nicole Hucks, Acting Children's Commissioner, does not agree with Minister Worden. Neither does Mick Gooda, who was co-commissioner of the Royal Commission in 2016. The reasons are simple: the failure to implement most of the recommendations of the Royal Commission. These recommendations were evidence-based.

How the government will make the huge leap required from what is currently happening with young people in detention to an entirely new approach – while at the same time largely ignoring the Royal Commission's recommendations – remains unclear.

The investments needed to bring about meaningful change, financial and otherwise, seem to be lacking entirely.

In the same episode of *Four Corners*, Mick Gooda said that we will be ashamed of ourselves in a hundred years' time. Our descendants will shake their heads in disbelief when they learn that we, our generation, used to lock up and torture young offenders.

This is the point I have tried to make throughout this book, using numerous stories about the prosecution of animals and inanimate objects. We should be ashamed right now.

We need to sit down and think; talk; and then take action. We need to look at other countries which do better. We need sustainable justice soon. It cannot wait another generation.

Endnotes

1   Minister for Police, Fire and Emergency Services; Minister for the Prevention of Domestic, Family and Sexual Violence; Minister for Sport; Minister for Territory Families.

2   ABCTV 2022, Locking Up Kids: Australia's failure to protect children in detention, Four Corners, 14 November. https://www.abc.net.au/news/2022-11-14/locking-up-kids:-australias-failure-to-protect/101652954?utm_campaign=abc_news_web&utm_content=facebook&utm_medium=content_shared&utm_source=abc_news_web&fbclid=IwAR1bq-0sY7PywnO8In4i_lpG89W1XTxqsoxKY7Xp2Q7b-4V3mFuV_y_SuLKYA

Table of Content

Legal page
Researched and written by
About the book
What is sustainable justice

Introduction

Truth and justice 12
One person! 14
How the issues are interrelated (Figure 1) 20
The problem 21
Need rather than greed 25
The causes 26
The triangle of crime (Figure 2) 28
Searching for solutions 29
What if? 30
Aims 32
Research questions 34
Scope 35
Perspective 36
Methods 36
Indigenous style research 37
Decolonising theory 38
Realist ontology 39

Consultation 49

The power of story 41

Centre for sustainable justice 42

A note on names and usage 42

Endnotes 43

The Telethon Kids Institute survey 44

Linguistic disadvantage 45

Mental impairment 46

Why do parents and Elders feel powerless to discipline their children? 48

Endnotes 50

The economic cost of crime in Alice Springs 51

Pre-tax spending 52

Table 1: NT crime statistics 52

Table 2: Estimated economic cost of crime in Alice Springs: total and per-capita 54

Example: A broken passenger-side window 56

How lawyers calculate pain and suffering 57

Domestic violence 60

Table 3: Domestic violence pre-tax spending 61

Domestic violence post-tax spending 61

Table 4: Domestic violence post-tax spending 61

Post-tax spending on crime (not DV) 62

Table 5: Cost of the justice system in Alice Springs 64

Endnotes 67

Chapter 1 Literature review

How we think about the problem of crime 70

The Elephant's Tooth 70

The narrative of the youth worker 72

A problem rooted in history 74

Free will and the law 76

Determinism 79

Harris and Dennett;

Two of the four horsemen of the new atheism 79

Sam Harris, Free Will 80

Benjamin Libet 83

Compatibilism 84

Dennett, The Nefarious Neurosurgeon 84

Dennett versus Harris 87

Dennett versus Caruso 89

Libertarianism 91

David Hodgson 91

Eastern philosophy and free will 92

Hunger for revenge and punishment 94

Belie in quick fixes 95

Signalling: Naming & shaming on social media
and prison architecture 96

Problems within the law 98

The concept of *mens rea* in criminal law 98

The division between criminal law and civil law 101

The age of criminal responsibility 103

Best interest of the child 104
The laws of complicity 107
Silence and gratuitous concurrence in legal
proceedings 111
Mandatory sentencing 112
Irrelevant factors on judicial decisions 113
Revolving-door justice 117
All-white juries 118 The closure of Bush Courts &
the steady defunding of community-based
mediation services 121
The lack of diversion out bush 122
Trauma 123
The relationship between harm and juvenile
detention 126
Trauma and neurolaw 129
Offenders' intergenerational trauma 129
Adverse childhood experiences of offenders 130
Trauma in police 131
Trauma in prison workers 133
Trauma and vicarious trauma in the Alice
Springs community 135
Trauma caused by the law and law enforcement 142
Volatile situations: The Rolfe Case 142
Victim trauma 143
NGOs and government organisations do not reach
the youth on the street sufficiently 149
(Vicarious) trauma in lawyers and judges 150
Kozarov v Victoria 151
Disability in offenders 153
Sustainable justice 154

A public-health issue 156
Ny Anstalt 157
The normality principle & principle of least
infringement 160
Animals as therapists 160
The arts in prison 168
A normal life 169
Endnotes 171

Chapter two – How we think about crime

The punishment of lifeless things, plants and
animals 191
Ancient Greece 191
Ancient Persia 194
In the Bible 194
Middle Ages – Europe 195
Outside Europe 198
Blameworthiness; a thought experiment 199
The punishment of humans 201
Endnotes 204
The thirty-one problems and three iconic
cases 205
The problems that we must overcome 205
How we think about crime 206
Problems within the law 206
Trauma-related problems 207
The Zak Grieve Case 208
The Dylan Voller Case 209
The Zachary Rolfe Case 216
Endnotes 220

Chapter three - The white elephant
Problems within the law

Mens rea and free will 222
The division between criminal law and civil law 225
Mandatory sentencing 227
Complicity 234
The age of criminal responsibility 235
Silence and gratuitous concurrence in proceedings 238
The impact of irrelevant factors on judicial decisions 240
Revolving-door justice 242
A white elephant 244
Legal Aid pulling out of bush courts in theNorthern Territory 245
The steady defunding of community-based mediation services 246
The lack of diversion out bush 247
Endnotes 248

Chapter four – Trauma

Offender trauma and neurolaw 253
Cultural trauma 256
Cultural trauma causes inter-generational and personal trauma 260
Parental incarceration 261
Adverse childhood experiences 262
Victim Trauma 263
Post-traumatic street disorder 263

Trauma in prison workers 269
(Vicarious) trauma in lawyers and magistrates 271
Trauma and magistrates 272
Trauma among the police 278
Endnotes 282

Chapter Five - Toward sustainable justice

Street-connected children and street-ism 286
Perceptions of 'them'; the feeling that the
problem is someone else's and not our own 291
It takes a village 292
The infantilisation of Aboriginal people 292
Community ideas 299
The lychee model and the principle of least
infringement 299
The Nosirp 300
The power of architecture to affect human behaviour
302
The proposal Centre for Sustainable Justice in town 306
The Nosirp - key words 307
The Sustainable Justice Charter revisited 307
Bi-partisan cooperation 312
Healing through caring 313
Hoeses 313
Pups in Prison 314
Furmentality 315 Endnotes 316

Afterword 317

Glossary A - Z

About the book – front matter

Adverse childhood experiences 262 130

Afterword 317

Age of criminal responsibility 103 235

Aims 32

All-white juries 118

Ancient Greece 191

Ancient Persia 194

Animals as therapists 160

Belief in quick fixes 95

Benjamin Libet 83

Best interest of the child 104

Bi-partisan cooperation 312

Bible 194

Blameworthiness 199

Broken passenger-side window 56

Centre for sustainable justice 42

Chapter five - Toward sustainable justice 286

Chapter four - Trauma 253

Chapter three - The white elephant Problems within the law 222

Closure of Bush Courts 121

Community ideas 299

Compatibilism 84

Complicity 234

Concept of mens rea in criminal law 98

Consultation 49

Cultural trauma 256

David Hodgson 91

Decolonising theory 38

Defunding of community-based mediation services 121 246

Dennett versus Caruso 89

Dennett versus Harris 87

Dennett, The Nefarious Neurosurgeon 84

Determinism 79

Disability in offenders 153

Discipline children? 48

Division between criminal law and civil law 101 225

Domestic violence 60 61

Dylan Voller Case 209

Eastern philosophy and free will 92

Economic cost of crime in Alice Springs 51

Elephant's Tooth 70

Free will and the law 76

Furmentality 315

Harris and Dennett; two of the four horsemen of the new atheism 79

Healing through caring 313

Horses 313

How lawyers calculate pain and suffering 57

How the issues are interrelated (Figure 1) 20

How we think about crime 171 206

How we think about the problem of crime 70

Hunger for revenge and punishment 94

Impact of irrelevant factors on judicial decisions 113 240

Indigenous style research 37

Infantilisation of Aboriginal people 292

Introduction 12

It takes a village 292

Kozarov v Victoria 151

Lack of diversion out bush 122 247

Laws of complicity 107

Legal Aid pulling out of bush courts in the

Legal page – front matter

Libertarianism 91

Linguistic disadvantage 45

Literature review 70

Lychee model 299

Mandatory sentencing 112 227

Mens rea and free will 222

Mental impairment 46

Methods 36

Middle Ages – Europe 195

Names and usage 42

Narrative of the youth worker 72

Need rather than greed 25

NGOs and government organisations do not

reach the youth on the street sufficiently 149

Normal life 169

Normality principle 160

Northern Territory 245

Nosirp 300 307

Ny Anstalt 157

Offender trauma and neurolaw 253

Offenders' intergenerational trauma 129

One person! 14

Outside Europe 198

Parental incarceration 261

Perceptions of 'them' 291

Personal trauma 260

Perspective 36

Post-tax spending on crime (not DV) 62

Post-traumatic street disorder 263

Power of architecture to affect human behaviour 302

Power of story 41

Pre-tax spending 52

Principle of least infringement 160 299

Prison architecture 96

Problem rooted in history 74

Problems that we must overcome 205

Problems within the law 206 98

Proposal Centre for Sustainable Justice in town 306

Public-health issue 156

Punishment of humans 201

Punishment of lifeless things, plants and animals 191

Pups in Prison 314

Realist ontology 39

Relationship between harm and juvenile detention 126

Research questions 34

Researched and written by – front matter

Revolving-door justice 117 242

Rolfe Case 142

Sam Harris, Free Will 80

Scope 35

Searching for solutions 29

Signalling: Naming & shaming on social media 96

Silence and gratuitous concurrence 111 238

Street-connected children and street-ism 286

Sustainable justice 154

Sustainable Justice Charter 307

Table 1: NT crime statistics 52

Table 2: Estimated economic cost of crime in

Table 3: Domestic violence pre-tax spending 61

Table 4: Domestic violence post-tax spending 61

Table 5: Cost of the justice system in Alice Springs 64

Telethon Kids Institute survey 44

The arts in prison 168

Trauma 123

Trauma among the police 278

Trauma and magistrates 272

Trauma and neurolaw 129

Trauma and vicarious trauma Alice Springs 135

Trauma caused by the law and law enforcement 142

Trauma in police 131

Trauma in prison workers 133 269

Trauma-related problems 207

Triangle of crime (Figure 2) 28

Truth and justice 12

(Vicarious) trauma in lawyers and judges 150

(Vicarious) trauma in lawyers and magistrates 271

Victim trauma 143 263

Volatile situations 142

What if? 30

What is sustainable justice – front matter

White elephant 244

Zachary Rolfe Case 216

Zak Grieve Case 208